I0534643

DEMON ENSNARED

DEMON ENFORCERS, BOOK 4

JENN STARK

You're always stronger in the broken places...

Angela Stanton has it all—the brilliant mind, the political job that can make a real difference, the townhouse full of strays she attracts wherever she goes. She's also got a secret that nearly destroyed her when she was a child. A secret she's buried so deep, it can't hurt anyone anymore.

Until now.

Gregori of the Syx, a gifted empath, has avoided all human emotion since he became a demon. Now he must convince Angela to trust him with her deepest pain, revealing a truth that could change the role of demons on earth forever. Unfortunately, the intensity of this particular human connection might also shatter what's left of his soul. But this time, he won't turn away.

Falling in love can utterly end you when you're a *Demon Ensnared.*

For those who know.

1

No.

It was such a short, unassuming word to carry this much weight, so quiet and small. But it roared in Gregori's mind with the force of rage, desperation, and despair.

He'd silently met every assignment given to him in his role of demon enforcer of the Syx with this same howling rebuke, yet never once had he given it a voice. Never objected, never begged off. Never turned aside from the horrific assaults on his senses that the Archangel Michael had forced him to endure, every time the Syx were ordered to dive once more into the world of humans, to rescue God's children from the worst of Gregori's own kind.

The luxury of denying that call had been taken from him, he'd reminded himself, job after job, year after year, century after century. This was his path now. This was where his weakness had brought him.

But...enough was enough.

"No," he murmured again, the word low and thick, rumbled in his deep voice.

Beside him, his fellow demon Hugh shifted up on his toes, and Gregori fought the grim smile at what the sly and silver-tongued demon enforcer must be thinking. No one opposed the archangel. Least of all the surliest, most taciturn member of their team.

Michael the Archangel, however, didn't move. His eyes remained ghostly white, his expression unreadable. "You cannot refuse this charge, Gregori. You know this as well as I do."

Gregori lifted his chin and intensified his glower at the archangel. The problem was, he knew far more than Michael had ever seemed to understand. Once an exalted angel of the heavens, Gregori had rashly agreed to become a Fallen, fully prepared to serve the children of God as a teacher and supporter, helping them navigate the magnificently complex planet on which they lived, guiding them as they reached for their highest potential. He could hear their cries all the way to heaven, could feel their frustration and their pain. How much better would he be able to serve among them, with such an attunement to their needs?

Upon becoming Fallen, however, he'd immediately realized his mistake. His sensitivity to mortal thoughts, emotions, and sensations had been magnified a hundredthousandfold. He was an angel who knew, who felt, and who *experienced* too much. Far too much. Every time a human would cry out for his aid, Gregori would practically be driven to his knees with their debilitating agony, crippled with despair.

He'd tried, of course. He'd served. He'd bent and toiled. Until at last the day had come when he'd simply—refused. Just once...just once he'd needed to turn away, to not accept the cup of the humans' pain, the cloak of their anguish. Just once he'd needed to take a deep and shuddering breath that was not laced with mortal cries.

And in that breath, he'd lost the grace of God and become a demon.

It wasn't fair. It was, perhaps, not even just.

But it was so nonetheless.

All these millennia later, Gregori could manage the pain humans caused him so much more easily, though it was always there. It dogged his crippled, shattered form beneath his glamorous façade. He'd never lost his prescient awareness of the agony that awaited him in the mortal space, lurking in the shadows, eager to strike—but he'd eventually learned ways to manage it.

To be fair, he was not normally the member of the Syx who was directly called, nor the demon who led an expedition. As a secondary set of fists serving another of his team, he could distance himself from what was going on directly in front of him. When he was called upon to fight under the direction of Warrick or Raum or any of the other enforcers, he could focus on the task at hand, ignoring the rest.

But now, everything had changed.

"You know what's been required of all the enforcers," the archangel continued, eyeing him more closely now. "You've been set on a path of redemption, like every member of the Syx. If any one of you refuses to walk that path, however, all will be lost. There will be no second chance."

"And I know that *you* are the one who created this path and these requirements," Gregori said, once again not missing the demon Hugh's shift of surprise beside him. One of the most elusive of their number, Hugh had rarely been called to partner directly with any of them until recently. His curse of deception had become his gift as a demon enforcer, allowing him to do his best work when he slipped alone through the most twisted of mortal throngs.

Gregori's sin—that of indifference—had no such silver lining. It also proved no impediment to his work, Gregori made sure of that. He would serve as he was demanded to serve, atoning evermore for the humans who'd died because he couldn't be moved to aid them, because he had not yet learned how to cope with the torment their needs kindled within him.

But, again, enough was enough. "There are many ways for us to find our redemption, many paths we can take," Gregori rumbled. "That you set this task before me shows either that you don't know me very well, or you know me so well, you deliberately risk the future of the Syx on their most tenuous member. Which is it, archangel?"

It was probably the longest speech he'd ever made to Michael, and by this time, Hugh was staring at him openly. Michael remained unmoved.

Resolutely, with no expression at all marring his eerily pale face, the archangel lifted his hand—and both Gregori and Hugh were gone.

A moment later, they appeared in the center of a crush of people who were practically vibrating with their riotously conflicting emotions and tangled needs, and Gregori drew in a sharp, agonized breath as he recalibrated himself. It was like this every time he was thrust into a human crowd, but he could manage it. He. Could. Manage. It.

"What the hell happened to you?" Hugh spun him around. "And I mean that quite literally."

Even the touch of his brother demon's hand upon him made Gregori stagger back. In an instant, he knew all of Hugh's thoughts, his emotions, his hopes and fears, a cascade of images and feelings that threatened to bury him alive. He nearly choked on the intensity of it, his lungs squeezing with alarm, panic searing his nerves.

Drawing in a ragged breath, Gregori forced himself not to strike out at his comrade—they'd worked together for six thousand years, and *none* of the other demons knew the full extent of his weakness—but it was a near thing. Hugh was tall and slender, sinuously built. In their present appearances, Gregori towered over him like a mountain. A fight between the two would not go well for the quick-witted demon.

"Seriously, since when did you become the biggest badass of the Syx?" Hugh pressed. "I've never seen *anyone* back-talk the OG like that before."

Gregori grimaced, compelling himself to remain upright, forcing his hands not to clench into fists, his voice not to build to a roar. Eventually, the screaming cacophony in his mind eased. "This isn't the right job for me to lead," he said gruffly.

Hugh snorted. "Well, it's pretty much the kind of job we always get. Lots of humans, lots of shadows, lots of bad shit on the verge of happening." He squinted, clearly trying to make sense of the main attraction in the stadium. "Any idea why there are a bunch of pickup trucks driving around inside the building?"

"No." Gregori took in the cheering of the crowd and the squeal of tires as trucks spun in the center of an enormous indoor stadium that had been inexplicably filled with dirt. The trucks were large, their tires larger, but it wasn't the *Monster! Truck! Extravaganza!*, as advertised on countless banners around the space, that had him worried. Not exactly. "There's a new kind of demon here," he murmured. "You can smell them."

"Maybe *you* can smell them, my brother. I can't," Hugh said, giving him a sidelong glance.

Gregori sighed. This was why he didn't lead expeditions. Even his most basic explanations of his abilities left his team confused.

"But I'm willing to roll with it," Hugh continued. "You tell me we've got a new rando demon breed to deal with, I believe you."

"You do?" Gregori shot Hugh a look, expecting a mocking grin, but for once, Hugh's ordinarily cheerful eyes were flat and serious.

"Yup. One of the benefits of being a consummate liar." Hugh shrugged. "I can always pick another one out. You suck at it, and you always have. Generally speaking, the rest of us use your mood as a sort of unofficial barometer. The unhappier you are, the more we're going to get beat to shit on a job. But, here we go. What's the story on this dirt palace?"

The completely incongruous sound of dogs barking barely reached Gregori over the roar of trucks, and he scowled. *Dogs?* No way. There wouldn't be dogs here. Not with all the noise and trucks—and demons. Dogs and demons never mixed.

"I don't know, exactly," he said gruffly. "Whatever these new demons are, however, they're closing in at the far side of the arena. See there? And there."

Hugh squinted in the direction Gregori pointed. "I do see. They're moving fast too, the scum suckers. Like they've scented their prey."

"Agreed," Gregori said, his eyes narrowing on a roped-off area near the midpoint of the stadium, where a group of incongruously well-dressed people milled about. "We need to move."

"REPRESENTATIVE STANTON! Angela—Ms. Stanton! What do you have to say about the president's latest—"

Junior congresswoman Angela Stanton turned and glared with such chilling reproach at the reporter that the man rocked back on his heels, his eyes going wide. She shook herself hard and managed a quick smile, the moment immediately passing.

"The president has a job to do, and it's not an easy one," she said. "But he's only one person in a government charged with moving the country forward at every level—federal, state, and local. And today, we're focused here in Atlanta, Georgia, Mr. Simms. Do you have a question that might be more relevant, a little closer to home?"

"I..." Simms recovered quickly enough from Angela's death stare, more flummoxed by the fact that she knew his name, she suspected. "Sure," he spluttered, not wanting to lose her focus on him. "What do you think about proposal 718?"

"I think I'll know more when I read it thoroughly. It was just introduced on the floor yesterday, and the speculation about its full impact is entirely premature. But I look forward to learning everything I can about it." She shifted her gaze. "Mary?"

It was another reporter's turn to blink in surprise. Mary Geary had been put on the political beat only three days ago, but Angela knew her name too. She knew all their names. Clawing her way back from an early trauma that still sometimes threatened to swallow her whole, she'd used memorization as one of the extensive coping mechanisms that had served her well through high school, college, and three years with the CIA before she'd joined the Frost Center, one of Atlanta's most advanced think tanks.

The fact that Washington had come knocking a few years later had completely surprised her. She'd never planned on running for a House of Representatives seat. She'd certainly never planned on winning. She'd definitely not anticipated getting assigned to a highly classified congressional committee only a few weeks into her term. It hadn't taken a rocket scientist to realize she was being manipulated into a completely unexpected position of power, but Angela didn't walk away.

She could have—should have, maybe. Instead, she'd stayed. And not just because she was curious to understand who was behind her sudden good fortune.

No. The truth was, after all these years and accomplishments and countless hours of therapy, she still wanted so badly to—

"Hey! Guys, stop it. I mean it!"

All the reporters and the arena's muckety-mucks scattered in surprise as a cacophony of barking burst from the opening of the nearby corridor, louder even than the roar of trucks far beneath them. A gaggle of bandana-wearing dogs came bounding out of the tunnel and onto the media platform, leaping into the space as their hapless handler dragged ineffectually against their leads. "Guys!" he wailed.

"Oh, you have got to be—" Her head of security, Joe Reynolds, didn't bother hiding his exasperation as Angela instinctively burst forward, dropping to her knees on the dusty floor and holding her arms wide.

"Well, hello there." She laughed. The small army of dogs scrambled over to her, baying, yapping, and howling with delight. "Why are you looking so fancy?"

"They're rally mascots," their handler managed. "Oh geez, sorry!"

The dogs collapsed in a scrum around Angela, licking and bouncing as she patted each of them in turn. None of the reporters had cameras on her, she noticed. As serious journalists, this kind of thing wasn't what they were after. Worked for her. Hell, if that was all it took to keep the media off her back, she should start having all her press conferences at the dog park. She never knew why she seemed to be best-friend material to every four-legged animal that walked the earth, but she didn't mind it. Animals made her happy in a way most humans never could.

"I'm so sorry—I'm so sorry!" the young man stammered as Joe and the team helped him peel the dogs away from the media platform. Angela rubbed the last dog's head, a bouncing Tigger of a Jack Russell terrier that reminded her far too much of Hey Mister back at home, her mixed-breed boxer whose entire world was on a spring.

"It's okay." She grinned, ruefully waving goodbye to the dogs before schooling her features back into her serious junior congresswoman expression. Beside her, Joe rolled his eyes. He, more than anyone, understood her preference for animals over people. He was one of the few in her close circle that she'd confided in. She didn't like most people. She trusted even fewer. She hadn't since she was very young. Eighty-seven days in a cage would do that to a kid.

Now Joe sent two of their security detail off to make sure the dog walker kept control of his truck rally mascots, and she turned back to the group.

"Mary?" Angela prompted, and—possibly flustered by the interruption—the reporter blurted a question that was a political softball, something about Governor Filmore. Angela smiled—the expression once more careful, practiced, and perfect—then phrased her response to contain a nugget of information that was sure to be carried on all the local news sites for the constantly churning news cycle, maybe even the national feeds. Since round-the-clock information streaming had begun ruling the internet, every outlet lived for the viral quote. Angela's suggestion that the governor of Georgia was in Washington to discuss his home state's investment in artificial intelligence would get everyone talking about something *other* than Angela Stanton and today's ill-advised side trip to a monster truck rally in the heart of Atlanta.

Or at least, that was what she hoped.

She heard the dogs start barking again—farther away this time, all the way down at the center of the coliseum. This time, their barks were rougher, strained, and the shouts that came after were...well, they sounded almost terrified.

Angela stepped sharply to the side, ignoring the next question as her heart began to pound. There was something eerily familiar about the panic in those distant cries, something that made her recall the trailing end of a memory. She didn't know if she'd experienced or maybe dreamed that memory, but it seemed to be another echo of something she'd long since buried. Whatever it was, it conjured up twin bursts of fear and anger so abrupt, it was like taking a physical blow.

"What was that?" she demanded of Joe, but he seemed equally perplexed.

"I don't know. Dogs get loose, you think? Hurt someone?"

"I can't think—"

Then the barking cut off, the shouting too. But Angela still ignored the new round of press questions. Her palms sweaty, she searched the crowd standing behind the velvet ropes, but she saw no faces she recognized, no obvious threats, only a sense of darkness rolling toward her like a deadly tide, grasping, clawing, and—

The thud of pounding boots burst over them. "Security," someone shouted. "*Move.*"

Two large men in dark jackets leapt over the velvet ropes to her right and rushed past her, exactly as that rolling tide of fear coalesced into the form of three other men pushing toward Angela from the opposite side, scattering people in their wake. It was as if the three men appeared out of nowhere, and the scream building in her throat barely got started when the two groups collided. But now, where there had been two security guards and three assailants, there were a dozen, no, *two* dozen assailants rushing the ropes, lifting what appeared to be guns—but of course, they couldn't be guns, because this was a gun-free zone, and—

"Gun!" someone shouted.

The first spray of bullets dropped the men to her right, and Angela's scream finally escaped her throat as one of the security guards twisted back from the line of ropes and barreled into her, taking her to the ground. The man's enormous body pressed against her—not intimately, not dangerously, but in such an act of total and absolute protection that it took her breath away...or maybe that was because he was crushing her lungs into her spine.

Momentarily stunned, Angela stared up into the face of the most beautiful man she'd ever seen in her life. Dark curling hair cropped short, brilliant green eyes so bright, they had to be the result of colored contacts, a broad, chiseled face, and lips that could've been the model for only the most gorgeous of Greek statues. Because he was pinning her arms to the floor, she knew the man was wearing gloves, which struck her as odd, although she couldn't at first figure out why. He didn't look into her eyes, however, and no sooner had he flattened her than the man was up again, diving back into the chaos of the crowd.

The instant he left her, Angela's own security detail swarmed in, practically lifting her from the floor and rushing her through the crowd in the other direction.

"Stop, wait!" she demanded, craning her neck to see what was going on. "Who are those people?"

"Terrorists," snapped Joe. "There's going to be fucking hell to pay. Move it! Move it, people, let's go!"

He shoved Angela into a corridor, piling after her along with the rest of their squad—then all seven of them came to an abrupt halt.

A dozen new men in Kevlar suits faced them, their rifles up and ready to fire.

"Careful, Hugh—" Gregori shouted. He turned and struck the beast closest to him so hard, the creature instantly dissolved into a spray of flying black goop.

"Got 'im!" A trio of demons had flanked Hugh, coming fast from multiple directions, but at the last minute, the enforcer unleashed a sort of spinning kick that somehow managed to take all three of the horde out in one movement. Once again, the effect was immediate and messy. Geysers of black goop—what passed as blood for demons—sprayed what few members of the audience were still in this section. Most of the humans had fled, at least those nearest to the fight. But Gregori was keenly aware of the slavering intensity that still surrounded them on all sides, pressing forward, eager for bloodshed, for carnage...and that was only the humans.

"*Oof.*"

In his distraction, he'd missed his own approaching phalanx of attackers, and he staggered to the side as they rushed forward with claws and teeth, shedding their demonic glamour as they did so, at least to his eyes. But then, it was difficult for any demon to maintain its glamour long around Gregori. It was one of the "gifts with purchase" his empathic abilities afforded him. He could pierce any disguise, see through almost any mask—human, demon, or otherwise.

Without warning, the image of the face of the woman he'd protected from an unusually focused onslaught of the demons flashed in front of his eyes. She'd clearly been the target of this attack, though he didn't know why. He'd been more surprised that she'd reacted to him not with the terror she should have, or even the anger and violation a more sophisticated mortal typically expressed when barreled into by a stranger. No. She'd studied him curiously, as if he was a puzzle to be solved, an equation to be followed to its end, then examined over and over from every angle. She was beautiful in a detached, remote way, and he'd carefully avoided looking directly at her. He couldn't afford to get lost in that inquisitive stare. Instead, he'd wrenched himself away to take out the demons clawing toward her, and the fight was on again.

A fight he needed to be paying better attention to, given the flash of white-hot pain that scored his side.

"Fire of *God*," he growled, grabbing the offending demon as it raced by him, gleeful in the success of its rushing attack. But Gregori was too quick for it. He lashed out with a powerful hand and grabbed it tight around the neck. With a rough jerk, he broke the demon's neck and used its body as a scourge, lashing it against another knot of the beasts. Something else he noticed: despite their intensity as attackers, these demons had curiously little durability. The moment Gregori connected with them, they shattered into gory pieces.

Unfortunately, another wave of them appeared almost as quickly as the first one fell away, and these were carrying the strange guns he'd noticed before. Guns that were not made of metal but... Glass? Plastic? Was that possible?

Yet for all their fierce appearance, these guns also only seemed useful for one round before shattering in the hands of the demons who wielded them, though of course the demons felt no pain. Guns couldn't take out a demon, not even exploding ones. In nearly all cases, only a demon could take out another demon, and Gregori was more than happy to do the job.

Opposite him, Hugh was making short work of his own mini horde attack, the enforcer's speed almost faster than the human eye could track as he dispatched beast after beast. For a demon best known for talking his way through anything, Hugh was a competent fighter, employing his vaunted strategy skills to the far simpler task of neutralizing oncoming threats with brutal efficiency.

Gregori, for his part, relied mostly on simply being brutal. He toppled another set of demons, punching them back beyond the veil as they exploded in a splatter of yet more goop. He slipped in the thick gore coating the concrete platform as another batch of demons leapt for him, his attackers wisely working as a group against him this time.

It didn't matter. When Gregori fought like this, deeply immersed in the glorious killing fugue that swept over him as he bent to the task that was now the sum total of his being, he could forget the clamoring world around him, the teeming mass of humanity in all its outrage and despair. He could focus solely on the ripping of skin, the exposing of sinew and bone, the disintegration of glamour and demon alike until all that was left was a steaming pool of goop. These demons were far more interesting than usual, because he hadn't been wrong about their different scent. They smelled...controlled. Held in check against their will. Was that restraint tied to their unusual dedication to their mission? The Syx were known as particularly vicious fighters, and they always got the job done. Typically, once the dark beasts realized who they were up against, at least a third of any given demon horde the Syx fought fled into the night. But this crew remained almost single-mindedly focused on their task...

...Their task.

Oh *no*.

The scream reached him almost at the same moment, a breathy, startled shout far more anguished than the blood-curdling howl of horror he'd heard so many times when humans finally grasped the true evil they faced in the demon horde. Nonetheless, it gave Gregori everything he needed to find his target. It was the woman. Of course it was the woman. The woman he'd left to her own team of security professionals, all of them bristling with weapons. He'd thought she would be protected among so many of her own people. He'd thought...

He grimaced with a new wave of shame. He knew exactly what he'd thought. That he couldn't—shouldn't—look at her, that he didn't want to know the truth she held in her wide and searching eyes.

Let this cup pass from me...

With a renewed burst of humiliation, defensiveness, and growing rage, Gregori turned and raced back through the now-empty, cordoned-off section of the stadium and practically flew into a corridor that was vibrating with dark energy. As he did, he took care to disguise himself heavily, blocking any sense of his nature from the demons that lay within. His efforts were aided, of course, by the woman's scream, wordlessly demanding his aid. While the archangel had sent Gregori and Hugh to this place, it was a human's desperate need that gave him power.

What he saw made his blood run cold. Thirteen demons in battle formation, holding the humans hostage. And it *was* a hostage situation, Gregori could tell immediately. Which meant there was something even worse in store for the humans who'd been trapped by the demons.

He quickly assessed the situation. A pair of security guards lay dead on the ground, while three others writhed in agony, their minds potentially shattered beyond Gregori's ability to repair, though...maybe...

With a swiftness accorded solely to the members of his shadow company of demons, he moved through the broken humans, touching them briefly, praying over them with swift and careful words. He couldn't heal the way he had once healed as a Fallen, but he did have some ability left. It wasn't up to him if these humans lived or died, but he would do what he could.

When he straightened again, he refocused on the remaining humans. The first, a security guard who was scared nearly to death himself, nevertheless remained steadfastly by his charge, using his body to block the same woman Gregori had dropped to the floor during the first wave of attacks. Then, she had surprised him with her stoic lack of emotion, but now she stunned him speechless. She was an empty slate. A cipher. The first human he'd ever encountered that he couldn't instantly read. She didn't seem catatonic, though. She was talking—talking in low, calm, and reasoned tones—and yet she was a complete emotional blank.

At least on the surface. It was impossible to tell what emotions she was hiding beneath that careful mask.

"It's okay, Joe. It's okay," she said, her voice low and steady. "If you walk, I think they'll let you go."

"I'm *not* leaving you." Of the two, Joe sounded far more legitimately human to Gregori's ears, and the emotions rolling off him—fear, anger, determination, horror—were appropriate. The woman, however...

Don't focus on the woman.

Gregori felt the urgency of the warning that formed in his mind, and he knew both it and himself too well to ignore it. If he wanted to stay upright long enough to help these people, he couldn't get sucked into the emotional morass of an individual human, especially a human who was so deeply blocked from feeling anything that, once her emotions *were* uncorked, they'd be damned near lethal in their intensity.

"I don't want you to get hurt too," the woman continued evenly, still the soul of reason. "They seem fixated on me. Like they're waiting."

"Yeah?" Joe spit out. "Waiting for what, Angie? What could possibly be worse than what these assholes did to Eric and Jim?"

Something shifted across the woman's face then, the briefest flashes of a deep horror that nearly took Gregori's breath away.

He bolted forward.

"Joe," he roared, and as if they'd already worked together dozens of times, the human security guard seemed to know instinctively what he needed to do. He turned and grabbed the woman—Angela Stanton was her name, Gregori realized in a rush, the male human as well as the horde repeating those words as if they were some kind of mantra—and shoved her to the floor, flopping his body on top of hers. At the same time, Gregori struck.

Whenever possible during fights where humans were present, Gregori preferred to work with a tool of some sort, a weapon. Mortals seemed to understand a man's ability to wield a weapon with great force, but they had a far more difficult time wrapping their heads around a man launching into a group of armed assailants using nothing but his fists. The guns these creatures were carrying were corrupted, however; some of them broken, some simply unable to fire, holdovers from the first wave of assailants. Demons could manifest themselves with any sort of glamour, but they couldn't manifest actual *weapons* into being. They could only wield what humans left around for them to use. Most of the time, even that wasn't necessary—not when teeth, claws, fists, and demonic fire were in play.

But these demons seemed determined to keep up the illusion of mortals wielding guns. Gregori had no problem working with that. Unfortunately, he was too close to the actual humans to use spectral fire against the creatures, and he too had no desire to let his glamour slip. So fists it would have to be.

Consumed once more with the glorious, healing rage of retribution, Gregori piled into the assembly before Joe and Angela fully collapsed to the concrete floor. There were twelve beasts to his one, but he had the advantage of surprise and the close quarters of the corridor to aid him. As the first group turned, he was already through them, exploding necks and shattering faces, breaking chests and loosing huge gouts of black goop. Demon blood showered the unfortunate Angela and Joe, but there was nothing Gregori could do about that—not and stay focused on the mission at hand.

But the demons didn't flee as he expected them to, not all of them. Roughly a third scattered, but then they came together again, only bigger—stronger. Gregori stumbled back, trying to get his bearings, and realized that these few demons were drawing from parts and pieces of their destroyed brethren. These were the same demons he'd sensed when they'd first arrived, the demons who were different. New. Profoundly wrong.

These weren't solely constructs of the Father, nor creations born of the pits of hell.

What the hell were these things?

"Gregori—what in the *fuck*?"

Hugh appeared at the front of the corridor, and that momentary distraction was all Gregori required. He'd only ever needed about two-thirds of his strength to effectively combat the horde, but now he loosed the restraints on his wrath more completely, glorying in the madness that consumed him, clearing out his mind, lighting his blood on fire. He blasted bodily into the first composite demon, taking it against the wall so hard, the stone buckled. Screaming in agony, the creature burst instantly into flames as Gregori head-butted it. Getting an idea from that, Gregori whipped off his gloves and bolted for the second creature, launching through the air with his arms outstretched to miss the side-swiping kick of the third.

"Hands!" he roared as Hugh joined the fight, but of course his fellow enforcer didn't bother covering his hands for interactions with humans. He didn't need to. Still, the move worked equally well for Hugh. The moment Gregori and Hugh connected physically with the new demons, they burst into flames. There was no black goop residue here, not anymore. In fact, the flames of these mightier demons set the demon blood coating the floor on fire, almost as if the black goop were fuel, and those flames raced along that fuel like an avenging wraith until they exploded into the corridor. Behind them, Angela and Joe screamed, and Gregori remembered that they too were covered in spatter. He turned to see them batting out the flames, but Hugh shoved him toward the final demon, who struggled for the opening of the corridor, trying to escape. Gregori lurched after it.

The demon raced down the concrete steps, flames spurting out in all directions, catching the VIP cordoned-off area on fire. Then it leapt and soared over the seats with an ear-splitting yowl. It landed in the center of the dirt-filled stadium as Gregori caught up to it. Gregori vaguely heard the roaring of trucks and the wailing of humans as the demon turned and spread its arms wide—

And was catapulted off his feet by an enormous truck. The demon's body flew directly at Gregori, who wrapped it in his arms and exploded it into black ash and smoke.

For a long, harrowing moment, there was nothing but silence.

Then all the screams started up again.

Gregori turned, blind with pain, but there was nowhere to escape, no path or exit immediately obvious to him. Worse, people were running toward him—running and shouting, bellowing even, their paroxysm of relief and joy no less agonizing for all that it was positive. Gregori couldn't get out—couldn't flee—

"Brother!" Hugh called, and Gregori felt the smaller demon's body next to his. Hugh threw his arm over Gregori and yanked him toward a doorway filled with shadows—

Then the archangel was there, his hand held high. Hugh of the Syx passed through Michael's misty form as if it was no barrier at all.

Gregori didn't.

3

"Go, go!" Angela railed, shoving Joe ahead of her so he'd stop trying to help her limp along and focus on the matter at hand. She didn't know why she needed to reach the fallen security guard so quickly, but she knew she had to, somehow *knew* his mind would shatter into pieces if she didn't.

It was a feeling she understood all too well, and she wouldn't wish it on her worst enemy.

But a small crowd had already formed around the man, who was growling at everyone like a cornered bear by the time Joe breached the outer group, Angela right behind him. She was pretty sure she'd sprained her ankle something fierce during the gunmen's attack, but she'd feel that pain later—much later, she suspected. Right now, the adrenaline she was riding was more than sufficient to keep her upright and moving.

"Get *away*," Joe shouted with impressive authority as he bounded up to the colossal security guard, who'd rolled over on his side, a mountain of a man who protected his face with blistered hands while he continued to warn people to get back, to get away, not to touch him. Though his words were earnest enough to carry real weight, it was the man's hands that were keeping most people back, as several were shouting on their phones at 911 about a burn victim. The backs of the guard's hands were bloody and raw, though she couldn't exactly get a fix on them to see how badly he'd been hurt. It was clear he'd been burned, though. His clothing was scorched and blackened, his boots coated with ash. How he'd even survived...she had no idea.

There'd been an explosion of fire back there in the mouth of the corridor, several of them, it'd seemed to her ears, and this literal giant of a man had continued to fight as if he'd felt no pain at all. She'd heard of such people, of course, their nerves deadened to any sensation. Once, long ago and somewhere else, she'd prayed to become one of them.

It hadn't worked for her, unfortunately, and she suspected it wasn't working for this man either. Because there was no denying that legitimate pain rolled off him, an almost physical wall of agony that shimmered and rippled in a wide arc. It also surrounded Joe, who'd clearly set himself up as the man's protector, a rat terrier guarding a Great Dane.

"EMTs are on their way!" someone shouted, and a cheer went up. The news seemed to have a galvanizing effect on the security guard too. He shuddered, then hunched over a little more before rolling to his knees.

"Whoa, whoa, whoa, there, buddy," Joe said, crouching down next to the man. Angela noticed he didn't touch the injured guard, and she wondered if that was in response to the man's pleas or an instinctual knowing to give the big guy his space. Probably both. Joe had managed to triage his entire team on the way out of the corridor with her, pronouncing two dead and the other three...

She frowned, glancing back. The other men of their company had been gravely injured. She'd seen them go down. But Joe had given them only the most cursory of glances as he and Angela had rushed by, promising to get them help. She recalled only one of her men had been conscious, his eyes wide, his face rapt with wonder. Probably going into shock, given what had just happened.

A current of unease flowed through the crowd as the security guard lurched to his feet, swaying a little. Nervous shouts of "Hey, man, take it easy" and "Help's comin', dude, you're good" emerged from the gathered group, but these died out as the guard shook himself like a wild bull, his hands still pressed to his face.

Angela grimaced. So far, she'd likened this poor man to a dog, a bear, a mountain, and now a bull. He'd saved her life, and he had doubtless saved the lives of her men. She owed him more than turning him into a cartoon character.

Then he dropped his hands from his face, and she gasped.

She wasn't alone. The crowd at the center of the dirt track was mostly men, but even they stepped back as the security guard turned to face them, his brilliant green eyes shining out of a face she belatedly remembered as being gorgeous enough to be a model's...if giants ever modeled. He stretched his fingers wide, his hands now decidedly less red and damaged, and smiled. He seemed exhausted and relieved at once.

"Who hit the man I was chasing? With the truck?" he asked, and his low, resonant voice flowed over the group with the impact of a barnstorming preacher, causing everyone to stand straighter and be prouder simply for existing in his presence. *Who is this guy?*

"I did." A wiry middle-aged man in a ball cap, T-shirt, and blue jeans stepped out of the crowd, his face somber and unapologetic. "Bastard had caught half the stadium section on fire, and you had the word SECURITY on your jacket." He grinned, deepening the lines around his eyes and face. "Figured I'd put my money on you."

Laughter rippled through the crowd. "I thank you for it," the guard murmured. He lifted his hand slightly as if to wave to the man. Angela didn't miss the way the truck driver rocked back a little on his heels, his eyes going wide for just a second before he recovered himself. She couldn't focus on that for too long, however, because the big security guard had turned and started moving for the exit.

"Hold up, there. You need the EMTs to check you out," Joe insisted.

"I don't," the guard said, slanting Joe a glance. "You do. She does." He jerked a thumb at Angela, though she noticed he didn't turn her way. Instead, he kept walking. He hadn't looked directly at her at all, actually, not even when he'd dropped her to the stadium floor during the first wave of attacks. Suddenly, she *wanted* him to see her, to focus all his attention on her, and her need for that focus was so strong, it caught her up short. She took a wrong step and landed awkwardly on her injured ankle, which rolled in her boot despite her relatively sensible footwear. Pain at last cracked through the box where she'd stuffed it away, and she cried out.

The burly security guard turned at once and seemed to be right at her side, though she would have sworn he'd been several steps ahead of her. He reached for her in one quick, flowing movement and caught her before she fell. His face twisted in a paroxysm of pain as his fingers wrapped around her arm, but there was no denying the surge of energy, the almost hysterical joy that flowed through Angela, seeming to trace every nerve ending with a blast of cool radiance. The pain instantly left her ankle, and she straightened, pulling away from him.

She didn't miss his expression of relief to let her go. Touching people genuinely seemed to hurt this man, yet he hadn't hesitated a moment to come to her side. Once again, who was he? At this point, she expected him to sprout wings out of his back and fly away.

Even as she thought that, he swiveled away from her, turning back to Joe.

"I'm sorry about your other men," he said, somehow managing to pitch his voice beneath the roar around them as they approached the opening to the stadium interior. Joe's bushy brows went up as if he'd just now remembered his fallen comrades, and he reached up to clap the man on the shoulder, stopping himself just in time.

"We'll send those medics up to them and get that taken care of," Joe said gruffly. "You say you don't need EMTs, then you don't need 'em. But don't go anywhere, okay? Because *I* need you, and that's a fact. You got someone with the stadium you gotta check in with, a report to make?"

The security guard's expression shifted again, a trail of emotions slipping across his face. Pain, resignation, horror, doubt—and finally, acceptance. He nodded to Joe as Angela watched him, spellbound.

"I'll wait for you," the big man said. He glanced to Angela but once again managed not to meet her eyes. "But you should know I'm not with the stadium. I'm not actually security here. I was just in the crowd."

"You..." Joe blinked at him, apparently dumbstruck for a second. Then he recovered. "Right. You got a name?"

"Gregori Stearns." Beyond the unusual way he pronounced his first name, with the emphasis on the second syllable making the words sound like Greg*ori* instead of Gregory, there was something familiar about his last name too. Angela's gaze flicked to one of the signs hanging around the inside wall of the stadium. Stearns Pharmaceuticals.

Right. Somehow, she didn't think this guy was the heir of a pharmaceutical fortune.

"Joe, go get the team taken care of," Angela directed as they stepped into the corridor. "I'm going to have to go through the motions of getting checked out by EMTs, though I'm fine. But there's going to be police and media descending on this place in the next ten minutes, if they haven't already shown up. They'll be all over us once the scene is secure. Mr. Stearns, we're staying at the Loews Hotel. If you would like, you could meet us there after the dust clears."

"Wait, what?" Joe swiveled his gaze between Angela and Gregori. Then understanding clicked. "She's right. Especially if you're not security here, you'll be detained and questioned if they can find you. Beat it."

For the barest moment, Gregori met Angela's gaze, his glance so penetrating, she fought not to take a step back. This was a man who could see deep into her very soul, if there'd been anything left for him to see. This was a man she didn't want to know her secrets.

This was a man she yearned to touch her with every breath of her being, to take her into his arms and—

What?

Jerking her glance to the side, she glared at Joe's profile

as Gregori stepped away. When she glanced back, the big man had disappeared into the shadows.

What followed after that was a public relations coup like no other. After Angela was removed to a safe location and secured, she weathered a media storm at close to ground zero of what the press was already calling a domestic terrorist attack. There'd been a total of five fatalities, including two of her men and three other members of the stadium's security detail who'd been guarding the VIP area, and countless injuries. None of the rally mascot dogs had been harmed, she was told. In fact, they'd defended their handler with completely unexpected fury when the attackers had gotten close. The footage of the grateful and hapless young man would be the lead segment on every morning show the next day, Angela was sure.

Everyone agreed that an unnamed man with a security jacket had been instrumental in stopping the attack, but no one knew where he'd gone, and they were waiting for the tape from the surveillance cameras to identify him. Interestingly enough, the several witnesses interviewed all had different ways of describing the man, which struck Angela as something important.

Still, it was another two hours before they were able to make a break for the hotel. There, to her dismay, she found yet more people who wanted to poke and prod at her.

"You need to stop asking me how I'm feeling," Angela growled at one of the doctors, though the man was only trying to do his job. She knew she should be grateful. After the EMTs had fussed over her sufficiently, she'd absolutely, categorically refused medical treatment at the local hospital. Then she'd learned that a medical team was being dispatched with the approval of Governor Filmore to attend to her in her hotel room, no questions asked. The governor of course knowing full well why Angela would never step foot in a hospital, even if she'd caught herself on fire. She wouldn't go anywhere she couldn't leave immediately. She'd never be trapped again.

"You've endured a serious shock," the physician pressed. "These medications—"

"Are unneeded. Thank you," Angela said. "You can take them and give them to someone who's in pain, or I can flush them down the toilet. Your call."

The doctor sighed but didn't push further, and he also didn't ask any more questions. Whether or not the governor had shared with him the particulars of her past, Angela didn't know, but the doctor had probably been given the broad strokes. That was usually all that was necessary.

Joe stepped into the room. "What's their status?" she asked quickly as the doctor turned, referencing her security team. She'd heard nothing of their condition, and it'd already been too long for it to be good news.

But Joe surprised her. "All three recovering in the burn unit at Atlanta General, by some miracle ending up with only second-degree burns. The bullet wounds are through and through as well. They're not going to feel great for a while, but they'll be okay. Eric and Jim were dropped by gunfire, according to the coroner. Any burns were post-mortem. They died instantly."

"Small favors," Angela muttered, her heart twisting. She'd already begun watching the coverage on the news, mostly featuring cell phone footage snapped right as the chaos broke out. Once the real fighting had begun, though, there seemed to be no good video to be found, which, in today's day and age, was almost impossible to believe. "Anyone taking credit yet?"

"That would be no, which has got everyone up in arms

as well. The Democrats want to blame white nationalists and the Republicans want to blame leftist crazies. The police aren't ruling out operators acting for no terror-related purposes at all, just the act of nutters, but even they have to admit the attack was too focused, too well planned for it to be that random. From what little they've been able to recover from the scene, the guns were ceramic and 3-D plastic jobs. Those are notoriously flaky, but with enough of them in play, you're going to hit somebody. They passed through the security checks like water through a sieve. So easily, in fact, that the running theory is that they were planted on-site over the course of several days. There's just no way that many weapons got through stadium security this morning."

"I'm inclined to agree with you," Angela said. She'd been puzzling over that same issue, the kind of puzzle she used to get all the time when she'd been working in the Frost Center think tank and dealing with insurrections and strike team tactics. Ordinarily, she liked to pace and work out the questions aloud, but there'd been no time for that. "The only problem with that explanation is that I hadn't made a decision to go to the rally until this morning. So, was the plan simply to attack any VIP, or could this group have seriously mobilized against me that quickly?" *And why?* That, she felt, was the most important question of all.

Joe blew out a long breath. "Unknown."

"Ma'am." One of her aides stepped into the room, and Angela turned, her entire body tensing with anticipation.

"He's here?" she asked.

"Mr. Stearns entered through the main lobby and was met by our team, who offered him the suite. He took it."

Angela's brows lifted. "Really." Beside her, Joe huffed his surprise as well. She'd expected that to be a fight.

The aide nodded, her own surprise evident. "Yes. He said he was available for the job you needed him for, but only on his terms. He just flat out said that to the staffer downstairs, where anyone could hear."

Angela glanced to the television again, which silently played the few clips of video they were able to salvage from the scene. "I don't think Mr. Stearns worries too much about what other people see and hear," she murmured.

4

Gregori studied the luxurious suite in which he found himself, struggling not to reach out and strangle Michael to death, especially with his boss standing so close to him. He didn't know if he could bring such harm to the archangel, who'd appeared as soon as he'd walked through the hotel room's door, but the more he had to work with Michael one-on-one, the more he was willing to find out.

"How can you not know what's going on here?" Gregori snapped instead. "You're the archangel of *God*."

"And these are God's children," Michael replied, unperturbed. He'd issued a variation of this statement three times already, and it still didn't make any sense. "They have the right of free will and the power to shield me from their thoughts."

"Fifty-dollar psychics can read people's thoughts," Gregori countered. He stopped short of saying that he could read them too. Mostly because it wasn't exactly true. He could feel others' emotions, yes, and he understood their pain as if it were his own, because it was his own. But riding the currents of that pain were generally thoughts and emotions and reactions that helped form the picture of whatever had befallen the unfortunate human to get them into such a state. It wasn't exactly the same as reading thoughts, but it was damned close—and Gregori was a demon of no particular renown. Michael was arguably the highest-ranked angel of God's army, and this wasn't a skill he possessed?

The archangel eyed him dispassionately, not responding to the bait of Gregori's very loud and disrespectful thoughts. A moment later, he continued. "Angela Stanton is a junior congresswoman who has very recently been asked to sit on a highly classified technology research and development committee. This committee is known in certain circles as being instrumental in pushing through legislation and even congressional approval for a series of dark ops and deep state initiatives. She has absolutely no military background, has worked exclusively as an analyst in the public sector and a think tank contributor in the private sector, and she is considered a political neophyte. She's only halfway through her first term and already significantly behind in her fund-raising efforts for reelection."

Gregori caught the archangel's emphasis on this last bit, though it seemed a minor detail. "Why is that important?"

"It implies she has no interest in extending her term as congresswoman. That is, of course, her choice, but it's not an easy thing in most cases to get elected, and for her to have reached her current pinnacle position at such a young age, you would think she would want to hold on to it. But she's taking no steps that would indicate that."

"So how'd she get elected in the first place?"

The archangel smiled, his expression still eerily flat. "A

very good question. One I expect you to ask, as her newest bodyguard."

Gregori made a face. They were back to this again. "I'm telling you this is a dumb idea," he grumbled. "Bodyguards are *not* automatically confidants, and she's already trying to figure out what I am. If she's smart enough to work in a think tank, it's not going to take her all that long to puzzle out the truth, even if she doesn't believe in demons."

"On the contrary. I'm hoping quite sincerely she figures it out almost immediately. I have reason to suspect that the government research being conducted under the auspices of Angela Stanton's committee involves the demon horde."

Gregori curled his lip, but he didn't say anything as the archangel continued. "In fact, I find today's violent demonstration particularly interesting. Congresswoman Stanton was caught completely off guard by a team of assailants that did not kill her, who, in fact, only resorted to gunfire when her security team recognized the threat and started to move her to safety."

Gregori winced. "You think if I hadn't entered the fray, they wouldn't have started shooting, and those people wouldn't have died?"

"Not at all." The archangel's tone was dismissive, and the tightness in Gregori's chest eased. "You're not the instigator of that action. It was due entirely to her security detail not going along quietly. Their alarm and Stanton's alarm were genuine. They were legitimately afraid. Which means a third party wanted to scare her into going along with them or was willing to take her forcibly. Who would want to do that, other than an organization whose own research efforts were being put in jeopardy by the course of Stanton's work in Congress?"

"She's pissed off the wrong people."

"It's the most likely situation. Interestingly, she doesn't realize that she's pissed off the wrong people, to use your terminology. She seems genuinely surprised at being targeted. Her response to both the police and the media was not one of a resolute fighter determined to continue championing her cause. It was a bewildered, horrified reaction to a senseless attack. That's important."

Gregori scowled. "You think she's a stooge," he said gruffly.

"I think it's possible. I think it's also possible that she's not yet been brought in on the full truth of the scheme in which she's becoming embroiled. Which takes us to our second option, which is that this little demonstration was orchestrated by the very people who want Stanton's vote."

"By killing people? That's hardly going to win them favor, especially with a junior congresswoman serving her first term."

"It is if they're trying to urge Stanton to recognize some security threat that US citizens face. If she's frightened, she may vote with her fear. That may have been the goal." The archangel spread his hands. "As you can see, we know so little that we're forced to speculate, and poorly. We need somebody on the inside."

"As a security guard."

"It's the easiest way to ensure your access to the congresswoman, even in delicate situations, without having to give you a complete crash course on American politics. You also tend to stick out, except in a situation requiring security."

Gregori narrowed his eyes. Though every demon had some say in their final glamour, there were elements to that glamour that were beyond their control. In his case, Gregori's sheer size had been accorded to him before he could even fully understand that he'd been transformed from a Fallen angel to a demon. It wasn't a transition that ever went well, and his had been particularly traumatic. But once he'd gotten past his horror, anger, and self-loathing, or mostly gotten past it, anyway, he'd used his size and strength to his advantage. Especially since joining the Syx.

A knock on the door had him turning, even as Michael whisked out of sight, for once not leaving Gregori with parting instructions. Gregori's thoughts were immediately diverted from that, however, as the door lock snicked open electronically and his room was breached. Who the hell had such easy access to his room?

Then again, he was a demon. It wasn't as if the humans could hurt him.

Right?

He stood at attention as a man and a woman in crisp military attire stepped inside his room, followed by Congresswoman Stanton.

Oh...no.

Gregori's knees nearly buckled.

Clenching his hands tight against the sudden, heart-wrenching surge of emotion that pounded him from all directions, he forced himself to keep his expression neutral. Sucking in a quick, choked breath, he desperately strove to clamp down his instant and confounding reaction and concentrate objectively on the woman in front of him.

No small task, given the roar of blood thundering in his ears.

Focus.

Angela Stanton was a deceptively ordinary female, tall and fit, with dark hair, blue eyes, and fair skin. The kind of woman who'd blend into any crowd, especially in the low-key gray sweater and trousers she currently wore. But her eyes set her apart. They weren't merely blue, they were a light ice blue that seemed a little too pale for her skin coloring, a little too hard, a little too knowing. They arrested your attention and drew you close, but not too close. The congresswoman would always put on the proper appearance, Gregori suspected, but there was an unquestionable reserve she carried about her person. It was completely at odds with the type of optics-obsessed media courting that was necessary to stage a successful political career. So why was she in politics? Who had gotten her there?

More to the point...what was it about her that pulled at Gregori so fiercely? It was all he could do not to cross the room and take her in his arms. She was attractive, certainly, but humans held no allure for him. Her spirit was strong and vulnerable at once, but how many of God's children had he encountered in the past six millennia who could claim the same? She was smart, capable, and shimmering with barely controlled pain, and...

And she flat out took his breath away.

Here, in this hotel room bare hours after her life was put in terrible danger, Angela Stanton stood with consummate ease, clearly prepared to execute some cool and calculated agenda she'd already constructed in her mind. Yet all Gregori wanted to do was roar with mindless, primal need and rip apart the entire seething demon horde who'd dared to try to kidnap her.

What was going *on*?

Behind Angela Stanton, Joe Reynolds bustled in, scowling as he waved the other guards back. "Stand down, stand down," he muttered before he met Gregori's gaze. The human's eyes immediately brightened. He seemed to physically restrain himself from bolting across the room and hugging Gregori, but his smile told the story well enough.

"You saved my men, Mr. Stearns. I don't know how, they don't know how, but that doesn't change the truth. I owe you everything for your efforts today."

The fact that he made this declaration in front of his congresswoman was a testament to the man's emotions, which struck Gregori like a rolling tide, finally shaking him free of his Angela Stanton thrall. He refocused on Joe, for once welcoming the pain of extreme human sentiment. After so many millennia serving mortals in the direst circumstances imaginable, he had learned to gird himself against the flow of ordinary human feelings. It was only when he was mired in a crowd in the midst of mass hysteria or handling a human whose grief was a keening cry that he felt flayed alive. Still, it wasn't easy managing any intense emotion, and there was no questioning Joe's loyalty to his men.

"I'm sorry for your loss of the other two," Gregori said, dipping his head slightly.

Joe straightened. "They were good men. Eric didn't have much in the way of family, but Jim did, and they'll be taken care of. That's all a man can ask for in our line of work."

The words were simple, quiet, but they struck Gregori with unexpected force, and this time, he did grimace, taking back a step as he physically absorbed the spear of human emotion that Joe had unwittingly thrown at him. The mortal believed his words through and through, and the image that attended them was unmistakable—Congresswoman Stanton.

Gregori refused to look at her, but he didn't need to. At this point, her essence had practically been imprinted on his soul. Nevertheless, he refocused on what he knew about the congresswoman.

According to the archangel, in addition to being a highly

skilled problem solver whose mental acuity was noted first at the college level, then the CIA, and then at a multinational consulting organization that styled itself as a market research think tank, Angela Stanton had also been a shrewd investor for the past ten years. Regardless of whatever insurance she carried, Gregori suspected she had personal funds to take care of the family of the fallen security guard. The fact that it was a foregone conclusion to Joe that Angela *would* take care of her own spoke more about the woman than any glossy campaign flyers ever would.

As if she was the one reading him, Angela spoke. "You told one of my aides that you wanted to take the job that I had to offer, but we haven't discussed any of the details of that job. How do you know I don't need an extra cook?"

Startled, Gregori shot a glance to her, only to find her studying him intently. He quickly allowed his gaze to slip past her and fix on the far window. "The better question should be, why are you willing to hire me without checking out my credentials? For all you know, I could be a plant, solely positioned at that rally to take advantage of your moment of weakness."

"Covered that already." Joe spoke up, waving his cell phone. "You keep a low profile, Mr. Stearns, but I have contacts of contacts, and they have contacts too. Took me a minute, but when the information started coming in, it was rock solid. Military service, contract NGO security, and some freelance work—not to mention some super questionable time with an organization called DEM Enforcement. Can't say I've ever heard of that group, which scares me a little bit."

Gregori lifted his brows. Though the members of the Syx rarely needed its help, Michael the Archangel's earthbound affiliate organization, the Arcana Council, boasted a sizable network of connections worldwide and had a computer genius on staff. Clearly that genius had been put to work this morning to set up Gregori's fake identity.

"I think it's safe to say that if you ever have to hear about DEM Enforcement, you're not in very good shape. So it's just as well you're not familiar." Gregori lifted a hand to rub his jaw. "Can't say that I've ever put that work on any of my résumés, though."

Joe cackled and waved his phone again, clearly pleased with his research work. "And I'm telling you, you don't work as long as I have in this industry without making some friends in both high and low places. Bottom line, we're good."

"So what would the work entail?" Gregori asked.

Angela's energy changed just slightly, alerting Gregori to the fact she was about to lie in some way as she began speaking. "As you know all too well, I've lost nearly my entire security team today, so we'll be gearing up on a couple of different fronts. But I assure you, I don't expect today's excitement to be a regular occurrence. Most of the time, Joe's bored out of his mind. I'll need you to accompany me to press events, steak dinners, traveling back and forth through Washington as needed, especially for the next little while until this all dies down. You're going to attract some attention because of your size, but I don't mind that so much. After today, I want people to have to think twice before they use my presence as an excuse to harm people."

Joe sighed. "Angela, it's not your fault," he said quietly, and she shook her head.

"It's close enough to my fault that it doesn't really matter," she replied, her voice clipped. "There's absolutely nothing that I'm working on that should have occasioned this kind of response. And I am not a touchstone for most hate groups. I'm very aware of my privilege and I'm grateful for the safety that has accorded me, but I am exactly what I appear to be: middle-class, overeducated, fortunate."

Gregori didn't miss Joe's eye roll, but Angela's attention remained focused on him. "Are you available right away?"

As if compelled, he met her gaze, and something shifted in his chest, hard and deep. He could barely breathe for a long, harrowing moment, but Angela blinked and glanced away first.

"I can start this second," he said.

5

A ngela waited for the security guard to scan her and Gregori, then continued down the walkway toward the nondescript series of conference rooms where she typically met with the members of the House Disaster and Defense Technology Committee. Like everything else in her freshman year as a representative, she'd been surprised to be tapped to join the committee, but she'd wasted no time saying yes. She'd waited for weeks after accepting the position to get some clue as to who had recommended her to the position, but no one had come forward. No one had called her phone, then mysteriously hung up after breathing heavily either, or eyed her oddly in the House cafeteria.

So she'd begun attending meetings, reading all the endless reports on the technological underpinning of federal disaster relief efforts and domestic terrorism defense case studies, while her mind remained on absolute overdrive to figure out the mysterious benefactor who was guiding her so obviously on this track. In truth, it was the obviousness of her positioning that made it the most intriguing. It wasn't a question of whether her suspicions were correct, it was only how long it would take until the next shoe dropped. And whether that shoe would be a stiletto or a steel-toed boot.

As he had since their first outing, Gregori walked a half step behind her. He'd assured her from the get-go that his best location would be behind her, not before or even to the side, because he could see what was coming toward her on three sides, while no one would approach from behind without him sensing it. She hadn't believed him at first, but a few run-throughs with Joe had quickly changed her mind. Gregori seemed to have eyes in the back of his head, and his speed in moving to her side to protect her from a flanking or frontal attack was astounding. He'd even managed to block Joe's laser-strike-simulated sniper hits, though he refused to wear Kevlar. She'd eventually stood down on that request. The assailants from the rally had never taken a shot at her. She decided it was statistically unlikely they'd do so if they approached her a second time.

They reached the outer lobby of the cluster of conference rooms where her committee met. There were already a half-dozen security personnel there, standing or sitting throughout the room. Not every congressperson felt the need to have twenty-four seven security, and before this week, Angela hadn't either. It seemed a little self-important to her, but she couldn't deny she felt more secure with Gregori on the team and with her people dogging her heels on the regular. Though no one realized it, not even Joe, the way the intruders at the rally had *moved* frightened her on nearly a soul-deep level, and she didn't know why. She'd endured far worse than being accosted by a group of thugs with guns. But something about these particular thugs had been...odd. Unnatural. And eerily familiar.

"You'll be okay here?" she asked as Gregori scanned the room. "I'll be in conference room B the whole time. Meetings can last up to three hours, or at least that's been the longest so far."

He grunted his assent. "No other exits?"

"No. If we need to use the restroom or take a call, we come through here. There's no Wi-Fi or anything available except for on a secured network." She grimaced. "I'm afraid it's going to feel like you're waiting an eternity out here."

A wry smile ghosted across Gregori's face. "I suspect not. Is there any threat from the people on your committee?"

Angela pursed her lips, considering the question. "It's a fair concern, but no. No weapons are allowed through security, no electronics. All documentation is strictly paper. I mean, someone could shiv me with a ballpoint pen, but they'd still have to escape through here."

"The guns at the rally made it through security," Gregori observed mildly.

"True, but our security is a little more exact here—fewer people come through these halls, any one of whom could turn out to be a deep-planted terrorist. That tends to make people pay more attention." She opened her leather bag and pulled out a thick file. "Here. I figured you might need some light reading while you were waiting."

She handed the file over, and Gregori took it. She noticed he wasn't wearing gloves. Immediately, she cataloged the instance in her running tally of his actions and behaviors. She'd thought at first he wore gloves constantly whenever they were out in public, but she'd amended that generality. It seemed he only wore gloves when they would be spending an inordinate amount of time in a truly public space, particularly one in which there was a guarantee of a lot of people. Walking through the park, for instance, or crossing the National Mall. Since it was June and the tourists were out in force, all the public areas of Washington, DC were particularly crowded. Angela had made a point of being seen outside as much as possible, underscoring her lack of concern about any further targeting by terrorists or whatever they were calling the assailants at the rally. Every time she did, Gregori had worn gloves.

But he wasn't wearing gloves now and typically didn't any time they were predominantly inside the Capitol building or meeting in places like this, where the flow of humanity dropped to a mere trickle. She'd noticed he didn't wear gloves during the execution of random errands or when touching weapons or food, though she hadn't seen him eat much. The sunbaked metal or leather of her limo didn't make him flinch either. Which meant that it was exclusively human contact he wanted to avoid. Which was...interesting.

"Ms. Stanton?"

She looked up and realized that Randall Severin, a senior congressman who'd chaired the committee for the past six years, was solicitously holding the door open for her. She smiled, barely catching Gregori's rumble of concern as she turned from him.

She glanced back. "What?"

"Nothing," he said, shaking his head. His expression remained neutral, open, so there would be no reason for Randall to feel judged, but Angela's neck prickled at the tone of Gregori's voice. "I get a sense of people sometimes, part of the job. He serves many different masters."

She lifted her brows. "Most politicians do, sad to say. We'll talk more when you've read through everything, okay? I value your opinion."

She didn't miss the surprise in Gregori's quick glance,

but she knew enough not to hold his gaze. For one thing, she couldn't police her own reactions when she met his eyes. Invariably, her heart rate increased, her face flushed, and her hands trembled for no good reason. But beyond that, meeting Gregori's eyes truly seemed to unsettle the man. She added that piece of information to her mental log as well. Perhaps he was on the autism spectrum? She'd never heard of a high-functioning military veteran with autistic tendencies, but that didn't mean one didn't exist. In fact, it would be an interesting discussion to see...

She shook herself as she moved toward Randall Severin, trim and somber in his well-cut suit and wing-tipped shoes, his crisp salt-and-pepper hair the perfect complement to his aristocratic, weathered face. She needed to stay focused on the issue at hand. "Randall."

"Angela. I'm so glad you're safe."

She murmured her thanks as he stepped back to let her enter the conference room. She'd heard a version of these sentiments many times over the last several days, Republicans and Democrats alike wanting to know the details of her assault. She saw a similar interest in the two other members of their committee, who both immediately started talking, each asking the same question in different ways.

"I don't know much more than what you've seen on TV," Angela said, raising her hands to cut them off. "Honestly, I can't imagine why I was targeted. There's been no follow-up, no credible party taking responsibility. There's nothing in my electronic trail of emails or social media notifications—and they've found no trace of the assailants, although it's obvious that some were taken down during the melee. It makes no sense."

"It damn well doesn't make sense," Randall said, taking

his seat at the head of the table. "We've all gotten calls about it."

Angela blinked, glancing first to Trudy Behns, a senior-ranking Democrat, and her unofficial mentor, then back to Randall. "You have?"

"You bet we have," Trudy answered for Randall, her broad Midwestern accent pitched with unusual strength, as if she was stumping on the campaign trail. Her bluff, open face, clear gray eyes, and no-nonsense helmet of dark brown hair came across as sensible and frank to her constituents—and oddly comforting to Angela. "Randall here, like the good Republican he is, is using it to strengthen his platform on international security threats. While Bob is playing the middle line, like he always does, waiting to see which way the wind blows before laying down his cards."

Bob Minnick chuckled. "And you've been squawking about gun control, rightfully enough," he said, his gentle tone taking any sting out of the words. Of all of them, he looked the most like what he was: a Southern gentleman with pale, rounded features, a body going only slightly to fat in his middle years, who probably was as comfortable on a porch drinking sweet tea as he was in this conference room. "Members of Congress get targeted. It's part of the job. But they don't often get targeted in such a strange way."

Angela sat up in her chair, unable to fully contain her relief. "So I'm not the only one who noticed how...weird it all was."

Trudy waved her hand. "I had my people on it as soon as I heard what'd happened, and Randall, I know you did too. They confirmed what you obviously already know, Angela. You didn't have that stop on your agenda until that morning. There's simply no way that some aggressor cell was able to mobilize that quickly and get people and weapons in place in a matter of hours through arguably tight security. I'm not saying it was the best security in the world, but we've all been doing this long enough that it was probably pretty good. So for some group to stage that deadly a demonstration and then just go poof? There's something more going on here, and nobody seems to have any answers. Not the local police, not our contacts within military intelligence, no one. There's been zero chatter from any of the usual suspects, and I don't like it."

"I pulled in a couple of favors as well to try to get to the bottom of it," Randall agreed, leaning forward. "The incident is attracting more attention than an ordinary strike, which is telling in and of itself. But I can only get so far and then everybody goes tight-lipped. And believe me, I've been around long enough that I'm not usually the guy they go tight-lipped on."

Angela nodded, hiding her surprise at Randall's candor. The Republican committee leader had always treated her with more respect than she honestly felt she deserved as such a junior member of this committee, but it wasn't as if he'd expressed any partiality toward her. On Randall's other side, Bob leaned back in his chair, swiveling slightly, a habit of his that betrayed his agitation.

"You want to know what I think is the most interesting part of all this? The terrible video," Bob said, his fingers rapping the table for emphasis. "We've all been caught on video so many times, you'd think we were Hollywood celebrities. You just can't avoid it. Phones are everywhere. And they were everywhere at that truck rally, I've got to believe. But have you seen any of it on TV or streaming on the web? No, you have not. Which, to me, says EMP."

"EMP?" Trudy was the one who spoke the word aloud, but Angela turned too. That was *not* what she expected Bob to say in his deep, gentle Southern drawl. "What are you talking about?"

"Something affected every electronic transmission going on at the time," Bob insisted. "We've got reports of the speaker system shorting out, then coming back online. We've got lights flickering while those godforsaken internal fireworks went off for the rally. We've got a couple of minutes of nothing. Then, all of a sudden, flash bang, we've got assailants and a whole hell of a lot of people taking video that mysteriously got scrambled. Hell, no two audience groups are even reporting the same things, to hear the police talk. It goes beyond typical eyewitness screwups to genuine outright confusion. Deliberate confusion, undoubtedly, because what they saw and what their phones *said* they saw are two different things. That doesn't smell right to me."

Angela blew out a long breath. Bob's theory wasn't as far-fetched as it might seem. "Well, I hate to speculate along these lines, but Bob does have a point. There was a project we worked on, a theoretical construct only, at the Frost Center. It posited the viability of a localized electromagnetic pulse device that wasn't intended to take down an entire network or grid, but merely to disrupt the flow of electricity within a highly defined space."

"To what end?" Trudy asked.

"To bypass security, largely," Angela said. "Which is why I didn't really think of it until now for this situation. Security had already been compromised at the rally. Gunmen were on-site. The only effect of a pulse in this situation would be to obscure the actions of the assailants, which, again, doesn't make sense. They were quite successful in inciting panic, and their assault was deadly. They were all wearing masks as well, so the inference is that they anticipated being recorded or at least seen."

She tapped her chin, her gaze drifting to the far wall, mapping out the logistics. She couldn't pace, but she still spoke aloud, and that was enough to order her thoughts. "I definitely was the target. We were cornered at the end, and two of my men died during that assault, while three others were injured. If security hadn't arrived when it did..." She let the words play out unstated, but that was more for self-protection than any attempt at drama. For all that she'd gotten a weird, eerie feeling of familiarity from these assailants, there was nothing to attach them to the men and women who'd assaulted her all those years ago when she was still a child.

Angela didn't like thinking of that experience—she prided herself on functioning incredibly well despite having endured that experience, in fact. But there was no denying she still had long-standing side effects from that event she couldn't quite shake. Her captivity in the metal crate had lasted eighty-seven days, she'd learned later. In some ways, she'd never quite come out of that box.

But despite the downsides, which were legion, there *had* been some positive outcomes from her childhood trial. Angela had developed the ability to compartmentalize and mask her emotions, as well as conceive and strategize in four dimensions. During her trips to and from her cage, she had mapped out and discarded hundreds of escape routes. It was this ability to focus on how she could escape from the chamber she had only known as the torture room that had helped her cope with her return to normal life. So had her resilience and resourcefulness.

Ultimately, it was the execution of plan #316 that had resulted in her eventual escape, a plan that had devolved into a series of pieces of other discarded strategies when her original calculations proved inaccurate. By then, she'd been able to create alternate solutions on the fly. She almost hadn't made it, but she'd a plan for that outcome as well. It sometimes shook her how close she'd come to enacting her final termination plan without remorse or emotion. And she'd been only eight years old.

Now she leaned forward, the lines of data in her mind connecting in ways she hadn't previously anticipated before Bob's suggestion triggered a whole new pattern, a pattern that seemed so obvious on the surface, it was strange she hadn't figured it out herself.

"This was a dry run," she said, her words sharp and certain. "Anyone prominent at that rally would have sufficed. The goal was ideally to extract the target at gunpoint and sow confusion and chaos. After that, I suspect we'd have been contacted—or some other committee, some other lawmaker would have been. They got the confusion part down, just not the extraction."

"Which means they'll do it again," Trudy said crisply.

"Which means they'll do it again," Angela agreed. She slid her glance to Randall. "You were right, Randall, to pound the pulpit on terror threats. Because unless I miss my guess, they're not going to wait long to get our attention another way."

6

G regori closed the file and settled against the wall, mentally reviewing the reports Angela had provided him. He could feel her energy straight through the wall. She and the others might not normally find their agenda given over to one long fraught discussion on a single topic, but that was definitely the case today. The emotions rolling from the room hadn't varied in their intensity since the opening words were spoken. Anxiety, anger, confusion, fearful doubt... But what disturbed Gregori most was how none of it included the kind of calculation or edginess that humans typically employed when they were being cagey. These politicians all believed themselves on the side of angels, which was particularly ironic given that they were up against demons.

But if none of them were in on the attempt on Angela, how did they figure into this? From everything the archangel had told him and the inference in the typed documents Angela herself had compiled for her file, the junior congresswoman's role on that committee had been arranged at a very high level. She'd detailed the timeline of her role in government with what seemed to be complete candor from the moment she'd first had an unexpected run-in with a local Democratic party official while she'd been eating at a café in Atlanta near the Frost Center's offices. The woman had asked quite generally about Angela's work, then proceeded to float the idea of Angela running for office.

It'd been so out of the blue that Angela had rejected the idea out of hand. The woman had gone off, and Angela hadn't thought anything more about it for another several weeks. The next time had happened at an event at Georgia Governor Martin Filmore's house, where he mentioned the possibility of her getting into politics as well. There was a seat coming open in the district where Angela lived, as it turned out. In the governor's view, the politicians vying for it were ill-informed extremists who were already in trouble with the national party for their incendiary comments.

Given Angela's family connections—her parents were long-time friends of the governor, and her father had worked for the man during her college years, after he and his wife had retired early—Angela hadn't felt comfortable simply laughing off the suggestion this time. She'd agreed to think about it.

That was all it had taken to set the wheels of power in motion. Within a few short weeks, Angela had found herself with a campaign committee, a fund-raising arm, and even policy planks listed out on a professionally created website. When she'd been asked point-blank by the media, she'd announced her run—and papers had been drawn up and delivered for her to sign, everything made as easy as possible. She'd recorded all this as if she was watching it happen from afar. It hadn't been the first time Gregori had gotten this impression about the nature of Angela's interaction with the world. She seemed almost withdrawn, hidden away, and of course, he could understand that sentiment too well.

But someone was forcing her involvement now.

He recalled her assessment of the recent committee documents she'd been asked to review. It was all very high-level, omitting any confidential information, but after a few entries, Gregori had to agree with Angela that her committee was, well...boring. There was nothing in the paperwork she'd been given to suggest that any sort of legislation would be coming to this particular committee that would tally with Michael's suggestion of a dark ops operation or deep state conspiracy. Yes, this committee was given over to concerns of federally funded high-tech security and defense programs at the state and local levels, but it mostly seemed to be the repository of every report ever made in a postcrisis action review. As a demon, Gregori didn't need sleep, but the descriptions of what Angela typically reviewed while sitting in committee damned near put him into a coma.

His keen hearing picked up voices lifting and chairs moving as the committee members finally stood, and Gregori straightened as the door to conference room B opened. Angela exited, her manner brighter, almost eager, her mind fully engaged—and Gregori watched her with renewed interest. A second conference room emptied at the same time, and the politicians all seemed to know each other. Their shared energy felt ordinary, uncharged except for Angela's heightened interest, and once again, Gregori got the impression that these committee conference rooms were not where the problem was. They should be, but they weren't.

What was he missing?

"I don't have anything until six p.m., so we might as well

go back to my condo," Angela said after she broke free of the knot of politicians.

"Is that your typical schedule?" he asked.

She eyed him with some surprise. "On committee days, yes. Why? Do you think I should vary it? There's been no untoward interest in me in the past four days since the attack at the rally. I don't believe I was specifically targeted. I was just handy."

He nodded, letting that go for the moment. He couldn't exactly tell the woman that the archangel of God had tipped him off about her security needs. Not yet, anyway. "Do you need any materials at your home? If you went somewhere else, would you be missing anything you need to work?"

"No..." She narrowed her eyes. "But I see what you're doing, and I'm going to overrule you. Joe's been taking prime on my home security. It's solid. My condo's in one of the newest, safest buildings in DC, and I chose it specifically for that reason. Plus, it's not like I'm alone there. I assure you my security there is very...noisy."

He didn't miss her emphasis on the word, but he pressed on. "You learned about it from the governor of Georgia, right?"

She lifted her brows. "Governor Filmore had heard of it being completed after I won the election, yes. But it wasn't the only place he recommended, just the one that best fit my particular needs. Why?"

Their conversation ended as they repeated the process to go through security. Gregori alerted the limo driver to come around to pick Angela and himself up, noting they had already switched out the vehicle for an SUV at his request. It was slightly more noticeable than most of the other town cars, but its size made his bulk much easier to manage and also positioned him higher, the better to survey traffic. He made no more objection to their destination, but the closer they got to Angela's DC condominium, the more nervous he felt, until they turned into the parking circle and his anxiety was running at a fever pitch.

Then he realized it wasn't *his* emotions he was feeling.

His gaze shot to the driver, but the man's jitters were based entirely on the level of caffeine coursing through his system after three hours of waiting at a coffee shop. Angela was going through messages on her oversized phone, resigned over whatever she was reading but not alarmed, which left only one other option. The anxiety was coming from whoever they were approaching.

He scanned the walkers on the sidewalk ahead, including those clustered around the entrance to Angela's building.

"Keep driving," he ordered the driver, who jerked his gaze to the rearview mirror, his eyes widening.

"What?" the man asked as Angela glanced up. Then her gaze skimmed by him and fell on a couple standing by the front doors of the condominium building, consulting their phones. "What in the world...? Stop the car."

"Angela—"

"Those are my *parents*, Gregori. What are they—" She pounded on the back of the driver's seat. "Stop!"

Her words were so authoritative, the man braked, and Angela was out the door before Gregori could move. A six-thousand-year-old demon, and he couldn't stop one impulsive human? Why had Michael ever assigned him to this job?

He exited the SUV as Angela embraced a stately older couple who greeted her, all smiles. They were exactly what he expected her parents to be—tall, patrician, upper middle class, modestly but expensively dressed in summer-weight clothes well suited to the heat of DC. The man swung away from Angela and lifted his hand in greeting—not to Gregori, but to somebody just beyond him, across the street.

And as he moved, Gregori realized the truth.

The man standing in front of him—Angela's father—was not human, not entirely, anyway. The demon possessing him was doing so with a sophistication Gregori had never seen before. Her mother was similarly possessed, both of the creatures seemingly directed by remote control, their demonic nature subverted beneath a crackle of electrical impulses. And as the possessed couple chatted merrily with Angela, they positioned their daughter with a full-frontal exposure to the building across the street.

Gregori dove in front of Angela exactly as the gunfire started, a strafing run that didn't spare her parents. There were screams, Angela's screams mostly, as all three of them fell to the ground, but she hadn't been wrong about the quality of security in the building. The front doors shot open, and two armed men and an armed woman ran out, one returning a *rat-a-tat-tat* of gunfire that sounded almost real, but Gregori suspected wasn't. More likely it was intended to scare away the gunmen without causing further loss of life.

The guards descended on the trio of Angela and her parents and pulled them inside the building. Gregori immediately felt the demon presence shrink back within the couple, whether the beasts were overridden by their fear and pain or they'd somehow been ordered to stand down.

He scanned the concrete building, noting the bullet holes, then pivoted and glared. He could almost see, almost sense...

"Stearns, you're hit. Jesus." Joe was at his side, having exited the building from his interior station after no doubt securing Angela and her parents. But Joe was good to have here. He could watch and protect Angela.

"Don't leave her side," Gregori ordered.

Then he took off across the street.

He knew instantly he was on the right track as the scramble of emotions inside the building he was running toward burst into chaotic frenzy. The structure opposite Angela's condo had a series of storefronts on the first floor, then offices above. It was also teeming with people. Based on the trajectory of the shot, the sniper had to have been positioned in a high floor, probably the top floor... No. No, he'd been on the roof.

Gregori didn't hesitate. He dashed down the next alley, and when he got a scant thirty feet away from the crossing street, he started climbing. He couldn't fully relinquish his human glamour in case anyone should happen to catch sight of him, but he scaled the wall as if he was scrambling up a ladder. Mortal constructs were never a barrier to his kind.

Demons weren't without their weaknesses, of course. You could capture and hold nearly any demon with magic, and you could outright kill a demon with the power of God at your back. But you couldn't contain a demon with traditional bars or walls. The traps needed to snare a demon were far too complex and arcane for ordinary mortals.

But something or someone *was* trapping the demon shooters here. They'd stopped firing and retreated, but he didn't sense that they'd gone.

He flung himself over the edge of the roof. Sirens rang out in the distance, indicating a police response to the shooting was already underway. Ordinarily, in the wake of most demon attacks, there'd be nothing left to see.

Only, here, there was. Three demons stood at the far side

of the roof, clearly held in place, their agonized and furious faces shifting in and out of their glamour. Just as with the beasts who'd possessed Angela's parents, something was controlling these demons. But who could *control* a demon, other than a witch? And why would she be using her magic to enable demons to possess humans, which most witches considered anathema? It made no sense.

As Gregori's mind churned, he was assaulted by the demons' emotions, a chittering cacophony of fear, confusion, hate, loathing, and recognition of what he was. These demons hadn't been brought here to be attacked by a Syx. They'd been brought here to shoot humans and flee. But the hand behind these demons remained hidden, holding them fast for some reason.

Not a witch, Gregori decided, or at least not *only* a witch. Witches could summon demons to do their bidding, but there was no spell of a traditional sort on these creatures. The restraint here was far more sophisticated in its style. Almost...almost electrical.

Gregori quickly traversed the rooftop, advancing on the trapped creatures. "Why are you here?" he ground out, realizing his mistake too late. These demons were still armed. In his quest to understand what was going on, Gregori wasn't racing to dispatch them, he was slowing down. As he did, all three of them raised their guns and fired.

Fury exploded through Gregori along with the bullets piercing his body. With a howl of rage and pain, he dove at the demons, realizing that only one of their number was a true demon, while the other two were possessed humans that'd been so far degraded that the human hosts were nothing but smoke, a husk no longer good for anything but sustaining the demon within it. The possessed mortals he dropped, though they were still waving their guns. The third he wrenched forward, never mind the blood pouring from the demon's nose and mouth. The outward manifestation of bodily damage to the demon's glamour would be enough to give any human pause, but Gregori needed information.

"Who sent you?" he demanded as the demon's lips peeled back, revealing long canine teeth in a deep red mouth. The demon gave another manic laugh, but he couldn't quite escape Gregori's gaze as the bullets started up again. It was only a momentary flash of revelation, but it was all that Gregori needed.

The demons had been summoned by a witch...but held by human technology.

He yanked the demon to the side and sent him sprawling across the rooftop, where he exploded into black goop as Gregori blasted him across the veil.

He fell on the two possessed men, but to his surprise, they were dead, bullet holes riddling their bodies. It was as if at the last minute, they'd given up on shooting him and instead had shot each other. Something about that bothered Gregori on a profoundly deep level, but he had no time to work it out.

He needed to get back to Angela.

He turned, but immediately stumbled, going down on his knees. Something... There'd been something in those bullets, something wrong. Or...maybe it wasn't the bullets, maybe it was the same energy that had trapped the other demons? Was he encountering a force field of some sort that limited his abilities? Had he simply been lured into a trap?

A brief, blinding flash of pain erupted between his ears and lit along every nerve ending in his body, making him howl. He lifted his hands to his ears and clamped down, trying to make the noise stop, but the voices continued, clamoring and raging and screeching at a level only he could hear, effectively fixing him in place. *So it's witches after all,* he thought grimly. Unreasonably powerful ones, using an ancient antidemon tool to drive their quarry to madness. Good to know.

Feet pounded toward him, and Gregori glanced up, bleary-eyed, to see a line of uniformed men rushing his way, guns up. For a split second, he thought they were going to attack him, but they raced by him to where the demons fell first, then circled back.

"You're Gregori Stearns?" the man in front asked, presumably the squad's leader.

"Yes," Gregori gasped as he finally shut down the howling voices in his mind, cutting them off completely.

"How the hell did you get up here? It's four floors."

Gregori grunted a laugh as he staggered back to his feet. "Climbed."

"Well, we will have to get you back down if you can walk. We've got a situation."

7

I t took them another fifteen minutes to get back down through the building, using more conventional means of travel—namely, stairs and elevators. As he moved, Gregori healed himself as best as he was able. The glamour was the easiest part, but also the part that needed to remain at least reasonably damaged in appearance. Healing his deformed demon body beneath took more energy, and he didn't have to feign his heaviness of breathing or grimace of pain as the security guards from Angela's condo building stopped to allow him to lean against the wall and catch his second wind.

Still, by the time he was back out on the street, he was walking more or less upright, which was more than he could say for the demons he'd dispatched. *Bastards.*

"What's the problem?" he wheezed. He knew it wasn't Angela. With her as his charge, he'd have felt her pain in the very marrow of his bones if she'd been harmed.

"Ms. Stanton's parents," the guard nearest to him said. "They've barricaded themselves in the corner of the lobby, won't let anyone near, and are screaming their heads off.

We're this close to tranquing them with darts just to get someone close to them without causing them greater psychological stress, but—hey. No. You can't go in there like that! *Stop!*"

Gregori wasn't listening anymore. He'd already picked up speed as the man started talking, and breached the doors to Angela's building a second later, never mind that he didn't bother opening them. He simply crashed through.

The scene in the lobby of a ring of people gaping in horror at Angela's parents was one he'd seen far too many times before, particularly in the Middle Ages when, for whatever reason, fear of demons had surged to an all-time high, particularly in Europe. Possessions had become almost commonplace then, causing havoc in villages and cities alike. The demon enforcers had been almost as busy then as they were now, and their work had been made easy for them by the fear the demons engendered. With fewer people, a less structured society, and a broader willingness to believe in the skills of strangers, the enforcers could usually do their work and be gone in a matter of seconds.

That wouldn't be possible here, but he'd work with what he was given. Angela's parents were huddled on the floor in their fashionable clothes, their legs crumpled beneath them, their fists up to their ears. He'd seen this reaction many times, though usually only *after* he'd identified the demon within the human host, a demon desperately trying to figure out how to escape without getting blasted beyond the veil.

In this case, however, Gregori wasn't here on a simple search-and-destroy mission. Not with Angela standing off to the side, watching with wide, horrified eyes, while her face remained carefully, painfully neutral. Too neutral.

Gregori strode forward, shaking off the security guards

and a man in a dress shirt and pants who exuded the air of being a doctor. Even Angela moved forward, attempting to block him. He lifted a hand and she stopped, clearly startled.

"I've done this before," he said.

She nodded, her mouth opening though no words came out, then Gregori pushed past her, focusing on her parents. On their knees, they keened in pain. Gregori opened himself up to the extremity of their emotion. He could feel their shock at everything happening to them as a tiny subset of the very real rage that racketed around inside their minds.

They were possessed, all right, but this possession had gone very, very wrong.

Typically, a demonic possession was a one-to-one proposition. A mortal makes the mistake of opening the door too wide to outside influence, or perhaps they are simply too weak or downtrodden to resist. The connection is made, the demon slips in, and the edges grow a little darker for the human every day. Getting the demon out takes an extraordinary effort on the part of the mortal, or, more often, the intervention of a stronger external entity, such as an exorcist or your friendly neighborhood demon enforcer. All the demon has to do is make sure the human stays alive. If the human host dies, the demon gets booted back beyond the veil. Not a good situation for the demon.

But in the case of the Stantons, this demon possession had a decidedly metallic aftertaste, and there was more than one beast apiece in their bodies. Hence the demons' ability to control the Stantons so thoroughly...but also the chaos once the demons realized they were trapped inside humans who were getting shot at.

Now, far worse, they faced a demon enforcer.

With one glance at the Stantons' rolling eyes, Gregori could identify the creatures inside them as if they were old friends. "*Shemael, Barzac, Mithra,*" he murmured to Angela's mother. Her father quailed back, his eyes peeling wide, and in them, Gregori saw all he needed. "*Mortain, Rickmalid, Zehim.*"

The demons shifted within the Stantons like coiled snakes ready to spring. These creatures were not former Fallen. They'd been born in the primordial evil that had been the unnatural afterbirth of the Father's glorious creation of the universe, and they were once and forever demons. So unlike those dark creatures who walked the earth in punishment, these walked in prideful glory that God so loved His creations that He wouldn't destroy a single demon out of hand, even though *they* did their level best to harm His most blessed of all creations, His children.

Now Gregori spoke to these demons directly, with the compulsion the archangel's blessing afforded him.

"Who are you beholden to?" He asked the question in sighing, rustling words, the sounds of wings upon the wind.

"*Borast! Menneilah. Zenoth. Ankar!*" they cried back at once. Of course, all the names were different. Gregori was not surprised. Whoever had coordinated this possession clearly hadn't informed these demons of what was to befall them. Which was unfortunate, because it indicated a level of planning that went far beyond anything the archangel had suspected. So Gregori let the answers go while filing the names carefully in the back of his mind, just in case they weren't total fabrications.

"What was your charge?" he tried again.

Once again, the response was fast and furious. At least in

this, the answers made sense. They were to guide the Stantons to Washington to see their daughter. There was nothing more important than that. They were not to make the Stantons do or say anything out of the ordinary, simply go to DC and meet their daughter in front of her condominium building. They'd been loitering in the area all morning, waiting for Angela to return home. Because that was her parents' expectation. Angela always came home.

Gregori grimaced. He was going to have to talk to Angela about her habits. He was going to have to talk to her about a lot of things.

"Then what?" he asked, bracing himself for another cacophony of responses. Only, the demons fell silent. They'd been given no guidance about what was supposed to happen after this pinnacle meeting. They'd only known they needed to make it happen. There was no joy within these creatures, none of the smug pride that typically accompanied a successful possession. Because the demons had not chosen the terms of this act; they'd been forced. They'd been thrust into the Stantons with almost the same level of violation the Stantons had experienced. Almost.

"You cannot remain within them. You cannot remain without," Gregori rumbled, turning over a problem in his mind. By all rights, he should return these demons beyond the veil as soon as he extracted them from the Stantons' minds. Leaving them to roam this earth was a liability, not only to other humans but to the demons themselves. They were supposed to die this day. Trapped inside their mortal hosts who were to have been gunned down in front of their own daughter, these demons had been intended to be a sacrifice offered by whoever was behind this attack. Gregori didn't know if that individual was human or demon, but that hardly mattered.

"Serve you, *serve*," the demons screeched and writhed. These were some of the new releases, he sensed, those members of the horde who'd recently been dumped out of darkness to sprawl across the earth. An older demon, one who'd had the experience of living upon this earth for any length of time, might not have been caught as easily as they'd been, but they'd been trapped. Ensnared.

That gave him an idea. If these pitiful members of the horde had served as stooges for the powers behind this attack on Angela's parents, they could also serve a purpose for Gregori. They could be bait.

Without further hesitation, he laid his palms upon the shoulders of Angela's parents. His large hands dwarfed their slender necks, and as he spread his fingers, he could feel the heat of the circuitry behind their ears. Bugs of some sort? Medical devices? If so, he suspected there'd be two devices per mortal, a fail-safe that spoke of a very careful planner.

"You will answer only to me," he cautioned the demons, who were now vibrating inside the Stantons with renewed hope. He didn't think for a moment they would follow this dictate, but as they keened with renewed excitement, he mapped their emotions, as unique to each of them as it was to every one of God's children. He would be able to find and follow them, he knew. He would need to.

A chorus of affirmations greeted his words, and he squeezed the shoulders of the mortals, using his nails to scrape the skin next to the electronic devices that had been implanted in them. Both of the older humans stiffened, and behind him, Angela spoke sharp, alarmed words. But his focus was only on the demons. No demon could leave a host unless there was an opening to do so. With the break in the Stantons' skin, he'd just given the creatures their opening.

The exodus of the demons was not a pretty thing. Both

Stantons convulsed and screamed in terror and pain. Only Gregori could witness the darkness that spewed out of them, the roughness of the demons' passage shorting out the electrical components of the bugs embedded in the humans' necks. Shorting them out, but leaving them in place.

Because Gregori didn't kill the demons infesting the Stantons, they appeared as nothing more than smoke even to his eyes and would be far less noticeable to those standing around, completely undetectable on video. They circled several times before exploding outward, shattering glass and leaving those they passed racked with chills and fear.

Despite himself, Gregori allowed a tight smile to curve his lips. He'd not thought to add the small finesse of the broken glass, but he appreciated it nonetheless. Perhaps having his own set of demon informants wouldn't be completely useless.

All this happened in a matter of seconds, and as the demons left the building, all the demons but Gregori, anyway, the elder Stantons collapsed against him.

Angela reached him first, Joe right on her heels. Gregori eased the passed-out couple into their arms.

"We're going to need them both checked for a mechanical device implanted behind one or both ears," Gregori said to Angela.

"*What*?" she demanded, her usual reserve momentarily supplanted by genuine horror as she hugged her mother close, then released her to the care of a security guard. "You think someone bugged my *parents*?"

Just as quickly, she ruthlessly schooled her features once more. "What kind of devices? Anything that could harm them?"

"Unknown. They'll need to check."

Angela cursed as she yanked out her phone and tapped furiously. That had been the first real outburst of emotion from her that he'd seen, and he rocked back a little on his heels, surprised by the almost physical jolt that it caused him. It appeared Angela Stanton's careful reserve cracked when it came to her parents. If the intensity of this snippet of emotional reaction was any indication...he wouldn't want to be there when her walls fully collapsed.

The building's security team came up to them as Angela shoved her phone back into her jacket pocket.

"EMTs arriving in two minutes, police right behind," the lead guard said. "We managed to contain the media after the shooting, but the blowout of the windows makes that a little more problematic."

"Incendiary device, released by one of the suspects," Joe said immediately. "Assailants fled the scene toward the back of the building, guards in pursuit."

"Done," the first guard agreed, and immediately, she and her partner took off toward the back hallway to make the lie credible.

Then a third security guard peered harder at Gregori. "You're the guy who went up the side of the building," he said. "You."

"Yes," Gregori said as Angela glanced at him, startled. Both police and medical personnel converged on the building at that moment, but the man didn't move. He only squinted at Gregori, shaking his head.

"I climb, man. You've got way too much bulk for what my guys said you did."

Gregori grunted a short laugh, then they were swarmed by emergency personnel, and he and Angela stepped back.

"There's no way you're going to get out of having to give

a statement to the police this time," she said tightly. "And I don't know who to trust. You really think my parents have been bugged?"

"I do."

"Well, that's flat-out impossible," she bit out. "My parents are friends of the freaking governor. Since I've become a congresswoman, they've had government security on them, courtesy of same. Official. Government. Security. They *couldn't* have been bugged."

Gregori returned her gaze steadily, despite the pain it caused him. He was almost getting used to it—almost.

Angela's lips twisted. "This sucks," she muttered. "We're about to get questioned by the damned police, and we don't have our stories straight. I don't know what you're going to say, you don't know what I'm going to say—we don't freaking know each other at all. And I don't know who to trust. Dammit!" She put her hands up to her temples, as if she needed to fight to keep her thoughts from pushing out of her skull. "We don't have time!"

"You could faint," he offered, the soul of reason. His suggestion had absolutely nothing to do with the sudden and unexpected desire he had to draw her into his arms, a desire he knew he should shove away...but didn't. Instead, he took a step toward her.

"I'm sorry?" She blinked at him, her expression of dismay far more immediate and real than even when she'd seen her own parents collapsed in his arms. "I could what?"

"I'm your bodyguard. You're my charge. You faint in my arms, I'm not talking to anyone until you're safely in an ambulance. After that, I'm not talking to anyone until they talk to you first. I'm not a suspect. I'm a guy doing his job. I did what I thought I needed to do in an unfortunate scenario. If you faint, you'll give us some time. You'll get the answers you need before you have to make up a story you may have to take back later."

Angela hesitated all of three seconds, then laughed with what sounded like genuine regret. "Nobody would believe I'd faint. I don't even know if I could pull that off. What else you got? Can we get wired up somehow in, say, the next thirty seconds? I really don't like how this is going down."

More police showed up, and men and women in suits too. Angela cursed under her breath. "Homeland Security," she muttered. "What the hell is going on here?"

Gregori felt the press of time bearing down on them both. "I can keep you safe, Angela, but you're not going to like how."

She grimaced. "Try me."

"You and I have to build a deeper connection. A more permanent connection."

She narrowed her gaze. "In the next thirty seconds? Unlikely."

"Permanent—that's not the right word," Gregori conceded. "But...I need to know your emotions more clearly, as your reactions are happening."

"So, a wire, but—"

"Not a wire." He exhaled a long, shuddering breath. This was going to hurt, but he had no time to come up with an alternative. And if he was being wholly truthful, he craved this deeper connection he was suggesting to Angela. Craved it more with every passing second. "If you'll let me show you, I think you'll understand. But we need to do it now, before you're sequestered by the police, so that I understand exactly what you're saying and what I need to say as well. Make sense?"

"Not even remotely," Angela said tightly, her expression once more unreadable. "But do it."

Gregori reached out and took her hand in his.

8

There was no hesitation. That was what struck Angela most when she gave her hand to Gregori —there was no hesitation on her part, no fear. She'd never quite accomplished that when she'd interacted with most people for anything more than a quick hand-shake or collegial hug, but then again, she'd known for a few days that Gregori was not most people. And the touch of her hand on his, the warmth of his skin, even the zing of response that fluttered across her nerves simply felt *right*. Her cheeks flushed and her heart kicked up a notch, as if they weren't standing in the middle of her condo building's central lobby while her parents were being treated on the floor—but more like, almost like...

Like they were flirting. Like he was a man and she was a woman and their hands were touching and there was nothing else in the world but her and him and their joined hands, his fingers long and strong, his palms calloused, his skin—

"Look at me, Angela."

She jerked back into focus, still staring at his hands.

Gregori had said the words almost as a plea, as if what he was asking of her was a far greater gift than she could imagine, but still nothing he would force upon her. She needed —wanted—to respond to him, but fear now laced her desire, as well as heat and excitement and...

And he was waiting for her to answer.

Slowly, laboriously, as if the mere act of rotating her head required every muscle in her body, she turned to him. And then she couldn't look away if she'd wanted.

The unending well of compassion in Gregori's eyes made Angela gasp with a soul-deep anguish. This was what she'd been guarding herself against for all these years, the reason she never wanted to gaze too deeply into the eyes of another. Not for the fear of any horror she'd encounter in their eyes, but to avoid any love and understanding that waited there for her, absolution she could never allow herself to feel.

Because she'd hurt others. She'd failed them. She may only have been a child, but that didn't change the reality of what she'd done.

There could be no absolution for her.

"No," she gasped, and though Gregori could have no idea of what she was asking, what she was silently begging him to help her avoid, he shook his head almost imperceptibly, his gaze never leaving hers.

"There's nothing you need to give up to me about anything you have experienced in the past," he said, his voice a tortured whisper. She blinked at him. Did he know? *Could* he know?

No, no. That was impossible. But he continued on.

"Every door is yours to open or close as your spirit wishes. If the spirit wants light, the breath of hope, healing...those doors can open. If the spirit does not, they stay closed. Your spirit, your doors, your choice. Always. The past, your memories, are a sacred gift given only unto you. I will not claim them."

"But—" Angela was trying to understand, she truly was, but what Gregori said made no sense. Then, somehow, his hands closed around hers, his big, meaty paws dwarfing fingers that had long ago been straightened, their bones reset into their proper lines, their constant ache as familiar to her as breathing.

So much pain.

In a flash, a flood of memories came piling back, along with the guilt. If only...if only she could do something to *atone* for everything she'd done. To make a positive difference in people's lives, to keep them safe. To believe that her mind, her intellect, her insatiable curiosity could help people—not hurt them, the way she'd hurt her family so badly when she was a child, not once, but twice.

It was beyond foolish to hold herself accountable for what'd happened when she was a kid, and yet...she should've been smarter somehow. She should've recognized the threat coming for her. She should have *known*.

And there had been so much pain. She'd fought and struggled every time they'd come for her, lashing out and striking against bone and brick and steel. She'd broken her fingers too many times to count because they would leave her alone then, at least for a while, until she healed. She always healed far too soon, far too many times for only being held for eighty-seven days. And then the torment would start anew, the terror and the screaming, until she had hardened herself enough to break something else.

In Gregori's hands, though, there was no longer any agony, no more broken bones, and she dropped her gaze again to his clasped fingers as he spoke in soft and soothing tones.

"What I do need, however, is your trust and your openness to share everything that's present today in your mind and in your body. Your emotions, your reactions, and the words that ride upon them, all shared with me, whether I'm standing next to you or if I'm across the room, or if I'm not even in sight. I need you to open a connection to me and let me *feel*."

"But how?" Angela's entire body tensed at this unexpected request, but it wasn't a request she wanted to deny, necessarily. It was simply one she didn't understand. Still, she once more met Gregori's soft green eyes, their hold both strong and compelling. He studied her as if there was no one else in the room.

He also didn't answer. She sensed that he'd made his request and waited only for a response from her. There would be no more words; there would be no more explanations. Not now, not yet. This was her time, her moment, and she either needed to give or withhold. The hows would then take care of themselves.

"Yes," she finally said, and Gregori gently, ever so gently, squeezed her hands with his. Not nearly enough to hurt, barely enough for intimacy and support, but no sooner did he do so than the world came crashing back around her, the lights and sound coming up as if the settings of the room had been brutally adjusted. Angela jolted in surprise, her gaze going immediately to her parents as they were being lifted up on gurneys, covered with thick blankets.

"Wounds are not life-threatening, from what I can tell, though they won't say anything for sure." Joe was beside her again, talking fast and low, as if he feared she might freak out in some way. She realized with some surprise she was no longer holding Gregori's hands. That he was, in fact, several feet away from her. When had he moved away?

"Where are they taking them?" she heard herself asking in her calm, stoic voice. Her fingers shook, and she didn't know what to do with them. They trembled uncontrollably at the ends of her hands like someone else's fingers, foreign appendages she needed to manage, as opposed to something that was part of her. She tucked her arms close to her body and snugged her hands against her rib cage as Joe kept talking.

"Georgetown. They've got a secured medical wing, and since your parents were the target of a potential terrorist threat, they're going to get the full treatment."

"There are bugs implanted behind their ears." As if suddenly remembering this crucial detail, when it should've been at the forefront of her mind this whole time, Angela swung away from Joe and rushed to the EMT who leaned over her father. "Please. I need you to tell the doctors this. Please have them check for mechanical implants of some kind behind my father's ears. My mother's too, I think. They would be fairly recent."

"Medical devices?" the EMT asked. "Something that's been compromised?" Then he frowned. "Both ears?"

He clearly didn't make the leap to the implants being surveillance devices or whatever the hell they were, but he didn't need to. He only needed to tell someone who could do something about them. "I don't know," Angela said truthfully. "My father mentioned something about them, and I worry they've malfunctioned, maybe contributed to what happened here today, their reactions—"

The EMT nodded briskly, though he hadn't been here to witness firsthand her parents' screaming rants and wild-eyed frenzy after getting shot. That was something she didn't think she was going to be able to unsee for a while. "We'll tell them at the hospital," he said, moving forward as Angela stepped back.

Two police officers were already there. Through the windows, she could see the first news van pull up. She knew they wouldn't dare to cross the cordon of protection the police currently offered her, but she'd eventually have to talk to the press, if only to have her own statement out and official before all the speculation could begin again.

A uniformed woman stepped in front of her. "We have some questions we need to ask you, Ms. Stanton. Do you need medical treatment before we do?"

Angela straightened. In truth, she hadn't been shot, had only been shaken up. "I can speak with you now," she said, her tone once again measured and calm, her face—she hoped—a careful mask of understanding and concern, and maybe a little fear, because that was what was appropriate in this situation. Ever since she'd come home after being abducted and held for eighty-seven days in a metal cage, emaciated and broken and so, so betrayed, she'd studied hard to learn what her appropriate reactions *should* be to any situation. She'd practiced them over and over again in her mind and on her face as she'd stood in front of a mirror, until she knew she could handle any surprise event. "I'm happy to give you whatever you need. I do need to get the hospital soon, though, to look after my parents."

"Understood. This will only take a minute."

The questions started up then, all of them strangely expected, almost comforting in their familiarity. Did her parents have any enemies? Did she have any enemies that she had thought of given the incidents of these past few days? What were her parents' backgrounds and medical history, what was her history within the condo building, her daily routine? The police didn't ask about any reasoning behind the attack. They didn't ask many follow-up questions at all, one of them taking notes on a small pad while their body cameras and recording devices worked in tandem. This would definitely not be a situation of he said/she said.

The interview took another ten minutes or so, then Angela's security team tightened around her once more. Joe was the only truly familiar face, even as her gaze sought out Gregori standing at the far edge of the room. He glanced at her only momentarily as she turned her gaze to him, then he returned to surveilling the room as if he could draw explanations from the shattered glass and scrambling people.

When she'd been cleared by the EMTs and the police, they'd taken her SUV to the hospital. Ahead of them and behind them drove two marked police cars, with neither their lights nor their horns blaring. After they'd hustled Angela into her car, the rest of her brand-new security detail had remained behind with her media coordinator, a fresh-faced, attractive man the press already loved. Yet another wall in the series of barriers that made her life possible.

Gregori sat next to her while Joe positioned himself in the front seat. Joe turned around and started talking quickly as the car sped away from her condo building. "No ID on the two assailants, though they appear to be the victims of their own mutual assassination contracts," he said, disbelief still strong in his voice. "There was absolutely no reason for them to take each other out after the disappearance of the third gunman, but they did. It's going to make figuring this all out that much more difficult without witnesses."

Angela grimaced. "Anything from the hospital?"

"Your parents have been admitted and are both in

surgery. Their prognosis is good. No word on the devices or implants or whatever they are." Joe's gaze slid to Gregori. "What are they again?"

"Unknown," Gregori rumbled, and his voice seemed to vibrate through her, shining a light on all the dark and frightened places she hadn't fully realized still lurked within her. "Depending on the technical expertise on staff at the hospital, I suspect they'll let us know if they recognize the device as standard equipment of some sort, although standard equipment doing what, I have no idea."

Something in Gregori's voice caught at Angela, but Joe seemed to accept his words at face value. "Fair, fair. And if they're devices of questionable provenance, they'll be handed over to Homeland Security for analysis. If we've got some sort of biomechanical terror faction in operation, sophisticated enough to get to a congresswoman's parents and stage this attack, we've got way bigger problems than everybody realized."

Gregori gave a fleeting smile. "I think that's a fair statement no matter what they find."

They rode in silence the rest of the way to the hospital, where Angela, Joe, and Gregori were taken to a private waiting room in the protected ward, the space discreetly tucked away from the main bustle of the hospital. There were no media allowed anywhere near, and she suspected they wouldn't be allowed past the front desk of the facility. Fine by her.

Gregori and Joe kept their heads bent together, with Joe continuing to grill Gregori over how he was able to scale the building so quickly, his experience in confronting the assailants, his interviews with the police, and a broad outline of how they were going to need to increase Angela's security. The brief respite she'd had in the wake of the Atlanta attack was clearly at an end.

To have been targeted again so quickly defied logic, though. If someone was trying to scare her into some sort of compliance, they were going about it in entirely the wrong way, at least if they were trying to be secretive about it. That thought truly nagged at her. Any legislation she'd approve would now be colored by her own personal experiences. And while that could be good, the opposition to any such legislation would be quick to point out that she was possibly suffering from some form of posttraumatic stress, and so could she really be trusted to help bring such legislation to light?

Then again, who better to champion an antiterror bill than someone who was personally touched by terrorist tactics? Particularly since she hadn't lost anyone close to her, other than her security detail, which was awful enough. Had someone somewhere assessed the optics of killing her parents versus killing a security guard? She shuddered to think.

She was about to suggest to Joe that the three of them go and get some coffee in the hospital's cafeteria or whatever passed for food options in this facility, when the doors opened again. A doctor walked in and glanced first at her bodyguards before zeroing in on Angela. He walked forward, and it was all she could do to steel herself for his words.

"Your parents are going to be just fine," the doctor said warmly, surprising her. "We did recover a medical device from the neck of your mother—not something I've ever seen before, but you can rest assured that analysis is currently underway. Removing it appeared to cause no other distress, so it could be simply a tracker. Obviously alarming, but not life-threatening by itself."

"And my father?"

"No device," the doctor assured even as Gregori stiffened beside her. "We did both X-rays and MRIs, even an incision. We were surprised, since we expected to find a device. There isn't even any scarring at the site where we would expect there to be, indicating a device had recently been implanted or removed."

"Okay." She had no reason not to trust this man, but given the intensity rolling off Gregori in waves, she suspected she should tread warily. She unexpectedly longed to hold Gregori's hands once more, to feel his cool and penetrating gaze. She didn't understand what was happening here, but she sensed *he* did in some way. She needed to know what he knew. "What are our next steps?"

"We're going to keep your parents here for a couple of days just to make sure they're recovering the way we expect them to, totally standard procedure, though that may change once the analysis of the medical device implanted in your mother's neck is complete. If we have reason to believe your parents' lives remain in danger, we'll suggest an alternative course of action, but otherwise, they'll be able to go home. Rest assured, they'll be safe here."

Angela pursed her lips. Up until last week, she'd felt safe enough that she'd become complacent. That complacency had been ripped away.

She needed to understand why.

9

G regori watched Angela closely as they entered the lobby of her luxury condo, having personally reviewed all her security measures and found them adequate, if not spectacular, no matter how ironclad she considered them. Angela was far more careful than the average woman, but if they were dealing with assailants who could implant her parents without their knowledge or consent, he wasn't all that interested in leaving a trail for them to follow. Especially if they were looking at a threat from somewhere within her government.

And that was beginning to seem a disturbing possibility. One of the benefits of being a demon was a thorough understanding of the physiological attributes of God's children. Human beings were perfectly integrated systems, and any alteration to those systems appeared to both demons and angels as glowing beacons—hip replacements, artificial hearts, even donor organs lit up like Christmas lights when a demon surveyed a human. A handy feature, since the technology for robotic replacement parts was becoming ever more sophisticated and ubiquitous.

Bottom line, however, Gregori hadn't merely *suspected* that Angela's parents had been implanted with multiple devices. There was no question in his mind. So for the smiling doctor to regard Angela with an absolutely straight face and tell her he'd only recovered one device...that was a problem. It meant that either the assailant group had infiltrated the hospital, or members of Angela's own government had done so, stepping in to extract the devices for their own observation without giving her complete information.

Gregori didn't begrudge the government its need to understand the terrorists in its midst, but he begrudged them the decision to lie about it. Perhaps Angela would be privately briefed later about the true nature of what was discovered when her parents were examined, perhaps not, but it was something Gregori would watch very closely.

He'd wasted no time informing the archangel of the developments, but he wasn't pleased on that front either. The fact that Michael seemed to be more or less in the dark about this newest splinter faction of strangely powerful demons was a very bad thing. He'd admitted to requesting the help of the Arcana Council to a greater degree and promised that help was forthcoming, but this was the Archangel of the Lord who'd been assigned dominion over both angels and demons since before the dawn of time. For Michael not to be in the know simply did not make sense.

"There's more security here," Angela said abruptly, nodding at the line of personnel at the reception desk. She appeared once more crisp and coiffed, not a hair of her dark ponytail out of place, the tailored business suit she'd changed into at the hospital camera ready. "That's your work?"

"Partly," Gregori said. "Joe agreed to it, as well as posting security personnel in any currently unoccupied units in the building. You're covered."

She shot him a glance. "You've done this before."

Gregori shrugged. "You could say I've had a lot of years protecting people."

"But you haven't been inside my condo."

"I have not." The truth was, he hadn't wanted to leave her side, even though he'd done little but hover at a distance as she'd conferred again with the doctors and then the police. But now they were back, and as they stepped into the elevator and moved up to the fourth floor, he sensed an odd energy in the building, something...out of place for the brick, steel, and glass condo. "Joe said he'd do a sweep before we returned."

She snorted, her lips curving into a wry smile. "Joe loves nothing more than being put on sweep duty, no matter how much he complains about it."

Gregori didn't understand what she meant, but then they were off the elevator and moving down the hallway, where the sense of wrongness intensified. The energy on this floor was—chaotic. Frantic almost. A whirling dervish of barely constrained activity.

He cocked his head, but he couldn't hear anything. In fact, the floor seemed almost preternaturally silent.

"You mentioned your security precautions before," he said, tension stealing over him as they approached the door. "What new precautions have you put in place since the attack in Atlanta?"

"None," Angela said simply, waving her key fob at him. "Brace yourself."

Then she opened the door—

And chaos exploded from every corner of the condo.

Gregori instinctively started forward at the wild, frenetic, and mindlessly joyful rush of life force hurtling toward Angela, his hands going up to ward off the demon horde—only to jolt with surprise as the cacophony of beasts seemed to freeze midleap, then scrabble back, howling and yipping in sudden terror. He had a sense of fur flying, ears flapping, and hind legs churning as a quartet of dogs hurtled out of the room as quickly as they'd rocketed into it, scattering a secondary assault of furry creatures—a trio of cats that hissed, snarled, and jumped straight up off the floor, landing variously on a counter, an overstuffed chair, and a couch while the dogs raced away.

And there, alone in the center of the room, staring up at Gregori with their paws tucked into their chests and their eyes as large as the world, were...

"You have *rats*?" he asked, aghast.

"Those aren't rats! How dare you! They're Teddy guinea pigs. Aren't you, sweet things? How'd you get out of your cage again?"

Throwing down her bag, Angela scooped something that looked like chopped-up weeds out of a glass dish on a side table and bent down as the furry-footed bean bags scurried across the floor. They nibbled at her fingers, which apparently was reason enough for the three cats to jump off their perches and head for Angela as well. The two grown cats immediately began twining around Angela's legs while the third...

Gregori froze as the miniature orange puffball batted at his pants leg. "What's it doing to me? I'll hurt it."

"Oh, you will not. That's Ginger. She's just a kitten, but she's very fierce. And she has her claws, so be careful." Angela stood with a large black-and-white cat in her arms, a gray one rubbing her calf. "This is Domino, and Ghost here doesn't come out much, but she clearly doesn't mind you."

"I can't say that for these idiots," Joe called from the hallway, and Gregori and Angela turned. Sure enough, the four dogs hunkered back behind the perplexed security guard, whining and straining by his legs. "You got a thing against dogs, Gregori? Because you're scaring the hell out of them."

Gregori grimaced. This didn't seem to be a good time to bring up the age-old conflict between dogs and demons.

"I'm big. It confuses them," he finally said, but he murmured a benediction under his breath, a half-remembered blessing from the dawn of time that spoke to all God's creatures. The whining stopped, and the boldest dog, a well-built medium-sized mix with a decided bounce to his step, scampered forward.

"Well hello, Hey Mister! There's a good boy," Angela crooned, and that was all that was needed. The remaining three dogs scrambled out after their ringleader, and Domino leapt from Angela's arms to avoid the canine assault. Then she and Ghost...ghosted.

"Hey Mister—he's a boxer mix, if you know your dogs," Angela said, petting the dogs with a genuine smile. "Elvis is a sort of a hound cross, while Old Sir here is a sweet greyhound, obviously." Her expression softened further as she stroked the tall, thin gray dog's white muzzle. "And...well, I see you've met Hellboy."

"The cat..." Gregori gaped helplessly as the orange kitten pulled herself up onto his pants leg, suspended by her tiny claws. But then he realized she was no longer alone in her assault. Beneath her, waddling from foot to foot, stood a squat, long-eared brown dog who gazed up at him with incandescently adoring brown eyes, his tale whipping violently back and forth.

Gregori looked from one animal to the next. "Hellboy?" he managed.

"I know, he's a dachshund, but it's apparently his favorite movie. A local indie cinema manager brought him into the shelter after the little guy kept breaking into the late show, and I couldn't resist. I think he likes you."

"Dogs don't like me."

"Yeah, well, this one does," Joe said, then turned to Angela. "Dogs are fed and walked, cats are fed, and the tribbles are...well, I threw some of that lettuce you're supposed to eat as a salad at them, and then they got out of their cage again. I can't believe you picked those two up. They're escape artists. Messy escape artists."

"What was I supposed to do?" Angela shot back with the air of someone continuing a long-standing argument, though Gregori had already lost sight of the guinea pigs. "Someone abandoned them in a cardboard box, right by the park. They would've gotten *eaten*."

"Yeah, yeah—hey!" Joe abruptly dove behind the couch, coming up with the two bean bags. "Back into the slammer, poop machines." He carried the animals out of the room, cackling, then reappeared a minute later. He pointed at Gregori. "Yo, watch that one. She's not quite litter trained yet. I'll be next door."

"What?" Gregori plucked the orange ball of fur off his leg, jerking in surprise as she flipped and wrapped her front paws around his fingers. "No. Take them with you."

"No can do," Joe chortled, heading for the front door. "Angela's governor friend got this place to bend the rules to let her house this horde—though she pays handsomely for the privilege. But they're only allowed in the condo or on the rooftop unless they're in their crates. So you're stuck with them, my man." He slipped out of the condo, still laughing as he headed down the hallway.

"I've got you, Ginger," Angela said, unpeeling the cat from Gregori's hand and toting her away. She left the room, the dogs following her—all except Hellboy, who remained at Gregori's feet.

Gregori sat in a wingback chair and scowled down at the dog.

"You don't like me," he informed it. "Even with the blessing. Have some self-respect."

The dog flopped down and rolled over, arching its belly toward Gregori. When Gregori made no move toward it, it rolled back upright with a faint air of bruised feelings, but still didn't leave his side.

Gregori passed a hand over his eyes, trying to get his bearings. The rest of Angela's security personnel were overseeing her rapidly expanding team, while he'd listened to her give her administrative staff enough work for a week on the drive over here. Even her spokesperson/chief-of-staff had more responsibilities than any single person could handle, tasked with media management both at the scene of Angela's condo and at the hospital.

So far, the media hadn't gotten hold of the parent angle, but it was only a matter of time. They were well aware that people had been injured and rushed to the hospital to be set up in a secure ward, and the fact that Angela had recently been attacked made for a scintillating story. Someone would get the idea sooner or later to check on her parents, and it would all come out. The fact it hadn't yet was a minor miracle.

"Gregori."

Gregori looked up to find that Angela had returned, still in her business suit, though she'd loosened her ponytail.

She regarded him with an intensity that would be unnerving in any creature, but triply so in a human. With the animals gone, her face was once again unreadable, and though Gregori's empathic skills could pierce her barriers, the fact that he'd have to work to do so endlessly fascinated him. She was a complete enigma to him, and a dangerous one. His job depended on him knowing what to do next, but in Angela's case, until he connected more deeply with her, he was at a loss. He'd started the process in the lobby—and had matched her story exactly when the police had questioned him—but he needed to finish it.

Then she surprised him again by beating him to the punch.

"I find I'm somewhat at a disadvantage in our relationship," she said, her words calm and considered. "I'd like to remedy that."

Gregori hesitated. "A disadvantage?"

"Yes." She sat in the nearest chair, barely three feet away from him. He could feel the heat rising from her body, the unexpected scent of lavender and cinnamon playing havoc with his senses. He was too attuned to her already, too aware. And it was only going to get worse.

"I need to know more about you," she continued. "Who you are. *What* you are."

Gregori settled back. It appeared he wasn't the only one getting more attuned. "What I am?"

"Yes, what. You performed some sort of mind-meld with me downstairs, and I want to know what you did and how. I don't believe in mutants, I don't believe in science fiction, but I do believe I don't understand everything about this world of ours. You're someone I need to understand better. You've already saved my life once, and I suspect you're going to have the opportunity to do so again."

It was a nice, tidy assessment, spoken in measured tones, but he'd watched the woman coo at an orange puffball and feed bits of parsley to walking floor pillows. He wasn't buying the reserved veneer so much anymore. "It's my job," he said simply.

"It wasn't your job until a very short time ago, and your first opportunity to save my life happened before you were even officially employed." She tilted her head, considering him. "I believe you're an insightful strategist, a warrior by any description, and a man...though not an ordinary man... with extensive emotional depths. I think you'll agree that those characteristics are not often found in the same individual. I think you'll also agree that the events of the last several days have been highly unusual for me. I don't often have the occasion to draw the interest of terrorists, nor do my parents. I also don't often have the occasion to necessitate evasive maneuvers from my own government regarding said terrorist acts upon my parents. I think you would further agree, I'm distressed by these developments. To the extent I can find some measure of understanding of what your role is in all this, I believe I'll be able to manage the developing situation with much greater success."

Throughout this meticulously worded speech, Angela's face never changed. But as she fixed on a point over Gregori's shoulder, he watched her eyes. And, for perhaps the first time, allowed himself to truly reach out mentally to the woman sitting so carefully still in front of him.

Pain. There was the swiftest flash of pain, a gossamer shimmer whisking out of sight almost as soon as he noticed it. There was anger too, bubbling rage that quaked beneath a barrier so thick that it would never explode outward on its own, never find a natural exit. A blur of other emotions roiled within that rage—hatred, bitter disappointment, and, of course, fear. But this fear had almost been calcified, a corked stone jug bobbing along in the frothing, spitting ocean. He wondered, briefly, what would happen if that jug would ever break, if it ever mixed in with all the rage, hatred, and disappointment that formed a stew around it.

And even seeing all this, Gregori knew he still wasn't grasping the full picture. Because he was afraid. Afraid that his own internal torrent was every bit as fragile and potentially lethal as Angela's repressed emotions.

Which made what he had to do next all the more dangerous. And here Angela was, practically opening the door for him.

"What do you want to know, specifically?" he asked.

She chuckled wryly, as if she knew she was asking the impossible but she didn't know why. "I want to know the information that didn't make it to your résumé," she said. "I want to fully understand the skills you bring to the table—all of them—and I want to know why you're here."

"To protect you," Gregori said almost automatically, and Angela gave him that same sad smile once again.

"I believe that's true, in part," she said. "I believe your charge is to keep me alive. However, I also believe that charge is ancillary to the real reason why you're here, why you showed up at that stadium in Atlanta for what I suspect was the first monster truck rally you've ever seen in your life."

Gregori quirked his lips. "What, I'm not the monster truck rally type?"

"On the contrary. You're exactly the monster truck rally type. I simply can't decide if you were chosen for this assignment because of that, or if it was just a happy coincidence for your employer. Because, let me be clear, I know this is an assignment for you. I appreciate it, because without that assignment, I'd very likely be dead or held in a circumstance that would be..."

She paused, and Gregori could see it again, that flash of pain, anger, and distress. There was no fear this time, though. It was as if she'd already noticed its appearance and had made adjustments to shove it farther back into her mind.

"Unfortunate," she finally said. "However, now this situation has expanded to threaten the lives of yet more innocent people, people who didn't sign up for the job of being a potential terrorist target. It has also become a situation that has attracted the interests of whatever branch of Homeland Security feels justified in lying directly to my face and not providing me with any sort of debriefing when it's obvious they're lying. As I said before, I find myself at a significant disadvantage. I'd like to rectify that situation."

It seemed that the more formal and measured Angela's speech became, the more obvious it was that she was drifting closer and closer to the brink. The brink of what, Gregori wasn't quite sure, but once again, he didn't think he'd like the answer.

"There are two ways to go about this," he said abruptly, before he could choose a safer course. "I could tell you what I am, or I could show you. But my personal nature is secondary to your other question, which is why I am here. So, let me start with that."

"Fine. Go."

"I work for an organization that believes in demons. Ah —that's DEM Enforcement. I'm still with them."

She blinked, but, to her credit, didn't interrupt him. On the floor beside him, Hellboy perked up.

"And yes," he continued. "I do mean actual fire-and-brimstone demons, which have existed since the beginning of time. The difference now, however, is that there's been a recent influx of the beasts across the globe. My organization is interested in eliminating as much of that influx as possible before more of Go—" He caught himself in time, and redirected. "Humanity is affected negatively. Granted, another person viewing the situation from a limited perspective might simply designate these demons as human terrorists. Accordingly, my organization is one of many that outwardly state that their mission is to help eliminate a new worldwide terrorist organization."

"But your group believes these are actual demons afflicting humanity."

She couldn't quite keep her disbelief from coloring her tone. Gregori merely nodded. She'd come to believe soon enough, but there was more information he needed to share with her before that happened.

"I was called in to mitigate one such threat at the rally in Atlanta, where you were accosted by several gunmen. Those gunmen didn't shoot you. They appeared more inclined to take you unharmed. Fortunately, the kidnapping did not take place. However, there are several anomalies within that event that I think you'll agree have not been adequately explained."

"The complete disappearance of all the assailants," she said flatly. "Even when some had clearly been struck down during the course of the attack. The disappearance of all that black goop that coated damned near everything in the midst of the battle but wasn't found several hours after everyone cleared out. It wasn't on my clothing or Joe's either. Even the samples of said black goop that the crime scene techs were able to recover from the scene strangely evaporated in their sealed containers."

Gregori lifted his brows. He hadn't realized Angela had

done additional research on the crime scene, but it didn't surprise him. "And the guns," he finished for her.

"And the guns. The guns that nobody can explain the appearance of in such numbers, given the stadium's security. One, maybe two such weapons could easily have slipped through, but not as many as there were, regardless of their construction. They were simply too big." She gave him a wan smile. "I will say, I hadn't thought of a supernatural explanation for the attack, but I can see how it certainly makes sense. Assuming, of course, that demons exist."

Gregori sighed. He lifted his gaze to Angela. Beautiful, perfect Angela, locked behind her walls of ice and stone. She'd carefully built those walls brick by brick, he suspected, after the horrors she had endured in her past, possibly far in her past. He'd only glimpsed a bit of her deeply buried pain, but she'd definitely survived something worth burying, to create the woman who sat before him now. He needed to know more about that time, but he hadn't earned the right yet to ask that of her. Not when he still withheld so much himself.

For one long moment, their gazes met, and he could feel the wellspring of Angela's emotion like a physical blow, pressing him back into his overstuffed chair. She wasn't revealing herself, but her seeking energy was so strong, so absolute, there was no denying it. And so, he simply...didn't deny it.

With a soft, shuddering breath, he let his glamour fall away.

Hellboy yipped and scrambled back—while Angela froze.

For a heartbeat, there was no breath, no thought, not even a quiver of energy emanating from her body.

Then, finally she spoke, her voice trembling with emotion.

"You *bastards*," she seethed, her hands coming up, her fingers arching into claws, her eyes wild. "I told you if you ever came back, I would rip you *limb* from *limb*. How *dare* you do this to me again!"

She attacked.

ngela was at the creature's face almost before she realized what she was doing, her fingers diving deep toward the hollow sockets, searching for the eyes she knew had to be there. The beast howled in pain and what sounded like genuine terror a moment before she touched it, but it let her strike anyway, only turning its head at the last moment to allow the bulk of her attack to rock its enormous, scarred, and twisted body.

"You said you'd done your worst!" she raged, clenching her hands into fists and continuing to pummel the monster. She couldn't breathe. She couldn't even think. Her lungs squeezed, her heart burned, and everything inside her turned to jelly. This was *exactly* like the nightmares she'd had when she was a little girl, after the eighty-seven days in the crate. Nightmares of ordinary-looking people having their skin fall off to reveal hideously distorted and grotesque figures beneath, leering at her, laughing at her, warding off her attacks with callous ease, whispering to her that it would never end.

They'd been right.

Intellectually, she knew there was nothing she could do to harm this creature. They'd taught her that as well. She'd broken bones, dislocated joints, ravaged her own skin across scales and teeth and horns and hide that burned like acid. But there was something deep within her that could never stop trying, could never accept the truth for what it was. And there was something in them, in those creatures, that'd kept letting her try. She'd known that was important; she just hadn't known how important.

And now they were back.

"Angela," the creature said with its ruined mouth.

"Don't you *dare* speak my name!"

She wrenched herself away from the creature. It didn't try to stop her. If anything, it seemed to hunch down within itself, glowering at her from its ruined face, somehow able to see without sight.

When she was eight years old, she'd never thought of the beasts as demons. She hadn't known what that word meant. She still hadn't made the connection when Gregori Stearns—or whatever his true name was—had started talking about the mythological creatures. Neither she nor her parents believed in anything so ridiculous as a Judeo-Christian god. That was for fools. Demons were no different from orcs or werewolves, part of the ever-evolving lexicon of humans desperate to believe in something outside themselves.

Now she scowled at the creature before her, still refusing to believe it. "Demon," she snarled, practically spitting the word. "Hallucination, more like."

Sudden pounding sounded at her condo door, Joe's nearly frantic voice barking in panic. "Angela!"

She jerked up stiffly, shooting her gaze first to the door and then back—to see Gregori appearing completely normal again. He sat in his chair, his back stiff, his hands on his knees...and the dog was back beside him, looking up at him with wide, adoring eyes.

"You *bastard*," she said again, hissing the word. Hellboy shrank back at her tone, which caught her up short, instantly piercing her mood.

"No, no, you're okay. You're my sweet boy."

She returned her glare to Gregori. "You, however, are a bastard."

Gregori grimaced with what appeared to be genuine regret, but he made no move to stand as she strode across the room, scooping up her phone as she did before shouting, "Joe! Enough."

Then she unlocked the door and pulled it open.

Her security team exploded through the entry—first Joe, then three more people whose names she hadn't even learned yet, all of them stopping short as she glared at them with folded arms.

"What the hell were you shouting like that for?" Joe demanded, his gaze darting around the room. "You sounded like the hounds of hell were after you, or you were after them. Where are the dogs?"

"The dogs are hiding. And all that was Gregori's fault," Angela snapped, jerking her thumb back to Gregori and then turning around to Joe again. Gregori had the grace to look embarrassed and wholly confused. "When I insisted he didn't need to hover, he accused me of not being able to defend myself appropriately even in the face of a surprise attack. Not two seconds later, he lunged for me and took me down—while hardly laying a hand on me. I didn't think someone his size could move so quickly, and I know Krav Maga. Needless to say, I didn't take my humiliation very well."

Joe squinted at Gregori. "You seriously did that? And then you let her get you?"

Gregori shifted uncomfortably in his chair. Angela realized for the first time that blood dripped down his face from the corner of one eye.

"Surprise works both ways," he rumbled. "She went down too fast, and I was so concerned about that, I wasn't prepared for her to rebound so quickly."

He turned toward her, though notably, he didn't meet her gaze directly. "Fighting back is sometimes more important than defending yourself in the first place. You can't always protect yourself from being taken, but you can always protect yourself from giving up."

Angela felt the surge of tears behind her eyes, and her throat burned as she lifted her hands to her hair, resetting her ponytail. She furiously knotted it back together, desperate to regain her equilibrium. How had he known exactly what to say? How much did he already know about her?

It took another ten minutes to calm Joe down, including Gregori being forced to give an impromptu demonstration of what he'd done to startle Angela. To his credit, the big man managed to catch Joe off guard as well by doing nothing more than turning and lunging while not moving his feet. The impact of so much bulk moving that quickly from a standing position was alarming to say the least. Joe stumbled back, then immediately burst into laughter.

"No wonder Hellboy likes you," he said, rubbing his chin.

Gregori glanced down at the little dachshund, whose tail was once more thumping the carpet, but nodded. "When the client is being harassed by idiots, scaring the idiots away is often the best measure."

"You got that right. You good?" Joe asked Angela.

She gave him the best smile she could manage. "I'm good. And I appreciate your concern, as always. I'll do my best not to scream like a banshee again."

"Scream as often as you want. But if you keep that door locked, you need to know that I've got no problem knocking it down if it's in my way. So you may have to add a little extra to your maintenance fee this month."

"Noted." She watched them as they left again, maintaining her cheerful expression until they were out of the room. Then she swiveled back to Gregori, folding her arms once again.

"Explain," she said brusquely.

"Which part?" he shot back. "The part of who and what I am and how I came to be that way, or the part where I tell you what actually happened to you every time you were pulled out of that crate you endured for eighty-seven days?"

She stiffened, stumbling to the side until she could collapse onto the sofa. Gregori continued standing, several feet away from her. She was okay with that.

"How do you know anything about that?" she whispered. "Were you there?"

"No." The word was quiet and absolute. "But you're right in that I have special skills. One of those skills is reading emotions, and sometimes those emotions are so vivid, they carry thoughts and words and memories along with them. When you attacked me, I...saw things."

She scowled at him. "You mean you're psychic."

"Not in the way you're thinking. I can't read minds. I can't predict the future. I'm an empath. I can feel what others feel, sometimes quite strongly."

"Do you feel it more when you touch someone?" she asked, her gaze straying again to his hands. They were uncovered. Had they been uncovered when she flung herself at him, scraping and clawing? She was pretty sure the answer to that was yes.

He frowned. "I try not to touch another person if I can avoid it, particularly in a crowd where I can't discern one person from another. If you've noticed it, though, others will too. I'll lose the gloves."

"You don't need to on my account—"

He gestured curtly. "It's not a problem."

Okay... She decided to push on. "Let's start with what happened to me when I was a child. What's your take on that?"

He didn't hesitate. "You were abducted by one or more of the Possessed. Humans who were taken over by demons. It's likely that one or more demons were attempting to possess you as well, but you resisted. Humans don't resist. It's not in their makeup, especially if they're weak or vulnerable. Which made you an anomaly the horde or their keepers couldn't resist. I suspect you weren't sexually abused in any way, though there was pain. Significant pain. But not defilement."

His expression had taken on a faraway cast, his face tilted away from her, his eyes on a distant point. "Even among demons, there are levels of degradation to which some will not go. Not all of them, but some. The group that held you had a mission to possess you, not damage you. Whether you were simply a novelty or there was something more to you, something important, I don't know. I can only gather so much from a flash of emotion. To learn more takes a much more focused attempt."

That startled her. "You can learn more?"

He grimaced. "I suspect that's why I was given this assignment, as you rightly stated. Because of my abilities, and because of something you know, something that's important to what's happening to you now. Something you may have thought you'd forgotten, but you haven't."

She blew out a long breath. "I've tried for a lot of years to forget what happened back then. I'm pretty sure I would have remembered something significant if there'd been anything to remember. There was no one else in any of the cages. I used to pray that others would be brought to fill them up, just so I wouldn't be so alone. Then I hated myself for thinking something so terrible. And then I hated myself even more for crying desperate tears when I would wake up again and realize I was *still* alone."

"How many other cages were there besides yours?" Gregori asked. "A dozen? Less?"

She shook her head. "More, actually, though most of them still smelled like animals. Almost like they were being prepared for people, but I'd come along too quickly."

"Or you hadn't been expected at all," Gregori said thoughtfully.

"Or that. But once again, it makes no sense. What did they want from me? I was never posed any questions. No one ever answered any of my pleas. No one spoke much to me at all. Most of the people I saw looked like people. There were only a few that appeared like...you just did. They tried to scare me, get close to me, and I fought back so hard, I hurt myself."

Angela realized she was rocking on the edge of the couch, but she couldn't seem to stop herself. "They seemed distressed when I hurt myself, actually. I do remember that. It was what I eventually realized could get me out of there, so I kept trying to...escalate. When I broke my arm in two places trying to escape, I was set free. Dropped off at the hospital, if you can believe that. I woke up as I was being rushed into surgery. Even as a little girl, I knew they had let me go, that I was free, but I was afraid to sleep. They always came when I was asleep. But then...I think I slept a lot. I couldn't help it."

"And your parents came for you in the hospital?"

"They did." She nodded. "We lived in a pretty small town outside Atlanta, and my disappearance would ordinarily have made national news, but there was something else going on. I can't remember what. In the end, when I went back to look, only a couple of articles remained, and they were all my old name."

"Old name?" Gregori asked. "You changed your name after the abduction?"

"My parents did, yes. Before the abduction, they called me Jane. Afterward, they called me Angela because they said I kept saying the word 'angels' in my sleep. They thought it was pretty and it seemed to give me comfort. I didn't know any of this until much later. The months after my experience are still a little blurry to me. And that wasn't the first time I sort of...lost time, I guess you'd say."

Something in her voice must have alerted him, because he stiffened. "What do you mean?"

"There was...another incident. I was barely five years old, being watched by my grandmother." She didn't know why she was telling him this, but with her parents looking so old and frail today, collapsed on the lobby floor...maybe that was it. She shrugged, more to herself than him. "She had a heart attack while watching me, and—well, I always felt it was my fault somehow. But I don't remember what I did to cause it, don't remember much of anything that night, really, or the weeks after she got sick. It's all just a blur."

"The mind protects what the heart can't bear," Gregori said quietly. "It's normal."

She snorted. "Well, it doesn't feel normal."

"If I'm going to help, I need to know the rest of the story about your past. But we can talk first about what I am, if you prefer."

"No." She straightened her shoulders, squaring them, trying to regain her habitual sense of control—though that was a losing effort. "I already know what you are. You're one of them, those people, but different in a way I can't really understand. I don't want to understand it, frankly. Right now, I mostly need to know that there was a purpose in why I was taken all those years ago, tested, and then left at the hospital. Or even what I did the night my grandmother got sick. I just...I just have so many questions. Can you help me at all with that?"

"I can," Gregori rumbled, his voice heavy with emotion. "I absolutely can. But I need you to look at me first."

She lifted her face to his and realized, to her shock, that he'd gone deathly pale. "I don't under—"

And then she met his gaze.

She...dissolved. There was really no better way to explain it than that. She vaguely had the sense of him approaching her, but that she'd already come apart. The pain was so swift and so all-encompassing, her entire body seemed to shut down. She couldn't breathe, but she no longer needed oxygen. She no longer needed anything but the touch of his hands on hers. She would have screamed if there was any breath in her lungs, any sound in her throat. She would have ranted and roared, but she couldn't.

She was crying. She knew she was crying, yet she had no control over her body any longer. She'd gone numb. She couldn't feel the tears on her cheeks, but she saw them dripping down, splashing onto her knees without causing any sensation. She hadn't fully realized that she'd dropped her chin until she swiveled her gaze back up, again not of her own volition, but because of the gentle pressure beneath her chin lifting her up. Gregori now knelt before her, his eyes infinitely gentle but his expression firmly steadfast, as if he was an immovable rock braced against the storm of her emotions. Her heart crumbled a little more, and she barely stifled a sob.

"Focus on me," Gregori whispered, his voice hoarse with effort. "You don't need to do anything more than that, O beautiful child of God, bright light of the angels, precious song of the stars. Just look at me."

And she was swept away on a soundless tide into a foreign, faraway night.

11

Gregori catapulted through a constellation of torment.

Lost in the pull of Angela's gaze, he was forced to experience each moment of her life as she'd experienced it, live each moment as she had lived it, from the cocoon of her earliest development to the chaos of her birth to the blinding fear of her realization that she was alone, separate in the world, destined to forge her way apart from all those around her. The unutterable despair of this moment was balanced only in part with the relief, the joy, the gratitude she felt as she was gathered into her mother's arms, comforted and cared for. Only in part, because even at that shockingly young age, this child had known the path she was set upon. That she would be taken, stolen, abandoned, lost. She *knew*.

A new explosion of terror burst into life before Gregori, hijacking his senses. He was seeing what a young Angela was seeing, but his reactions weren't those of an eight-year-old girl, the age at which Angela had been abducted. No. This little girl was barely five years old, her mind already a ceaseless flurry of activity, her hands nimble, her eyes sharp. She trailed around after anyone who had an appetite for answering her endless questions, whether they be her mother, grandparents, neighbors, or babysitters. She never rejected anything that was told to her, even when it was patently false, the made-up stories of mortals trying to humor their young into silence. Though she was bright and cheerful and enthusiastic almost to a fault over her newfound treasures of information, she rarely argued or showed any negative reaction when adults were condescending, dismissive, or outright untruthful. She simply absorbed everything that was spoken, testing and verifying and categorizing the eventual results into a strictly coded order in her mind. She was, by all accounts, a gifted child, and she learned to read far earlier than anyone realized. Too early for the books she was exposed to.

"What...what did your parents do?" Gregori gasped, watching in horror the scene playing out before him, a scene he knew without a doubt Angela didn't consciously remember. A scene he also knew had led her inexorably to all the trials she now faced.

Angela, caught up in the trance of her connection with him, answered without hesitation. "They were professors. Anthropology, study of societies and cultures. They went everywhere, brought home everything, studied it all. The house was always filled with books, so many books..."

Either her voice trailed off or it was Gregori's turn to be caught up again in the scene unfolding before him, where the young Angela crept into her parents' study when they were out and her Nana thought her fast asleep. In all the tomes and manuscripts crowded into the warm and inviting space, she had stumbled on one with pretty pictures and symbols and words. She shouldn't have been able to read the words, except there was a translation on a scrap of paper tucked into one of the books—and her mind quickly identified and ordered and codified the letters the same as she had done months earlier with English. She couldn't understand what she was reading, but of course, she didn't have to. The only thing required was for the words to be spoken.

The mist that had filled the room was enough to pull the five-year-old Angela from the book, but as she blinked around her, there was still no panic in her eyes, no fright. Only curiosity. She was the beloved only child of two academics, living in a comfortable, solidly middle-class home in a comfortable, solidly middle-class suburb just near enough to the local college to be interesting but not so close to be dangerous. She would have no understanding of the demons that roiled and writhed in the smoke, moaning and chittering and calling to her to finish the spell. She would have no frame of reference for the evil that seethed from them. The Serbian spell book was a very old, very corrupt dark grimoire, not at all the usual fare for the *vrac*, the spell casters, witches, and shamans responsible for the care and healing of the villages. This was something altogether different.

Angela barely even noticed when the door opened beyond the roiling mass of demons, and her Nana poked her head in, saw what was in the room, and promptly collapsed. Then the five-year-old Angela, frightened for perhaps the first time in her life, leapt up off her chair, abandoned her book, and ran straight for the old woman... directly through the snarl of demons.

The pain was cataclysmic.

With his empathic abilities caught in the furor of the scene, Gregori recoiled at what his brother demons were feeling in this moment, their wild, desperate need. This was it—this was their chance!

The horde leapt for the mind of the child, scratching and thrashing, desperate to catch hold of her light, her soul, anything to bind them to this earth for long enough that they could escape the darkness from whence they sprang. The old woman, unconscious before she hit the floor, they couldn't reach. But the girl—the girl! This they could take. This they could hold!

Angela never stopped, never wavered as she raced across the small room toward her grandmother, but the demon horde tried their very best to trap her. Their claws slashed out, scoring deep gouts into her psyche, exposing her to all their terror, making her heart bleed. Their screams rang through the night, a hundred thousand voices, insane and cruel, slavering and wild, filling her ears with the horrors of their kind. She burst into tears by her third step, was trembling violently by her fifth, and by the time she reached the old woman and wailed in fright and terror, she had seen more darkness at the tender age of five years than most mortals could stomach in a lifetime.

But she hadn't stopped.

She still didn't stop.

With a strength well beyond her years, she scrambled over her grandmother and yanked the tiny woman out of her parents' study, then, to Gregori's continuing shock, returned. Returned! And she leveled the demons with her own fury-filled screams, her outrage so incandescent that it took the horde by absolute surprise. She spoke back the words she'd read at the start of the grimoire, the words of binding and banishment, and even with her untutored voice and her broken Serbian, the ancient spells were of such power that they emptied the room with a hiss of centuries-old magic. Until finally, Angela—who was still Jane at this time, sweet and unwittingly powerful Jane—was left alone.

She crossed the room to her parents' books. Righted the stacks. Stood back, surveying the place critically with all the severity a five-year-old could muster. She stood there another long moment, even when her grandmother called out in a confused, wavering voice. Then she nodded and turned on her heel, and left the room.

She no longer cried.

She told no one, not even after she'd used her grand-mother's phone to call first 911, then her parents, remaining huddled on the floor next to her grandmother while the operator kept her on the phone. Her grandmother, who'd fainted clean away again when Angela opened the door of the study, remembered nothing. She didn't have to. Angela remembered enough for both of them.

Gregori convulsed with the weight of the decades-old terror that the little girl still carried around with her, the shock so great on her young, impressionable mind that she could only wall it away and cement it over so it only came out when her defenses dropped, like when she slept or got too tired. Every dream, every nightmare from that time, he assimilated. Every horror, he took into his own mind. Every terror, he took into his heart. He felt each moment with her and raged and shivered and whispered and shuddered and wept. His empath nature was created to hold every drop of another's pain, and Angela's river of agony ran deep and wide for all she'd seen and all she believed she'd done to her grandmother and to the world. Because, to a little girl who didn't believe in a heaven or hell, there was nowhere for those creatures to go when they left her but into the world itself.

She believed she'd set them free.

Gregori's mouth moved in the imperfect litany of healing that was all he was still allowed to pray over the shattered and the lost. He'd prayed it many times over the past millennia, whispering to mortals who'd long since given up on ever finding their way back to joy. Some already in the midst of crossing over, most wishing they could just end the suffering. And, with his help, they did. And, with his help, so too did the young girl who trembled in the dark, desperate to be strong, burying herself in books and learning, anything to keep her mind busy, focused, separate, apart.

He bowed over that precious broken little girl, words of restoration dropping from his hushed lips, even as he watched her age to six, to seven, until another beautiful summer's day, when she was eight years old—

"Gregori."

The sound of Angela's voice brought him back to the moment with a brutal jerk, and he blinked, momentarily bewildered. Ordinarily, once he'd begun the process of healing, nothing could draw him from it until he was done, and he was nowhere near finished with Angela. Her spirit still cried out from all she had seen and experienced, and he'd not yet begun to break down the walls she'd built around what had happened to her at age eight.

But her voice wouldn't let him focus.

"Gregori," she whispered again.

His gaze cleared, and he realized that Angela was leaning back in his arms, arms that were wrapped around her, not tightly, not oppressively, but creating a circle of protection to allow his healing energy to pour through her. The flow of that energy had been cut off, but her eyes were wide as she gaped at him, her expression not one of peace but of shock—and something approaching fear.

He stiffened, preparing to lean away, but her arms came up and around his broad back, her hands pressing flat against him. "No—please! Please don't leave me," she begged, her words tight and fierce.

The wave of pain and need and desperate loneliness struck Gregori so hard, his knees buckled, and it was only through sheer willpower that he broadened his stance and bowed his shoulders against the onslaught of emotion. It spilled out of Angela in an almost physical wave, cascading forth in mute testimony to a lifetime of denied connection. Her hands trembled against him, her whole body shook, in fact, and though she bowed her head forward, he could feel each tear as it fell from her eyes to drip onto his shoes. The hissing of each drop against the leather spoke to the depth from which those tears emerged, and even Angela gasped as she saw the wisping smoke rise.

"What's happening?" she whispered.

"Allow it," he rumbled, his voice resonant with the remains of the ancient gift he'd been accorded at his creation, the gift that had so often felt like a curse. It didn't feel that way now. As Angela crumpled against him, her shoulders shaking as she sobbed, he murmured prayers, not for the child she had once been. He would need to return to that girl soon, to finish what he started. But at this moment, his priority was the woman he held in his arms. A woman whose raw, naked pain opened up a yawning, answering ache within himself, an anguish so great that he wanted to spread his arms wide and cry out to the heavens in horror that any one human should be forced to carry such a weight within their frail bodies, grinding down their fragile bones.

But he didn't spread his arms. If anything, he gathered Angela closer to him, his breath whispering over her hair, speaking in English the words barred to him in all things except in the care and healing of God's beloved children. And gradually, her shaking subsided. Gradually, the burning sting of her tears slowed, until her breathing evened out and she sagged against him. The emotion that emerged from her then was tinged with both confusion and embarrassment, and he held her a little more gently as she cleared her throat.

"Ah..." she finally managed. "So...right. I'm...I'm okay. Really. I'm good."

She straightened, and he let her step away from him, the rapid wash of her words helping him return to normal as well. Strangely, it wasn't as difficult as it usually was. Healing humans, taking on their pain, always exacted its toll on Gregori, but Angela's pain had been...different. Taking it from her had been as much a grace to him as a gift to her— and it had been a gift. One she probably didn't fully realize yet that she'd been given. He found himself aching to take her back into his arms, to complete the trials still remaining before them both, but she took another wobbly step away, once more reaching up to smooth her hair back into its beleaguered ponytail.

"You should rest," he suggested, and she flashed him a sudden, startled look, a flush of embarrassment slashing her cheeks a moment later. Gregori blinked, still so attuned to her thoughts that he knew what she'd been thinking. And for the first time in all the millennia he'd served as a demon enforcer, he wanted it as well.

A rapid thumping started up four feet away, and he turned, blinking in surprise.

Hellboy raced across the room and leapt for him.

"Whoa!" Gregori caught the dog automatically, then tried to fend off his assault, but it was a losing battle as the creature wriggled and yipped and scrambled up to reach his face, licking him with frantic affection.

Angela laughed shakily, and the unexpected sound nearly cleaved his soul in two. He gasped as Hellboy pressed his little body against him, quivering with all his might.

"I think he really likes you," Angela said, her voice breaking a bit.

Their eyes met over the dog's head, and taking in her tearstained face, her wobbly smile, something new shifted inside Gregori. Something far more dangerous.

He needed to leave. Now.

"I'll make a search of the building, make sure you're safe," he said.

Angela nodded a little too quickly.

"You'll stay here tonight?" she asked, then bit her lip, her cheeks flushing at the need they both heard in her voice.

"On-site, yes," he agreed. "You'll be safe. I swear it."

"Safe..." she echoed, and the first hint of awareness of her changed circumstances seemed to skate along the edge of her words. "Safe."

12

Angela smoothed down her suit and kept her expression carefully neutral as she walked up the stairs to the House committee conference rooms, Gregori only a few feet away. To any who cared to look, she appeared exactly as she always did when arriving at the center. Professional, feminine, tough, accessible. Intelligent without lacking common sense, no-nonsense without being gruff, practical without appearing uncaring. The exact combination of personality traits you'd want in a junior congresswoman.

Inside, she was a morass of conflict.

A nervous giggle cropped up from somewhere deep, and she gritted her teeth to keep it contained. But the truth was, she wanted to burst out in wonder-filled laughter every time she drew a breath—until that emotion was choked off by a bone-chilling need to scream. She wasn't sure which reaction was going to win out, but her money was on the scream.

That was especially unfortunate considering how much work Gregori had done to heal her. She'd felt ridiculously *good* since the moment he'd touched her the day before, as if a weight of seismic proportions had been lifted from her shoulders. He hadn't explained what he'd done either, but there was no denying the truth.

Gregori Stearns was a demon.

Even thinking the words sent Angela's internal pendulum swinging back toward the edge of hysteria, because of course, he couldn't *actually* be a demon, for all his insistence. He might believe he was, and there were certainly things she'd witnessed that made him appear to be one, but a real demon? Banished by God to wreak havoc upon the earth? No.

There had to be another explanation. She'd long ago decided that she'd been under the influence of drugs when she'd been incarcerated as a child, and it seemed like those same drugs were in play again, even if unintentionally. Some sort of organic hallucinogen pumping through her system, maybe emotionally triggered, that made Angela see things that simply weren't there. That had to be what was going on. It had to be.

Because she could never feel for a demon the way she felt about him...right?

Angela pursed her lips. After sleeping like the dead for several hours in her condo, surrounded by her menagerie of pets, feeling actually *safe* for the first time in longer than she could remember, she'd popped awake with a sudden clarity of memory. A door had been opened that she'd kept firmly shut, a door she'd opened before the terrifying events of her later childhood, a door she hadn't even known she'd deliberately closed.

Her nana, lying on a hospital bed, her face serene as she explained to Angela the effects of a mild heart attack, and that she was going to be all right. Her nana had been so sorry to have frightened her granddaughter, but she recalled not one thing other than walking upstairs to check on her, then coming to as EMTs hovered over her.

Angela remembered, though. She remembered her nana's wispy white hair, perfectly styled even against the too-white pillow covers of the hospital room. She remembered her too-tidy house, a place that felt curiously empty for all that nothing had changed. And she remembered her parents' study, the chamber of horrors that no longer held any horrors at all because Angela had released evil into the world. Or so she'd believed for far too long, until she'd buried the memory altogether.

Now a nervous giggle did leak out, and Gregori glanced at her sharply. "What is it?"

"Nothing," she murmured smoothly. "I feel amazing, frankly. Hopefully, nobody picks up on it, or I'll fuel suspicions that I'm either hopped up on painkillers or I just got laid."

The words were out before she could stop them, and Gregori's reaction was perversely pleasing to her. He drew in a sharp breath, his chin lifting as if he'd been struck a glancing blow, and he fell back a half step as if to give her space to breathe. Probably not a bad idea. She'd become acutely aware of him as a physical person, in a way she simply didn't normally, especially with staffers. Or unfamiliar men. Certainly not demons.

Gregori Stearns was a demon.

No, she refused to believe it.

Even without the horns and a tail, though, it wasn't as if Gregori didn't have his own set of matching baggage— something she usually avoided in any relationship, friend or otherwise. After all, while he might not be the fell beast he believed himself to be, he *had* gone through significant trauma in his life. His ability to horrify and intimidate coupled with whatever psychotropic drugs he'd oozed out of his pores that'd allowed her to see his body as withered and decayed was not exactly something she wanted in the guy she'd bring home to her parents. Then again, he'd already saved her parents' lives, as well as her own, so she supposed that evened things out.

She needed to get to the bottom of the hallucinogen he'd been infused with, though. There was no doubt in her mind it was the same hallucinogen that'd been applied to her when she'd been kidnapped, possibly the same one she'd stumbled into when she'd imagined she'd been summoning demons. It was dangerous stuff, because Angela'd had zero problem attacking anyone who looked like the freakish beasts she now realized she'd seen in her parents' study some three years before her own abduction.

What had she done to create those images? She didn't believe she'd summoned them with the sheer force of the words she'd recited from the scrawled Serbian text, but there had to have been some trigger. Had she knocked over a vial of poison? Had she released some type of gas by opening the pages of the ancient book? Did her parents have any idea what they'd had trapped in the room with them during all those days and nights of research?

She doubted it. They never would have left the room unlocked if they'd thought there would be any danger to Angela or her grandmother. And they never mentioned anything about the room. For all these years, some secret part of Angela's mind had thought she'd released something truly horrific into the world. That latent fear had fueled her desire to fill her mind up with any other information she could find—facts, figures, absolutes, and equations to solve esoteric problems that had nothing to do with fire-breathing demons. But the demons hounded her all the same.

And Gregori Stearns...was a demon.

A demon she thought was *hot*. And not for any of the reasonable fire-and-brimstone reasons, but because he made her smile. He made her laugh. Because she straight-up wanted him.

What was *wrong* with her?

"Congresswoman Stanton." The security guard nodded to her, and, fighting back her blush, she went through the protocols exactly as required, as she had for so many weeks. Only today, Gregori was behind her, murmuring his responses to the security guard and allowing himself to be searched. It was an almost laughable exercise given how imposing he was. This wasn't a man who needed to rely on guns to protect her. This was a man who'd thrown himself in front of her to stop flying bullets, a man with whom she'd already shared her innermost secrets, secrets she hadn't even realized she'd been carrying. He was plenty intimidating on his own, no weapons required.

A few minutes later, they were in the holding room of the conference center, the lobby that already housed other bodyguards and congress people, drinking coffee and catching up. She hadn't had a moment alone with Gregori since their, ah, conversation, or whatever that had been yesterday, and she regretted that. There was no possible way they could have a conversation here. The place was undoubtedly wired for sound, and an aching wave of loss swept over her.

Why hadn't she pushed for time alone with him? Why had she allowed herself to go through her normal routine? She'd woken up, showered, eaten breakfast, reviewed the day's paperwork, scanned the news feeds...when all the while, somewhere in the same building was a man who'd shone a light on her past, so bright that it'd chased all the shadows away. Shadows that had crowded around her so closely, she hadn't even realized they were there, that the darkness was not simply part of her past and present, absolutely normal.

But she hadn't reached out for Gregori, hadn't sought him out at all. She had hidden behind her paperwork and her coffee and her routines, and now it was too late.

"For your signature." Gregori handed her a notebook with a rich leather casing, and she frowned at him, taking both the notebook and the pen he proffered when she'd given him nothing to review or prepare for her. She'd never even seen this notebook before, actually. Still, she gamely opened up the pad and saw the single line of text scrawled on the crisp paper.

What's wrong?

Her eyes popped wide, and without thinking, she penned a quick note back to him. *Want some time with you.*

Immediately, she grimaced. Okay, that was the height of unprofessionalism, but she wasn't going to scratch it out, and she'd written it with his fountain pen, the smooth slide of ink seeming to take on a life of its own. She snapped the folio shut but tucked it under her arm instead of handing it back. She would take out the paper as soon as she had a chance and throw it away...or eat it or something.

"Same routine as usual," she said, smoothing her hand down the soft leather of the portfolio. Her fingers looked neat and straight against the dark background, as if they'd never been broken. She was proud of that. "All good."

Gregori's next question broke through her reverie. "Why all the animals?"

Her head came up with a snap. "What's wrong with having pets?" The response was too sharp, almost audible to the nearest congress people milling about, and she pursed her lips as if she could recall them.

Gregori simply shrugged. "Pets are two matching lapdogs or a cat. You have a herd. Why?"

"Does there have to be a reason why?" she challenged.

"With you? Yes."

The words were easy, without censure, but they cut through Angela's bluster like a fan through whipped cream, scattering her carefully parsed thoughts and her media-friendly sound bites regarding her affection for animals, dedication to the vulnerable, and all-American-girl sensibil-ities. Instead, she could only blink at Gregori, fighting the flush rising in her cheeks and failing.

"I like them," she blurted, blushing harder. "They don't judge. They—they let me help them."

"They needed you," Gregori agreed. "Joe says they were all pretty sick when you found them, even the orange thing. You helped them a great deal."

She lifted one shoulder, but the tightness around her heart softened as she thought of Old Sir's toothy smile, Hey Mister's bounce. "Not as much as they help me."

"We should talk about—"

Staccato alarms sounded around them, and everyone froze for a second. Then instantly, security entered the room, their guns visible, their orders blunt and autocratic.

"Fire," one of them said briskly. "Saw it even as it happened, electrical short in a bank of circuits scheduled to be worked on next month, but they caught while mainte-nance was not five feet away. Protocols require we evacuate, but you'll be back soon, I promise. We won't even need to take you out on the street, only into the courtyard. You'll be completely protected."

"Of course," Angela murmured as she filed out with the others, Gregori right behind her. She didn't exchange glances with him, but she felt the flush crawl up her cheeks as they moved. It was too much of a coincidence that the fire alarm had hit mere seconds after she'd regretted not having more time with him, right? But how could he... How could anyone...

Their security detail dumped them out into the courtyard as promised, a borderline charming space that Angela had used many times over the past several weeks to relax and collect her thoughts. Shelter from above was achieved through a healthy canopy of tree limbs and strategically placed awnings, making the space the safest area available outside while still allowing open air to circulate. Gregori gestured to the table, and they sat, and without thinking, she handed the portfolio to him.

He set it aside without glancing at it. "What's wrong?" he asked again.

"Did you do that?" she shot back, her voice low. "Did you know that was going to happen—? What am I saying? I'm sorry."

She sat back and drew in a deep breath as he studied her without expression, his eyes retaining their habitual concern without straying into obvious worry that she was losing her mind. She appreciated that.

She also appreciated that she'd just gotten what she most wanted in that moment, and it seemed churlish not to take advantage of the serendipity. "I never got a chance to thank you properly for what you did yesterday," she said quietly. "I don't know exactly what you did, but it seems I'm able to tell you things I haven't even been willing to tell myself. If you don't work out as a bodyguard, you definitely have a future as a bartender."

That made him chuckle. "All part of the job, ma'am," he said with such an incongruous drawl, she blinked at him.

"Why are you really here?" she blurted, then flushed, glancing away. "I'm ashamed to admit I forgot all about pursuing that line of questioning in the wake of everything that happened."

"You had a lot to process."

"That's as may be, but I need to understand—"

Gregori gestured slightly, and for a moment, she thought he was going to lay his hand over hers. Instead, he kept his hand lifted slightly until another congressperson passed them with a cheerful word for her. Then Gregori dropped his hand lightly back to the table, near hers but not touching it. She found herself staring at his large, capable fingers, the size of them dwarfing her own, and fought a nearly impossible urge to reach over and graze his skin. She balled her fingers into a fist.

Gregori started talking again. "I told you this before. You came up in my company's research as a potential target for terrorist attacks, and they've gotten quite successful at predicting the timing and nature of such attacks. They had me in place at the right time, and I was able to achieve my goal of keeping you safe."

"Why would they care about my safety?" Angela asked warily. "What's their agenda?"

"Their predictive models indicate you'll be faced with several opportunities to impact legislation that aligns with their goals. They are in no way attempting to influence your decisions on that legislation. They merely want you to have the opportunity to guide it as you see fit."

"What legislation?"

Gregori gestured again, dismissively this time. "I don't know," he said with an air of frankness that she doubted all the same. "They're not in the business of providing policy guidance. They're merely in the business of predicting outcomes of said policy and doing what they can in the private sector to ensure the world is prepared for any...untoward eventuality."

"And these are the people who think that the threats you referenced yesterday are actually real, breathing, sentient beings. Not illusions."

"Would you say I'm an illusion?" he asked wryly.

"I would say you've gone through significant trauma, and that you very likely have been...enhanced in some way to serve as both a protector and a weapon." She grimaced. "I guess you could say the same about any soldier of war who's been trained well enough to be released to the front lines. But you're not a soldier, you're a civilian. And I don't understand what happened to you, or the effect you're having on me." It had to be some sort of hallucinogen, right? It simply had to be.

Gregori smiled. "I can't help you with the second part, but what happened to *me* was the result of actions a long time ago, nothing that you or your government can be held accountable for. And it's not relevant to the issue at hand. What's most important is that you're safe enough to do your job. That your mind is clear of fear and your body protected at all times. That's what I'm here for."

Angela tensed, his reference to her body completely innocent and almost sterile, but still affecting her in a way she couldn't seem to control. In fact, once again, she almost desperately wanted him to protect her body in a very up close and personal way. That was *not* going to happen.

"Okay! We're good to go." An official-looking staffer stepped out into the courtyard, holding the door open as Angela exhaled sharply. "Sorry about the inconvenience."

They all stood, and she ruefully noticed that Gregori had picked up the portfolio, though he handed the pen to her.

"Keep it," he rumbled. "I'll be waiting for you when you finish with your meetings."

13

Gregori stood with an air of cool, detached interest as Angela entered the room. He looked detached, anyway. Inside, he was a roiling morass of sensation that was completely outside his realm of understanding. When he'd seen what Angela had written on the pad in her crisp, exacting hand, he shouldn't have been surprised. He'd known her thoughts easily enough with the strength of the bond that was developing between them. But seeing the tightly worded request written out, not just as an emotion, a thought, but as actual *words* gave it tremendously more weight. He'd carefully ripped the page out of the portfolio and folded it up, transferring it to an interior pocket. He didn't know why he did that. It wasn't like he was going to forget her request anytime soon. But that didn't stop him from tucking the slip of paper away.

Now he could hear the murmuring of voices through his earpiece, thoughtfully provided by the archangel and commissioned directly from the Arcana Council's resident tech expert, the Fool, along with the transmitter pen. Both devices were completely undetectable by normal mortal scans, and his glamour rendered his earpiece imperceptible to the human eye. He didn't really need the augmentation of traditional tracking devices in order to hear Angela's thoughts, as vividly as her emotions were expressed. However, he didn't have that bond with the other members in the conference room, the congressional representatives who were today going to be discussing the legislation that had brought them to this point. He could tell by the set expressions on their faces, the rigidity of their movements, that two of the four congress people had already been briefed on the nature of the day's revelations, while the other two remained blissfully unaware. Angela was one of the ones unaware, but...

Gregori frowned. How would he exactly describe Angela's current mindset? She seemed more at peace than she had when he first met her, relieved almost, which was typical for a human whose pain had finally found an outlet for release. But she wasn't as relaxed as she should be. He hadn't finished the job. She still retained all the horror of her abduction at eight years old, horror and something more. Something important, the archangel believed—and Gregori now concurred. He'd need to finish his process with Angela sooner rather than later.

"Angela, your thoughts?" Hearing her name startled him back to focus, and Gregori narrowed his eyes. It was the older congressman who spoke, Randall Severin, one of the two already in the know.

"My thoughts are, primarily, that I am concerned that this research and development has gone on for so long without the oversight of this committee. I understood when I took this position that all new research and development activities were at some point funneled through our office.

This initiative has gone on for a full year, and this is the first I'm hearing about it. How is that possible?"

"It was ongoing, yes, but we haven't received an update in the nine weeks since you joined the committee. Simple oversight."

Even to Gregori's ears, the explanation sounded too pat, but Angela appeared to accept it. "Why them?" she asked instead. "Why did this..." There was a rustling of paper, "... AugTech International receive funding and approval to move ahead when there are literally stacks of applications awaiting our consideration, some that have been in process for several months? And yet they're already to stage two of their development process, and ready to give us a demonstration. That speaks to a level of progress that, once again, should have required an update in the past several weeks."

"Well, I, for one, say it's about time," came a smooth, older woman's voice in a Midwestern accent. Trudy Behns, Gregori surmised. He could tell from her energy that she also knew what was going on, at least in part. "While I can understand your frustration, Angela, I'd also mostly forgotten about this company since we hadn't heard from them in so long. It happens. Even with congressional support and funding, experiments frequently fail. When that happens, most of these organizations creep off to try to sort things out until we show up, asking questions."

"Or they fold altogether," said another man, apparently Bob Minnick. "But Randall, you seem to have the inside track here. This briefing is pretty basic. What else are we missing?"

"Besides that we may find ourselves in the position of having to notify other departments depending on what we see later today," Angela pointed out.

"That's not at all how I would characterize the nature of this test," Randall said hastily.

"I, on the other hand, can absolutely see Angela's point," Trudy replied. "If AugTech has reached a level that's anything close to what they're suggesting, it's time to escalate it through the proper channels. That includes Homeland Security, NSA, FBI, DOD. The whole lot."

"How much of this initiative are they already aware of?" Angela asked, her voice distracted, as if she was searching through paperwork.

"Gregori."

The sudden sound of his name caught Gregori completely off guard. His hand was halfway to his temple to adjust the speaker when he caught himself, shifting his fingers to adjust the lapel of his suit. Why would anyone speak his name? And even weirder, the earpiece was in his right ear, and the voice sounded distinctively like it was coming from his left.

"Gregori," the call came again, and he stiffened. He wasn't being summoned by someone in conference room A, but his boss. Great.

Gregori could feel the tug of the archangel's compulsion to leave his post, but he resisted, scowling. Michael, more than anyone, should know that mortals didn't simply disappear into thin air. That meant he couldn't either. He needed to remain here, guarding his charge. Exactly what Michael had asked him to do.

A second later, Gregori was ripped out of the conference center waiting room, his arms going wide as he found himself in the center of an entirely different room, this one perched improbably high over Las Vegas.

"I'll be missed," he growled.

"Yo, dude. Only for a millisecond."

The unexpected voice made him blink, and Gregori realized he wasn't alone in the room with the archangel. At least half the Arcana Council was present, from the Magician to the Devil to the Fool, their resident tech genius. Even Sara Wilde, Justice of the Arcana Council, had put in an appearance. She slouched in her chair, her fists driven into her pockets. Their eyes met briefly, and she nodded.

But it was Simon, the Fool, who kept talking. "I've hijacked one of the cameras to project, not simply record," he explained. "What that means is you're currently a hologram there. Yes, if somebody comes up to you and spills coffee on you and you don't notice, that's a problem. But so long as people give you a wide berth, which I kind of suspect they do on a regular basis given the givens, you should be good for the few minutes we need you."

"Fair enough," Gregori grunted. He trusted Simon, at least in this.

In appearance, the Fool was one of the youngest members of the Arcana Council, and he seemed barely more than a boy, with his long legs and spindly arms, his unnaturally pale face and large eyes that tracked computer code incessantly, a skullcap pulled over his mop of dark hair. In his typical glamour, Gregori looked like he could twist the Fool into a pretzel, but he was well aware of the power every Council member wielded, from the tech wizard Fool to the pale and ghostly archangel.

He glanced to Michael. "What do you need?"

Sara Wilde interrupted. "We're tapped into the same information feed that you are from the congressional conference room. AugTech is a new organization to us, at least by that name. But what they've been messing with is something that's definitely been on our radar. Several months ago, there was an attack on a coven of Serbian witches, you remember?"

"We did not intervene in time. It was a massacre." Gregori winced as he said the words, but the Syx had had no idea of the power behind the horde that'd been unleashed on the unsuspecting witches, one of the oldest covens in the world.

"That's not the worst of it," Sara said. As Justice of the Arcana Council, it was her job to hear the cries of the afflicted in the Connected world, particularly those who were being abused by their own kind. Psychics, magicians, and sorcerers who'd taken it upon themselves to oppress those too feeble or too ignorant to get out of their way. "We'd thought that most of these witches were dead, like you did. Only now, they're starting to show up in other places."

Gregori straightened. "They're unharmed?"

"Oh, they're harmed, all right. They self-destruct before we can get close, but it seems clear that they're a conduit for control. They were kidnapped, abused, and forced into service to control demons for their abductors. They're behind the demons' actions, but not by choice. They get their orders through some sort of implant—we haven't figured that part out yet—and then convey it to any demons on the frequency nearby. They're getting pretty good at it too. The attack in Atlanta? There's a Serbian witch behind it, mark my words."

"Did you know this?" Gregori directed this question to Michael, who'd remained uncharacteristically quiet so far.

The archangel grimaced. "I didn't. I knew about the attack on the Serbian coven, of course. The massacre in the name of demon overlord Ahriman. I hadn't heard that the witches were not uniformly killed and burned, which was bad enough, but that they were taken for these...experiments. This subjugation. It's a level of debasement I still can't quite grasp."

Gregori scowled. "You've had millennia to get used to the depths to which humans will sink when properly motivated. If you can't grasp it, you haven't been paying attention."

He ignored the archangel's glare and turned to Sara. "So what do we do?"

"From what we can pull from Simon's bug, this AugTech group is staging a demonstration of a new brand of supersoldier later today. Very intense, very hush-hush. The congressional committee Angela Stanton sits on will be seeing it at the same time as Pentagon brass and the Joint Chiefs of Staff. Not the President, though."

"Plausible deniability." Gregori nodded. A failsafe he'd seen in nearly every government since the dawn of human history. "What's the test?"

"That's the question of the hour," Simon piped up. "From what we can gather, it's some sort of battle, but it's almost gotta be demon on demon. And demon on demon..."

"That's not a good idea. Push the right one too hard, he'll kill on command." Gregori didn't bother slanting a glance to the archangel. The demon enforcers had certainly proven that demons could be pushed pretty damned hard and not break. But they'd been vetted for their position, and they'd all been Fallen. Ordinary members of the horde were a far different breed. "Push the wrong one too hard, and he'll kill everything in sight."

"Hugh will join you at the drop site, wherever it is," Michael said. "You'll intervene if necessary, but I would prefer it not be necessary."

Gregori grinned mirthlessly. "What, you don't want to

treat the Joint Chiefs of Staff to the sight of demons getting sent back beyond the veil?"

"Could be cathartic for them," Simon offered. "Evil gets its due and all that."

"Unless they realize that evil's getting routed by creatures they also consider evil," Michael said sharply. "The witches' involvement is an unknown. Can they force demons to drop their glamour? Can they force them into killing each other for the sake of a demonstration? The horde is made up of two distinct groups. Those who have fought long and hard for their place on this earth, surviving in the shadows for millennia, and then the new influx of demons that were released in the midst of the battle against the pagan sorcerer gods."

Sara muttered something under her breath, and Gregori glanced her way. She hadn't always been Justice of the Arcana Council. When he'd first met her, she'd been the only human strong enough to carry Gregori and his fellow Syx out of the bolt-hole they'd been lured into by another member of the Council, the Emperor. They'd agreed to the Emperor's terms—to remain until summoned by him, guarding a group of children he'd abducted—on the archangel's say-so. But the moment Viktor had left them in an oubliette outside the veil, they'd realized the truth. The Emperor never planned to release the children. Never planned to release the Syx either. The archangel, never much one to care about their personal comfort, had given them no indication how long this exile would last. In the lifetime of an immortal, it hadn't been all that long—a scant ten years—but it'd still chafed. Then Sara had arrived to reclaim the children that Viktor had stolen from her hometown when she herself had been a young girl, and the demons had seen their chance for escape. They'd forced

Sara to give them safe passage back to earth and only a few months later met their overseer, the archangel, in the flesh. Sara had been none too thrilled to play taxi driver to six demons, but that was nothing compared to her horror at inadvertently loosing legions of the horde across the earth, a side effect of her battle against the intruder gods.

She blamed herself, but Gregori knew better. He shifted his focus to Michael. The archangel held his gaze, the tension between them almost a physical thing. It wasn't Gregori's place to correct Sara Wilde. Eventually, she would learn the truth. Until then...

"Humankind has known worse than this scourge of demons," he said quietly to no one in particular. "It will all make more sense when it's over."

"We're done here," the archangel snapped. "You can return."

"I'll warn Angela," Gregori said.

"No." To his surprise, the archangel's response was echoed by Simon and even Sara.

"We don't know for sure what they have planned, and Angela Stanton is trusted by them. She's believable in her role. We don't want to jeopardize that," Michael continued. "Keep her safe, but don't tell her about the demons' involvement. There's still too much we need to learn, and we won't if we act too soon. Go."

The archangel's directive was dismissive, but Gregori waited a second longer, simply because he could. Then, however, as his kind had been forced to do since the moment they'd been pressed into service as enforcers six thousand years ago, he went.

He replaced his hologram seamlessly in the conference room. As Simon had promised, barely a few moments had passed. Gregori lifted a hand to his ear, checking the earpiece nonchalantly, but the congressional committee members droned on, their attention shifting to several contract organizations which were rumored to be testing similar weapons to AugTech, though with no real progress or success.

Of course they wouldn't have, Gregori thought. They didn't have witches on their side.

His lips twisted as all the ancient lore sprang up in his mind, seared into his senses over the millennia of his time with humans. Witches had real power over demonkind. When summoned into the circle of a witch, a demon was bound to do her bidding for the duration of whatever spell she put on him. Demons that'd previously been Fallen were not as susceptible to witches' orders, but most of the horde would be. Still, how had this group of humans at AugTech managed to subvert not one but several of the most powerful coven of witches? What sort of technology had they developed to accomplish such a thing?

The doors opened, and a row of congress people strode out, including a tight-lipped Angela. She gazed across the room at him, and his heart tugged hard. She was afraid of what they were about to see, no question.

From what he'd just learned, she had reason to be.

14

A ngela stood at one end of a grassy field they'd reached after a long and winding drive through Virginia forest. They were easily two hours outside Washington, DC at this point, but given the nature of the "test" she was about to witness, that was a good thing. AugTech had promised a three-wave exposition of the intelligence capacity, efficiency, and ferocity of their new weapons, which had been disturbing enough.

More disturbing by far, however, were the assertions they were making, their words at odds with the cheerful sunshine and light breeze playing through the trees of the pleasant glade where they'd set up tents and refreshment tables and chairs, a summer garden party of death.

"We believe that the following demonstration will impress you," the AugTech rep was saying, his military-perfect bearing well-earned through the US war machine. "We know it will disturb you. What you're about to see isn't like something out of a Hollywood movie or science fiction book. It's not about showy explosions and scorch-the-earth warfare. It's far more minimal than that, and far more effective. We'll only be showing you a very basic attack, far less sophisticated than what these units are capable of, reminiscent of wartime tactics we've long since abandoned. But rest assured, these units are equipped for far more sophisticated campaigns as well. Importantly, however, we're not alone in developing this technology."

"You said as much in your report," Randall cut in. "Before we go further, explain that." To his credit, there was a new edge of concern in his voice. He'd been AugTech's largest advocate, but he wasn't a monster. He was having as much difficulty as the rest of them wrapping his head around the concept of AI war robots that were so humanoid, they bled and appeared to suffer pain.

Will Granger, the AugTech rep who'd retired from military service with full honors and the rank of Colonel three years earlier, had already shown them detailed schematics of the insides of the robots—you didn't get to anything approximating a circuit board until you were deep inside the torso. He'd also offered a live dissection demonstration with an AI battle unit, and the committee had turned him down flat. There would be time for that later, but none of them had the stomach that morning to watch surgery on a functioning humanoid figure, even if it was a robot. As it was, Angela's head throbbed with all the medical and human-rights ethics violations inherent in this process. Did AI war machines have rights? Did it make a difference that these machines looked like humans and reacted like humans, to the point of screaming and dying with credible effect? AugTech had shown them a short video of those deaths, and the subsequent process to repair and return the machines to the front lines. It was...impressive.

And deeply wrong.

Now Granger grimaced—not quite a smile; the information he was sharing was too important for a smile—but not a scowl either. It was the expression of a confident man who believed in himself and his project, no matter how unsettling it was. "Russia, Korea, China, Japan, Iran—not Iraq yet, but they're exploring it—United Arab Emirates all have R&D underway. So far, we've seen no sign of development in South America with government contractor groups, but it's happening in North America and there are also several private sector labs in the US currently undertaking this research. And they're moving fast, without needing to worry about congressional oversight."

Issued by another man, those words would have come across as a rebuke, but Granger kept his voice carefully modulated. His company's efforts were being funded by the US government, and from what Angela could tell, Uncle Sam had given AugTech plenty of leeway to develop his machines as quickly as possible.

"What's your assessment of the threat level of these various operations?" she asked, her voice carrying on the brisk afternoon breeze.

"We don't believe the Russian, Japanese, or Iranian operations will be viable for another year. They're too far behind the curve. The Chinese effort, though, is robust and well funded, and the regime is motivated by the amplified political unrest of its citizenry. The idea of deploying a security force that appears human but that puts no more of its actual personnel at risk while quelling uprisings is very compelling for them. Dubai's operation is moving quickly, but with a level of specificity that is different from ours. They want to create assassins and private bodyguards for the sultanate, not a massive police force."

Angela winced. "That's still incredibly dangerous."

"Agreed. If one or two of these highly developed

machines worked their way through our border security, they could infiltrate the personal security of high-level targets in the public or private sector. They could, in turn, also serve as a lone gunman in a mass shooting, though that is more problematic."

"Autopsy reports."

Granger nodded. "Detection after the fact remains the largest exposure for the use of these units. The mass hysteria that would result could potentially lead to bans and politically charged fearmongering that would, at a minimum, delay additional development and, at a maximum, shut down the operation entirely. No one in the business wants that."

"So if you're going to use these, um, robots...your best bet is to use them in active theaters of war."

"Yes, where 'casualties' can be removed from a combat scene without detection. All units are programmed to simulate death on the battlefield on command—there won't be any hostage taking. That would also result in detection. But Congresswoman Stanton, I would encourage you not to use the word 'robot' when referencing these units. The term robots conjures up images of mechanical constructs that are easily discernible as not human. That's not what we're developing. These units look, smell, feel, communicate, and react like humans."

The deep sense of wrongness continued, and Angela scowled. "Then how can you tell them apart?"

Granger smiled and held up a slim device, like a remote control for a hotel TV. "Human beings, no matter how well trained, can only be directed, not controlled. AugTech battle units are different. Their programming is ironclad, and though they appear to be sentient, with thoughts and emotions and worries and feelings—they aren't. Any reactions they display are merely one of dozens of precoded subroutines we developed for any units deployed in social environments where they'd be expected to interact with civilians or even in close contact with US soldiers or enemy combatants. Underneath that veneer of artificial humanity, however, is a machine. And machines can be controlled by other machines."

Angela pursed her lips. She'd been forced to relinquish her cell phone and all writing devices and paper before exiting the vehicle, and the security detail for all congress people had been forced to remain behind. She was surrounded by the top brass of the military, so it wasn't like she felt exposed or in danger any way. Still, she wished Gregori was hearing this—not just sensing her emotions, which were likely all over the place—but receiving this intel directly.

There was a rustling of activity at the front of the tent, and Granger straightened. The five screens flickered on, showing various views of the field in front of them, but Angela moved forward to the table that held binoculars. She didn't want to see whatever was about to happen on a screen. Atrocities on monitors afforded their watchers a certain sense of remoteness, and she didn't want that.

"The first test will be a simple skirmish, with two lines of enemy fighters coming together, both with orders to shoot to kill," Granger said crisply. There was a low muttering from the congressional pool, and he held up a hand. "Remember, ladies and gentlemen, these are machines. There's no difference between what you're going to see and a video game. They do not feel pain, even if they've been programmed to express pain. They do not feel remorse, even if they've been programmed to express remorse. Which none of these units will do."

He hit a button on the remote he held, and before anyone appeared on the field below, on the screens, Angela could see two lines of soldiers moving through the heavy forest at a fast trot. Behind each group, a trio of three uniformed officers followed, two men and one woman in both cases.

"Who are they?" she asked.

"Military and technicians," Granger said, his eyes shifting from the screen to the field. "Pay attention, this won't take long."

It didn't either. As Angela watched through her binoculars, the two lines had no sooner broken free of the tree line when one-third of each party dropped to their knees and began firing their M4s, while the rest raced forward, guns out. They shot without hesitation, but it still took nearly a half-dozen rounds of ammunition before the first soldier fell, his body a mass of bloody flesh, his eyes wide in death before he hit the ground. After that, the two lines converged, and it was swift and brutal carnage, a combination of guns, fists, knives, boots—

"Enough." The order was sharp and powerful, and Angela recognized the four-star General who uttered it, his keen eyes fixed on the field.

Granger hit a button and—only because she had swung her binoculars that way—Angela noticed how one of the female techs jolted. The woman raised her hands, then corrected and pulled a remote from her pocket, and a second later, the men on the field peeled away from each other, staggering into ragged ranks.

Granger answered Angela's question before she had a chance to ask it. "Part of their programming allows them to appear as normal soldiers would in the wake of bodily damage. In most cases, there will be no outside witnesses to any military incursions that involve these units. However, in the event that someone is watching, we have designed them to ensure they comport themselves in a manner consistent with that of a well-trained soldier."

"They got that down," muttered one of the military types, someone whose name Angela didn't know. She glanced swiftly down the line of senior officers, but most of their expressions remained stoic, unreadable.

Granger pushed on. "The second illustration is an extraction of a hostage in hostile territory—"

"Wait," Trudy said, saving Angela the trouble. "Why aren't they getting up? The units on the ground. Why aren't they reanimating or whatever you call it and exiting the field?"

Granger turned back to watch as another group of soldiers burst out of the trees, sets of men carrying stretchers between them. They raced to their fallen comrades, then systematically began loading them on the stretchers, before retreating back to the tree line. "I think you'll agree that the sight of half a company of grievously wounded soldiers suddenly standing up and brushing off their uniforms would eventually be noticed and remarked upon," he said. "All units are programmed to remain down until they're removed from the field. It's only when they return to a safer location that those who can return to active duty do so. Bear in mind too, these are still machines, and much as you can shoot up a motorcycle to the point where it no longer works, some of these units have sustained a level of damage that will take time to fix. But what's important to notice here is that there's been no loss of life."

"No loss," Angela echoed, once more beating back the dread she felt watching the field being cleared with precision. Could that possibly be true? Was that what she was seeing with her own eyes?

"What problems are you facing?" one of the brass asked Granger. "What keeps you from being able to deploy these units immediately?"

Granger nodded briskly. There was no denying the flare of excitement in his gaze as he turned it to the senior officer. "What you're seeing here are prototype units, whose programming we have tested and trust. In addition to the money and supplies it would take to scale up this operation to create a meaningful quantity of units for military purposes, we also need to ensure the programming doesn't degrade once the units are put into operation. We have not been a hundred percent successful in that regard."

Angela lifted her brows. She wasn't used to anyone admitting any problems when they were seeking government funding and expansion of their programs.

"Meaning?" the senior officer pressed.

"Meaning, some of the units have assimilated their human veneer of personality and that personality programming has, on occasion, overridden their base programming. We have identified the likely subroutines that are causing the issues, but at this point, we have been trying to ensure the viability of using these units in social situations, not just straight combat. So rather than abandoning the personality programs altogether, we are seeking to refine them."

"Show me what a failure looks like," the four-star general demanded.

"Of course." Rather than turning to the field, however, Granger directed everyone's attention to the screens. "This was a recording from three days ago that I believe you'll find instructive."

The screen filled with an image of a hunched-over man

sitting in what appeared to be a concrete bunker, his head in his hands. Armed guards stood around him, though he made no move to attempt to break the shackles that were locking him to the floor.

"Is that a man, or...?" Angela didn't realize she was the one speaking until Granger turned to her.

"That's one of our most advanced models, deeply embedded with personality programming along with military tactical programming."

"He's sweating," Trudy said, her voice hushed. "How is it that he's sweating?"

"As I said, we've created the most-humanoid-possible units," Granger said smoothly. "We also have been pleased to report a ninety-eight percent success rate with the programming. This is part of the two percent that did not go according to plan."

The man glanced up, his dark eyes shining desperately beneath heavy dark brows, his brow glistening with sweat. His lips twisted as he saw something beyond the plane of the camera—and went absolutely wild. He leapt to his feet with so much strength that one of the chains broke, while the other was half torn out of the ground. He used the trailing edge of the chain as a whip and managed to disarm two of the four guards in less than five seconds. But even more alarming than his speed was his face and body. His jaws stretched wide, roaring in agony and anger, and his entire body shifted. It was as if the skin wouldn't stay where it was supposed to over the muscle and bones, but shuddered and slipped and bulged. The man lurched forward directly toward the camera, and it was clear what he was trying to yell: "No!"

Another of his chains broke, then, with a barrage of

gunfire, he was down. Bleeding out very effectively on the cell floor as the guards converged on him.

"That was a machine," Angela said shakily.

"That was a machine," Granger confirmed. More personnel rushed into the bunker and surrounded the figure on the floor. In less than thirty seconds, they stood back again, and Angela got a glimpse of the body. The man's sternum had been flayed open, and there was no denying the circuitry that gleamed beneath the muscle and tissue and all the blood.

She gritted her teeth, trying not to be sick. *A machine,* she told herself. *A machine.*

"The next demonstration is ready," Granger said, his voice crisp and cool. "If you'll direct your attention to the field..."

15

G regori leaned against the shiny black metal of the military-grade SUV and peered thoughtfully at the men with rifles who guarded the entrance to the demonstration area. He'd heard the shots and shouts of the first round of attackers rushing through the forest. They all had. But he'd heard something more too.

A plea.

It was faint, uncertain, as if the cry was coming from someone trying to fight their way through a fog, but it was there. Too diffuse for him to get a fix on without really focusing, and it didn't last. Had he imagined it?

He glanced over to the far edge of the security details, where a long, sleekly muscled man lounged against a tree, his aviator shades masking his features and his face schooled into a permanent half grin. The demon enforcer Hugh eyed him right back, then lifted one shoulder. Maybe, maybe not. He'd heard something too, but it'd been too faint to constitute a true cry for help the first time around. The afternoon wasn't over yet, however.

There was a buzz of activity toward the gates, and the

men stood aside as a new vehicle approached, this one a heavily armored van. Gregori heard the term "hostage" and watched with interest as the vehicle trundled past the checkpoint and toward the demonstration area. Something shifted at his side, and he glanced over to see that Hugh had abandoned his position by the tree to draw closer.

"They do keep things interesting, don't they?"

Gregori grunted. God's children never found themselves short of ways to perpetrate atrocities against themselves. As a Syx, Gregori had waded into more than his fair share of battlegrounds, which were homing beacons for the worst of the horde. Even demons who'd been doing a good job keeping to the shadows for millennia were tempted by the siren call of gunfire, the scent of blood. They were creatures enslaved by chaos and pain—of course the battleground would draw them.

But what would draw them here?

"You sense it, I assume?" Hugh drawled, and Gregori nodded. They both shifted slightly to the side, drawing even with the trucks. No one was watching them, and this area wasn't under surveillance. The only cameras were at the checkpoints into the demonstration area and the one where they'd exited the main road to head to this facility. "This place is crawling with demons."

"They're trapped," Gregori agreed.

"Ayup. Couldn't happen to a nicer group."

"It shouldn't be happening at all."

Hugh had nothing to say to that, because of course, Gregori was right. Tech or no tech, demons couldn't be controlled by any humans other than witches, and even then only within a very limited set of parameters. They also couldn't be truly harmed or killed by humans other than members of an elite group of human-angel hybrids known as Nephilim. The American military was undeniably impressive, but Gregori was pretty sure they didn't house any Nephilim in their ranks.

Witches, however...

Gregori filled Hugh in on the information he'd gleaned from the Arcana Council, and the typically laconic demon stiffened further with every word. "The Serbian attack? Ahriman?" he grunted, squinting now. "That's great, but what the hell are these witches doing to control that many demons in the wild? They shouldn't be able to do that without a sacred circle, and I didn't see anyone handing out chalk at the checkpoint."

"Agreed," Gregori said. "But it appears they're controlling them all the same."

Hugh stretched his arms high over his head, as if he was knocking the kinks out of his back, then resumed an easy lean against the truck.

"So, what're you going to do about Angela?" he asked.

Gregori shot him a look. "Don't even think it."

Hugh grinned. "Dude, anyone with eyes in their head knows you've let her get to you. And why not? She's beautiful, smart, brave. So long as we care for the children of God and they come to us willingly..."

Gregori snorted. "You would know about that better than I. No human is safe with me, Hugh. I'll hurt them."

"You'll hurt *yourself*, maybe. A human like Angela? Nah."

"Stop it," Gregori growled. "Your lies have no place—"

He cut himself off, drawing in a sharp breath. In his heightened empath state, Hugh's words were striking far too close to home. He of course felt deeply for Angela, but he'd told himself it was merely the side effects of their intense empathic connection to each other, nothing more. It couldn't be anything more. She was a child of God, beautiful, broken, and unbearably strong. She was uncannily smart, vulnerable and uncertain, while he was...

He was...

He grimaced, too attuned to any emotion, even his own, not to see the truth. He was already half in love with her. Fantastic.

"Told ya," Hugh chortled. "You suck so bad at lying."

At that moment, the air became electric with tension, a tension even the ordinary security personnel noticed. These were highly trained soldiers, skilled at reacting to the tiniest nuance of danger. Now they shifted toward the entrance to the demonstration as one. The guards at the gate straightened as well, pulling their hands up to position their guns more prominently.

The gunfire started seconds after that. No one from the AugTech remote viewing tent moved, and there were no human screams that Gregori could discern, but three rapid bursts of machine-gun fire strafed the area beyond, and then there was the indisputable sound of men rushing through the trees, exactly as they had before, only this time, a much smaller group.

"Extraction of a hostage," one of the AugTech reps called out to the security personnel, his voice grimly amused. "Violent extraction, but extraction. Your people are safe. Maintain your positions."

Compelled beyond his own personal safety to learn more, Gregori reached out, stretching his senses to find Angela in the area beyond—horror. Fear. Dismay. All the ordinary emotions of a person forced to watch something distasteful, but not a hint of personal danger. He widened the net of his reach, though, and he heard it again.

"Please." It was a woman's voice, high and intense with panic, not spoken aloud, but uttered so strongly in her mind

that it practically pushed Gregori back a step. Beside him, Hugh rocked up on his toes, ready for action. *"Please, I can't —I can't let him die. He didn't know! He didn't know. Fallen Angels of God, he didn't know."*

The outpouring of emotion that accompanied this cry was so passionate that Gregori was smothered in a wave of pain and remorse, the woman practically suffocating on true regret. She was begging for God's grace, not for herself, but for someone—for some*thing* trapped in this test. He knew it in his bones.

"A Fallen?" Hugh murmured, but Gregori shook his head.

"Only a demon at this point. No single human can hold a Fallen against its will. But probably...probably once a Fallen." He shuddered to think of it. They came across such demons, of course—there had been scores of Fallen charged by God to train humans to explore his creations faster, better, quicker. The lessons of the Fallen had led to breakthroughs in science, magic, mathematics, animal husbandry, agriculture, and navigation, language, the arts—so many things. But the temptation to the darker side of humanity remained ever present, and the Fallen had not been well prepared for that. Some sinned without even realizing their loss of grace before it was too late; some willfully turned away from God's call; some acted in a moment of passion, overwhelmed by the vibrating energy, the intense need for growth, for change, for *action* these humans represented. It didn't matter what the reason was, of course. The moment a child of God was harmed by any other creature born of God's hand, that creature—whether angel or Fallen —was condemned. And so it was, so it always would be.

But this Fallen-turned-demon had apparently struck a chord with a witch.

"She's used him before, worked with him, gotta be," Hugh grunted. "She may even have summoned him without realizing it this time around, or, worse, he followed her, thinking she was in danger. We go in?"

Hugh was already vibrating with the need to move, but the mission was technically Gregori's to command. There was probably some sort of strategy he should apply to this moment, but strategy wasn't his game. Emotion was. And there was so much emotion pouring out from the battlefield beyond that he was drowning in it.

Gregori nodded. "We go in."

They moved more swiftly than any human eye or technology could track, cutting back through the trees and blowing past several blockades set up in the forest, manned by heavily armed soldiers. AugTech was clearly not taking any chances with its AI battle units, and Gregori knew why. You lose control of a demon horde, especially one you've figured out how to entrap and abuse, and you were dead men walking. He wondered idly if the human foot soldiers had any idea of the danger they were in, or if their leaders had been wise enough to keep that information to themselves. Probably the latter. These soldiers showed no fear, merely interest, and he suspected they weren't idiots. Which meant they didn't know they were about to become lunch meat.

Gregori and Hugh burst into the clearing a moment later, moving swiftly. In the center of the field, angled so that the watchers in the tents and the drone cameras could have the best viewing angle, was the large panel van that had driven by them minutes earlier. Both sides were open, and on the near side, easily a half-dozen demons crouched, barely holding on to their human glamour. The pain that held them in stasis was breathtaking in its severity. Even Hugh sucked in a sharp breath. "What the hell is this?"

"That's not the worst of it," Gregori gritted out. "These aren't just demons. They're the Possessed."

"Oh, for the love of—"

They reached the van, generating no reaction from the horde, who were so transfixed by their pain shackles that they had no time to worry about a visit from the Syx. If anything, a few of them turned misery-locked eyes their way, begging for release.

Gregori scowled. You knew you were having a bad day when the prospect of returning to damnation across the veil was your best alternative.

Still, Hugh and Gregori accommodated them, and in less than fifteen seconds, nothing but black goop remained on the battlefield behind the van. That would get noticed, but not until the AugTech minions checked the video stream from the remote drones. Nobody was watching the back of the van now.

All the action was in the front.

It was outright chaos. A human—a real human, neither possessed nor merely a demon in excellent glamour—cowered in the center of the field, guarded by three Possessed soldiers who were systematically taking out waves of demons racing out of the trees. Both sides had guns, but the Possessed were simply better at shooting. They were the ultimate hybrid, bent to single-minded focus, and when Gregori opened up his senses to them, he could easily see why. They had implants in their skulls—several of them, and in a line down their backs. So not only Possessed, but controlled, with a combination of AI and a witch's touch. And they were winning.

"The demons getting shot by the Possessed aren't going

to die," Hugh muttered as they maintained their glamour against the truck, blending in against the bulky vehicles. "They're debilitated by the pain they're feeling, enough to knock them out, but they're not going to die."

"Nope. Instead, they'll be collected, stored, and released again for the next demonstration." Gregori's lip curled. He had no affection for the worst of God's creatures. Demons were the basest form of what humans called evil, with no morality, no choice, no option in most cases other than to seek out and destroy all that was good and bright. They lived for horror and blood, and it took tremendous willpower for them not to attract attention to themselves with their depravity. They had to learn that willpower in order to survive on earth all these millennia. But the recent influx of the horde was a different story. They'd had no time to learn the ropes, no time to understand the balance that must be struck between ravaging and restraint. They had been herded, trapped, and enslaved by someone even more diabolical than they were, and certainly a hell of a lot smarter.

But while all demons had the power to possess humans, they could only be compelled to the act of Possession with any level of success by a witch. Gregori narrowed his eyes on the three soldiers standing over the hostage. These Possessed also vibrated with pain, pain and something more. Outrage. Even the most heinous of creatures knew when they were being exploited, it appeared.

"Please," moaned the witch again, the voice in his mind getting louder. Gregori turned and saw the small knot of AugTech technicians gathered at the edge of the field. Two men, one woman. The woman held a slender device in her hand. Some sort of remote control, Gregori knew, but that wasn't where the real power was coming from. It was coming from her other hand as she raised it and played with the currents of energy surrounding this field of death. This was a very powerful witch, and one also encased in shackles of pain...but not so much pain that she couldn't raise at least her voice in defiance, even if she couldn't raise her fists. *"Please."*

"Go," Gregori muttered. He and Hugh materialized from beside the truck, their glamour morphing to take on that of so many faceless demon soldiers who'd been attacking the three hostage defenders. Startled, the Possessed humans turned, but Gregori and Hugh didn't give them much time to react. Even with the incredible electrical surge of the artificial circuitry of the Possessed, the enforcers reached inside and yanked the demons free from the mortal bodies they were violating, dissolving two of them immediately into ash. Those demons would find themselves on the other side of the veil, and there it would be God's choice as to what happened to them. But no longer would they be held in the thrall of humans who would bend them to such depravity.

The third demon was something different, something new, and it took both Hugh and Gregori to remove it from its human host. When they did, the beast glared at them with eyes as blue as starlight. It was one of the most powerful demons they'd ever encountered, someone who could give any one of the Syx a run for his money, and they stood for a moment, staring at each other as the rows of demon soldiers dropped to the ground and a net of human soldiers raced onto the field, guns firing. Gregori made the call.

"Fly," Gregori whispered. "Fly."

The one-time Fallen didn't need more encouragement. With an inhuman cry, its wings unfurled, tattered ribs stretching, and it lifted itself toward the heavens and out of sight. Hugh and Gregori turned as one of the AugTech technicians ran up to them, fear rolling off her body—and they realized she too was not exactly what she seemed. She was a witch, right there on the battlefield. *Of course,* Gregori thought, *to control the demons within the Possessed.*

"Please," she gasped. "You must help us."

ngela had surged forward without thinking, her hands clamped around her binoculars, as soon as she'd seen Gregori and another man race around the van in the center of the clearing, clearly catching the hostage team by surprise. Only...Gregori was now dressed like one of the AugTech soldiers, the same as his partner. As if they'd been part of the demonstration the entire time, a secretly embedded duo of destruction loosed to create havoc at the last moment.

They certainly created havoc in the tent, though immediately controlled havoc. Every screen had blanked, and Granger had started snapping apologies about technical difficulties, loudly calling into his walkie-talkie to hold the mission. Smoke bombs went off in front of the hostage group, and there seemed to be more fighting, which several keen-eyed military officials watched through their binoculars. But Angela tossed her set on a table and dashed forward, directly into the smoke.

"Congresswoman Stanton," somebody barked, probably Granger. She didn't stop. She knew Gregori was in trouble by the van. She knew it with every fiber of her being. She just had to—

A nightmare erupted in front of her, one of AugTech's soldiers snarling in rage. Not Gregori—she was still too far away from him—but one from the outer perimeter of attackers. The soldier staggered out of the smoke, eyes wild, arms flailing. Then his skin—shifted. His face sagged and his jaws extended, and in the disorienting haze and smoke, he looked...well, he almost...

He struck. Angela's arms went up protectively, but she was no match for a hundred and ninety pounds of solid muscle and flailing arms, hands—claws, fangs. Her mind blanked in absolute terror, and then she started screaming back words and lines and passages so buried in her psyche, she'd long since forgotten them. Passages from an ancient book buried in her parents' study. Passages of protection and power.

The creature heard them. His head swung around, his eyes snapping to hers as he hissed in surprise, scrambling away from her to leap back into the smoke. His pain-crazed eyes had seemed almost *relieved*, she thought as she struggled to her feet. She had no idea what she'd told him, but he was away from her, and that was good enough.

The smoke cleared, and as someone shouted over the intercom to *stand down, stand down, civilian on the field* she realized that civilian was her. But by then, she was almost to the van. Gregori and his partner—whoever that had been—were no longer present, but three bodies lay on the ground, and another huddled in a heap in their center. A woman, she realized with renewed horror.

"What's happening here?" she demanded as she dropped to her knees to help the woman, blood seeping into the material of her expensive pantsuit. "These people are hurt. Where are the medics?"

"No one's hurt." A man ran up to them, his voice a little breathless, almost desperate, and even as Angela reached for the crumpled woman on the ground, she felt herself roughly pulled up and away.

"Hey!" she growled.

A second voice followed directly behind. "Get your hands off the congresswoman."

The low, steely voice reverberated with such strength, Angela could practically feel the van rocking beside them in reaction. She turned with as much surprise as the AugTech employee—and staggered to the side when the minion released her and straightened out of pure, animal instinct.

Gregori stood beside her, once again dressed as a security guard, though he seemed bigger. Rougher. And he glared at her assailant with such an outpouring of hatred and barely restrained fury that the man took another step back. Other people ran up, these looking far more official, and Angela dropped to her knees once more, her arms going around the woman, who was just returning to consciousness. Small, fine boned and pale, with soft blue eyes and ghostly blonde hair, she looked like a fairy fresh out of Middle Earth, not a highly trained military technician.

"I'm fine," she said. "Perfectly fine. Really."

Her words sounded steady, but her gaze, when it connected with Angela's, conveyed the depth of her lie. She wasn't afraid, exactly, but she was outraged and mortified and deeply dismayed. What was this woman to AugTech? Why was she here?

"Ms. Green," a new voice behind Angela rang out, hard

as granite. "You're all right? And you, Congresswoman Stanton?"

"No thanks to your man, yes," she said stiffly, taking in the newcomer. He was compact, square jawed, and tough-looking...which put him in good company with most everyone she'd met today.

"My apologies for that. I'm Zachary Howard. I run this division of AugTech. Janice Green is one of our best testers, but admittedly, this was an extremely heightened demonstration. We did not take the appropriate precautions. The blood you believe you see is not human blood. It is a tinted and viscous liquid meant to simulate real-time situations."

"And these guys?" Angela gestured to the men sprawled around Janice Green, as she recategorized Howard. Not a minion at all, then, but one of the men in charge of this mess. Good to know he was so hands-on.

"Knocked out by the gas," Howard said without hesitation. And to be fair, the EMTs were administering oxygen masks to all the soldiers scattered on the ground, many of them responding with convulsions and gasps. "We can't always be sure soldiers will respond to verbal commands in the heat of battle, not when they've been given their orders."

"But I thought you said these men weren't soldiers," Angela snapped.

"The units, my apologies," the man amended easily. "We work hard to approximate real-life conditions, including how we reference the battle units. And we anticipate that the eventual utilization of the security measure will occur almost exclusively in battlefield conditions, with other soldiers who *are* human. We needed to be prepared to stop the demonstration even if verbal commands were overwritten or not heard. We did that. The gas is extremely localized, released at each unit's collar. It takes them down quickly and completely, without harming anyone around them. As you yourself can attest."

Angela made a face. She hadn't been dropped by any gas, that was true enough.

"Congresswoman Stanton?" Gregori's low voice had her turning her head, and she met his gaze. It was so forceful, she nearly stepped back, but not because of his anger. Instead, she felt as if she knew exactly what he was thinking, exactly what he wanted her to do. And that was to stand down. To act like she accepted everything that was happening in front of her and even be complimentary about it. That message in her mind was absolutely preposterous, yet so strong that she couldn't deny it.

"I'm solid, thanks." She turned back to Howard and offered the man her first smile of the day. "I apologize for entering the field of your demonstration, Mr. Howard. I appreciate how quickly you responded to a civilian on the field, and I must say, I'm impressed with the level of your operation here. From everything I've seen, this is truly a security measure—even a weapon to be reckoned with."

Howard's eyes shifted slightly, as if he was assessing the veracity of her comments. As well he should. Angela poured it on a little thicker, stepping toward him.

"What's the timeline here? I know there are probably two dates in your head, one you feel confident about suggesting to the congressional committee, which I certainly appreciate. But I need to know what the other date is as well. When could we deploy these units if we needed to? If you had sufficient funding and support?"

It was the word "funding" that did the trick. The intensity of Howard's expression eased, his mouth even twitching into his own smile. "For an emergency deployment situation, we can ramp up in a matter of weeks. For smaller units, such as an extraction like the one you just saw but with much less fanfare, we're talking days. Some of the units have been sufficiently tested to qualify for that. I wouldn't want to trust them ordering coffee from Starbucks, but they could go into the store and get somebody out with no loss of human life."

"Excellent." Angela kept her expression open and enthusiastic. At this point, other members of her committee were approaching, carefully escorted by AugTech representatives. She turned toward Randall and noted his excitement and something almost approaching hope as he glanced at her. She could feed that hope easily enough.

"So what do you think?" she asked. "Because I thought this was the most extraordinary thing I've ever seen."

Trudy responded first. "There seriously was no loss of human life in any of that carnage?" she asked shakily.

"None," Howard confirmed, his gaze returning to Angela even though she hadn't asked the question. His eyes were assessing, hard, and more than a little curious. There was no way he could have known she'd screamed out ancient Serbian demon injunctions while getting accosted by one of his "battle units," but the man clearly sensed something was up.

Angela peered all around, but Granger was no longer on the scene. Now that the situation had escalated to the point of meeting the big guns, there was no point to him anymore. She suspected he was little more than a glorified babysitter.

Howard continued. "All units except for these employees will be extracted and repaired within the next forty-eight hours. We may need to give our employees a little more time off to recover."

"Well, this is very impressive," Randall said, and several murmurs of agreement came from the military brass in the crowd beyond them. Nobody seemed to have any concern about the mechanical glitch in the screens or the necessity for issuing gas to take out the drone soldiers, but Angela was pretty sure they'd agree to just about anything with the idea of a military force that could be repaired, not buried. "When could you deploy test units into our military installations? With the approval of military leadership, of course."

"We'd work with all parties on the standards and protocols needed to be put in place," Howard said smoothly. He nodded deferentially to the row of brass lined up beside the van. "It's too early to speculate what standards we'd need to meet, but I can assure you that as soon as you have a need for these units, they'll be ready."

"And if we needed them next week? Tomorrow?" asked one of the brass.

Howard offered a red-carpet-worthy smile. "We'd do everything in our power to accommodate you. Depending on your needs, tomorrow might be pushing it, but I can guarantee you the results will exceed your expectations."

The demonstration broke up shortly after that, with all the requisite glad-handing and promises of follow-up documentation, and the congress people dispersed to their own vehicles. Angela was more grateful than she could possibly express to realize that she and Gregori would be alone in a state sedan, whisked back to DC without the need for conversation. She had no doubt the interior of the vehicle was bugged, so there'd be no point to that conversation regardless, but at least she didn't have to keep up appearances. Merely having Gregori's solid, reassuring bulk beside her did more to settle her nerves than she was brave enough to admit.

"You're okay?" he prompted as soon as they cleared the last checkpoint and were back on the highway. She blinked at him, surprised because, of course, he knew the car was bugged as well. But his steady gaze once more seemed to convey far more than his words. He wanted this conversation between them recorded and logged.

"Completely," she said, pitching her voice between relieved and intrigued. "I shouldn't have left the tent."

He snorted. "No, you shouldn't."

"You shouldn't have entered the demonstration field either."

"AugTech approved clearance after you left. One of their reps approached me, gave me a briefing," he said, surprising her. She had a feeling there'd be techs somewhere scrambling to corroborate that, but if it gave her permission to continue this ruse with Gregori, then so be it.

Still... "Why?" she asked with credible wariness.

Gregori shrugged, his eyes crinkling at the edges, though he didn't give her an outright wink. "Because of my military service and a few of my other contract positions. They did their research, wanted me in the know."

That sounded incredibly unlikely, but she wasn't the one who had to prove it. "And what was your assessment?"

"Tactically, these units are more capable than they honestly should be. I don't know how they advanced robotics that quickly."

She leaned forward. "Agreed. If I hadn't left the tent, I never would have seen how these units perform in the heat of battle. It—it's extraordinary. I know AugTech is worried about assimilation into social settings, but I think that's the least of their concerns. I wouldn't glance twice at most of them. Setting aside the direct military engagement I know the company is seeking out, they could transform safety concerns in public settings. With no loss to human life..."

She allowed her voice to trail off, as if she was stunned by her own words. "No loss."

Gregori nodded again, apparently pleased with her performance, and they fell silent. But as Angela stared out the window at the unbroken line of forest that made up so much of the Virginia hills outside of Washington, DC, she realized that not all her wonder was feigned. A security force that was completely dependable, unhackable, and that delivered on the promise that AugTech was making actually *would* transform security in America. How many mass shootings could be eliminated with a robot who had immediate access to all criminal data and all camera feeds with facial recognition software instantly recording and uploading data on every person in the area? That sort of identification tech was already in place. The question remained only on how to use it effectively. She didn't know what AugTech was doing specifically, but if it actually was implementing its stated mission...wouldn't that be something?

Sighing, Angela reached for her briefcase. They had two hours of downtime before they arrived back in DC, and she had hundreds of pages of reading to do, emails to respond to, and texts to return. She needed to use the time wisely.

Across from her, Gregori settled back in his seat and, to anyone not watching closely, seemed to fall asleep. She knew differently, however. He studied her from beneath his hooded eyes as she worked, the brilliant green missing nothing as she plodded through report after report. He watched her hands, her mouth, her gestures. He studied her so intently, it was almost as if he was gazing deep inside her, searching for answers to questions he hadn't yet asked.

She felt herself flush, her fingers tightening on her pen.

She wanted him to ask those questions, she decided, the

realization both a certainty and a surprise. She wanted anything he would give her, if she were honest.

Whether he was a demon or human, empath or soldier or creature of magic—it simply didn't matter anymore. Her path had led her to this point from the moment she'd first opened the witch's spell book in her parents' study and seen the cloud of magic burst out. Now, sitting here with Gregori, she felt more connected to another being than she ever had in her life. A crackle of fire burned through her bloodstream and made her heart pound faster, an awareness of power and possibility that called to her like a siren's song—because of Gregori. Whoever he was, whatever he was...

She wanted him.

17

Gregori eyed Angela with concern as they reentered her condo. While they'd been at the demonstration, Joe and her security team had temporarily removed her menagerie of pets and swept her place for any surveillance equipment, friendly or otherwise. Then they'd installed the best tech Simon and the Arcana Council could offer. Her place had also been swept by the Syx for any residual demon energy lurking in the ductwork, but they hadn't found anything. Gregori shifted as Angela shut the door behind them, excruciatingly aware of her proximity.

She tossed her bag on the couch, running her hand through her hair, some of which had slipped free of her elegant hair clip. "Joe texted that he's setting up a perimeter detail on the building, but I asked him to keep the gang for a bit. They're at the vet's for wellness checkups under duress, but I've needed to get them there for a while. I...I just want to be alone with you, if I could. For just a little while."

Gregori braced himself as another wave of her need washed over him, need he was pretty sure she hadn't fully identified yet. But he had. Partly because he was a former Fallen, a member of the Syx, with the heightened awareness and sensitivity that brought. And partly because he was a natural empath already bonded to Angela. That elevated their connection to a searing intensity, making her every thought, every emotion, every shift in heartbeat and breathing pattern as familiar to him as his own, down to the very dilation of the woman's blood vessels. It was maddening, overwhelming, and it carried him along on a tide he not only welcomed but craved with every last ounce of his being.

Gregori sighed out a long breath. Hugh had been wrong. He wasn't ready for this. He wasn't ready for any of this.

"Gregori?" Angela asked uncertainly. She sat on the couch beside her briefcase, her hands clasped on her knees, seeming so oddly alone in a space normally filled with all the animals she cared for, desperately clinging to the reserve she needed to project in public...the reserve she was losing more and more by the day. She had easily explained away her flashes of anger and the completely foolhardy dash across the battlefield during AugTech's demonstration, but her hair was no longer caught up in its ruthlessly tight ponytail, her suit was no longer so crisply pressed, and she seemed to not even realize she'd scrubbed off all her makeup and not reapplied it. She didn't need it, of course, especially not with her emotion riding so high, flushing her cheeks and brightening her eyes. But the fact she didn't notice its absence was telling.

If he gave her enough time, she would. She'd pull back on the mantle of studied and calculated calm, present her expression of self-assured control to the world, and carry on. It was what she wanted, he knew—what she probably believed she needed.

And he, as a member of the Syx, dedicated to protecting Angela Stanton and keeping her safe, should give her what she wanted. Should allow her to keep shoring up the walls she'd so carefully built to protect herself from the world around her. Should allow her all the rationalizations and intellectual rabbit holes she could manage to chase down so she could keep the desperate agony she'd buried deep inside her from swallowing her whole.

He should.

He wouldn't—couldn't, at this point. But he should.

He crossed the short distance to the couch and wing-back chair, but instead of taking the chair like any rational human would, he lifted a boot and shoved the coffee table out of the way with a sharp, swift motion.

Then he dropped to his knees in front of Angela.

"Oh!" she managed, pulling back a little on the couch, her hands dropping from her knees to grip the cushions on either side of her legs. "What are you doing?"

Gregori leaned closer, his eyes dark and intent. "You know I'm an empath."

Sudden awareness zipped across her expression, and her cheeks colored. But to her credit, she didn't back down. "I do," she said.

"And you know what that means?"

She started to speak and couldn't, then cleared her throat to start again. "It means you can feel the emotions of anyone around you, particularly somebody with whom you have, um, bonded. Which I assume we have."

"Not only the emotions. The sensations. The reactions, every nuance of change to your breathing, your heart rate. I can sense your pain the moment you're injured—"

"And you can sense how I'm feeling, if I'm not injured. If that's not what's hiking my heart rate or making my hands shake," Angela whispered. Her eyes had sheared away from his gaze to drop to his mouth, which caused a responding urgency to well up inside Gregori, a desire twin to Angela's own. He let his mouth open slightly while leaning yet closer, and could practically feel Angela's eyes dilate.

"I can sense all those things," he rumbled. He was close enough to feel the touch of her breath on the skin of his neck where his shirt was open at the collar, feel each of the tiny hairs on his arms prickle with awareness of Angela's every shiver. "And I can imagine what it would feel like to hold you, kiss you, because those thoughts are so powerfully etched into your mind that they have become one with your emotions. But I'd rather you give me permission to take you into my arms so I can experience that firsthand."

"I..." She swallowed, and her cheeks went scarlet as a new thought struck her. "You're not just doing this because I want you too, though, right? I mean, as much as I want you to—"

That was all the permission Gregori could stand to wait around for. With his own blood pounding in his ears, he closed the distance between them, his arms going around her as he pressed her back against the cushions. Though it wasn't the first time he'd kissed a woman, it might as well have been for all the millennia he'd walled himself off from feeling any emotion for anyone else.

The touch of her lips detonated something within him, driving his need with such startling intensity that it blanked out everything else. All he could do was just allow himself to be carried along on the tide of it, his mind blown by the sheer wonder of how strongly he felt and how perfectly right it was for him to be here with Angela in this moment.

She responded hungrily to his kiss as well, leaning up into him, her hands reaching to curl into his shirt, pulling the material out of his trousers until she could slide her hands along the length of his abs, laying her quivering fingers flat on his chest.

Gregori hissed with the contact, and Angela immediately pulled her hands back, breaking her kiss to peer at him worriedly. "Did I hurt you?" she gasped, and he shook his head, leaning away only long enough to pull his shirt over his head and wrench off his belt.

"You can't hurt me, Angela." Not exactly true, but he wasn't about to explain the finer points of human-demon interaction. Right now, all he could focus on was the way his own body was changing, not just the glamour of his humanity, but the demon form beneath, the crippled, misshapen husk he'd been cursed with the moment he'd turned his back on God's children and sinned. Even that broken body was caught up in the glory of both the emotions and feelings that poured through him. The basic connection between two creatures of energy in light and darkness, in need and want, in love and hate. That one had been born to walk in the light and one was condemned to eternal darkness didn't matter anymore. They were together in this moment, and this moment would be enough. This moment was everything.

There was a pressure at his waistband, and he glanced down to find Angela's hand tugging at the rest of his clothing. He knew he should stop, or at least that he should make sure this was what Angela truly wanted. She had gone through much at the hands of the worst of his kind, and even though he didn't want to be a demon, he knew what he was. He should ask—

"Gregori," she implored, turning her face up to him again. Her eyes shone with a need so strong, it was bordering on panic, her mouth set in a determined line. "If you don't take the rest of your clothes right off right this instant and make love to me, I swear I'm going to rip them off with my bare hands and then I'm going climb right on top of you and screw you blind."

ANGELA CLAPPED both her hands over her mouth, but it was too late. Gregori, his jaw clenched tight against emotions she could only guess at, tilted his head back and laughed as if the weight of the world had been lifted from his shoulders.

He stood up just long enough to kick off his boots and wrench off his trousers and boxer briefs in one quick movement. Wrenching off her own clothes, Angela gaped in astonishment as Gregori slung his clothing against the wingback chair. She'd never seen anyone so perfectly formed. In some small corner of her mind, she knew all of it was glamour, but that didn't matter anymore. The man who regarded her with such open adoration was like something out of a dream. Easily over six foot five, Gregori towered over her. The muscles she'd always known were there under his clothes now stretched and glistened in the muted light, drawing her eye inexorably down to the apex of his legs, where his shaft was full and ready...and definitely proportionate to the rest of his body.

Dear God in heaven above...

And then he was on her again.

This time when Gregori kissed her, there was no hesitation, no uncertainty. He cradled her, pressing his lips to hers as if he was coming home. With just the hint of his gentle pressure, she opened her mouth to him and accepted his tongue as it ran over the seam of her mouth and tucked inside, generating a whirlwind of sensations unlike anything she'd felt before. She was no virgin, she'd had plenty of sexual partners, but always before, she'd given of herself with the understanding that there would always be something more that she could hold back, a barrier she could place between herself and whoever she was with that would allow her to remain in control.

Not only was that barrier not there with Gregori, she didn't want it to be there. The raw excitement of being with this man, knowing that he felt every emotion, every sensation as she experienced it and that he wanted, craved even more, made her feel like she was inhaling the most addictive drug in the universe.

"Gregori!" she gasped as his lips left hers to drag a trail of kisses across her cheek and along her jaw, every new inch he explored setting her on fire. "How—"

"It's you—and me—together," he groaned back. "Loop."

With that, she finally put it together. What she was feeling wasn't just the physical sensations between them, but everything else as well—and not just what she was feeling, but what *he* was too. The experience was entirely shared. Her every desire was reflected back to her, reinforced with the power of Gregori's needs and desires. As he drew his lips along her jaw, he opened his mind to her, swamping her with images and feelings, colors and sounds, and music and words of light and magic. A thousand years, two thousand years and more of terror and tears, sorrows and joy, everything that had overloaded him for so long that he had never been able to share with anybody else, he poured into his every kiss, his every sigh. He turned with her then, sinking back against the cushions as he pulled her up on top of him. Her legs spilled over either side of his broad thighs, but she pushed his hands away to take the lead.

As intense as her need was for him, she didn't want to rush this.

Gregori hissed as she leaned forward to run her hands down his trembling abs, but he didn't stop her. When she wrapped her fingers around his straining cock and leaned into him, he went mute, and she didn't dare stop for fear that he might ask her not to go further. She drew her tongue along the edge of his shaft. He bucked in response, his hands clenching into fists on either side of her. In that moment, she knew anything she asked of him, he would do. Any boon she demanded he would grant, whether it was within his power or not. He offered himself completely and utterly to her, she had only to take what he was giving.

So she did.

Shifting her body up, Angela slid down over Gregori's cock, seating him deeply inside her. The pressure was extraordinary, stretching her almost to the point of pain, but she wouldn't stop. Couldn't stop. Not now. He reached up to touch her face gently—so gently—as if she was a revelation of some deep and arcane mystery that had eluded him for centuries, then she was caught up in her own sensations once more. Placing her hands on his broad chest, she braced herself and began moving. Slowly at first, and then with gathering intensity, until Gregori's hands came up on either side, bracing her hips, then driving her even harder, faster. The way their bodies were positioned, she could feel her own release building impossibly fast, spiraling up within her as she clenched her hands into fists. She was determined not to finish before him, wanted to see him tumble over the edge, when the expression on Gregori's face shifted. He withdrew one hand from her hip, keeping her tightly braced to him with the other as he dropped his fingers between her thighs and brushed the bundle of nerves there.

Angela jerked in response, but he didn't let her go, instead rocking her forward, lifting his hips to meet her forward thrusts, absorbing her every gasp, shudder, and tremble as he quickly ratcheted up her own responses until she teetered on the brink of release. But she couldn't...she wouldn't...

She grabbed his wrist. "Together!" she demanded.

"Together," he agreed, and he rotated his hand until their fingers interlaced, and he lifted his other hand so that those two hands could join as well, and they moved forward together, sharing each breath, each sigh, their gazes locked on one another as the need built once more within them and crested over, built and crested and rose again, until there was no going back, there was only going forward...and then...and then—

She dropped off the edge of the world.

18

G regori came back to his senses in a rush, barely able to stop himself from catapulting off the couch. But he instinctively sensed more than intellectually registered that there was a woman sleeping soundly on top of him, curled safely within the protection of his arms. He stared down at Angela, his mind racing, his overloaded senses taking a moment more to fully process what had happened between them. The intensity of their shared release had gone beyond the physical to the emotional and psychic, and Gregori drowned in a sea of emotions he could no more stop than he could understand.

As he moved to gather Angela to him more closely, she shifted as well, and he smiled as she instinctively stiffened. It wasn't as if either of them hadn't been aware of what just happened, yet it already felt like that experience had occurred a million years ago in a faraway place. Behind the torrent of his own emotions—now strangely evening out with Angela's awakening—he couldn't even fully recall the details of what had passed between them. Only that he wanted, more than anything, to do it again.

His body instantly reacted to that thought, and he shifted just in time, easing Angela off him before she could detect the change in his glamour—his *glamour*, which technically was supposed to be under his control at all times. The inconvenient reaction went the rest of the way toward refocusing his mind, however, and when Angela turned to face him, he thought he was more or less prepared for the blast of emotion that would accompany her first glance.

Instead, he gasped, his hands coming up so quickly that Angela flinched back. "What?" she demanded.

"No—shhh, wait..." His words were barely more than a whisper, infinitely gentle, and that, perhaps more than anything, convinced Angela to remain still as his hands settled on either side of her face. She gaped at him with wide eyes as he brought her chin up, his gaze finding and holding hers.

"There is more that you want to share with me," Gregori murmured, and Angela's expression softened, a smile flickering to life on her lips.

"I'd say we just shared an awful lot—even if..." The smile slipped away again as quickly, a furrow of surprise forming between her brows. "Why can't I remember the details?"

"I don't know," Gregori said frankly. "It's been far too long since I've attempted more than a conversation with anyone other than the Syx. I don't know what is ordinary."

"The who?"

Gregori shook his head. "There'll be time for that, later. Right now, I need you to focus on this moment, my eyes. Let me see what you want to show me."

"I—" Angela cut off her own protest as her gaze lifted again to Gregori's, and she drew in a startled breath, but she didn't break eye contact this time. Instead, she lifted her hands to cover his, gripping them tightly. "I don't know what you want," she finally said, but that wasn't true either. Gregori could see the initial slip of her control as tears rose in her eyes and spilled over her lashes, trailing down her beautiful cheeks. She appeared not to notice, caught in the thrall of his gaze, but with each tear, a part of the wall she'd so carefully built and reinforced for so long crumbled.

The first wave of pain came after that, so much outrage and despair that it turned Gregori's bones to ice. It was all he could do not to rush the process, but this course couldn't be rushed. Humans were both infinitely strong and shockingly fragile. They could endure the most incredible pain for weeks, months on end, and then, years later, the slightest word or snatch of song or even a scent could send them into a downward spiral of madness. He knew he couldn't push Angela beyond the precipice of her own control. She needed to be the one to take that step. She needed to be the one to willingly fall back into the embrace of her memories. He knew it—and she knew it too.

The fact that she was willing to try to do exactly that humbled Gregori and drove him to push his own discomfort away, his own panic at the way his senses were expanding, opening, absorbing her pain as it cascaded over him in sheets.

"It hurts," she finally gasped, and Gregori breathed out the softest sigh he could manage.

"I know," he said. "But it must be your choice for me to help you. I cannot take what you won't give."

Angela nodded quickly, several times, as if she was ratcheting up her own inner fortitude to continue breaking down the wall. Her breathing became little more than a racking sob, and her hands clutched Gregori's, clammy with sweat.

"I remember," she managed, the words brittle with pain as the tears stopped and her eyes widened, incandescent with horror. "The day they came for me. That was what I couldn't understand, how I'd let this happen, how I'd been so stupid, so foolish to be in a place where strangers could abduct me without my parents realizing it. I was eight. I knew better than that. I knew!"

Gregori stayed quiet as Angela railed on, making no indication that she had started speaking not in the cool, measured tones of the junior congresswoman, but in the heated rush and querulous tone of an eight-year-old girl yelling at herself. Her entire body was shaking now, but there was no more fear left. It was all anger and indignation, directed inward.

She *hated* herself for what she believed she'd done, releasing demons into the world willfully and without outside help, and that hatred was worse than any pain Gregori had ever endured. God's children were not made to hate, and especially were not made to hate the perfection of their own creation. That emotion was beyond anything the Father had ever intended, a byproduct of the free will He'd so carelessly and beautifully bestowed on mortal souls. But as Gregori'd had the opportunity to learn over and over again through the past six thousand years, any gift can turn into a weapon in the hands of the determined, none more so than the gifts of the mind.

"I should never have opened the book again," Angela seethed. "I knew what was in it, I hadn't forgotten *everything* about what happened to my grandmother. I'd known that something terrible had happened because I'd opened that book and I knew something terrible would happen again. I knew it! Yet I couldn't stay away, wouldn't stay away. My parents never realized I kept track of their anthropology collections, offering to help them shelve and sort, not because I was kid of the year but because I wanted to *know* where those damned books were at all times. They were like a drug to me, and I didn't even understand what drugs were at that age. I only knew that if I kept track of where they were and didn't touch them, then everything would be okay. Until the day that I wanted to touch them. Until the day that I wanted to open the book. Until the day..."

She blinked, focusing on Gregori once more. "I wasn't kidnapped that day in the university library. The school had never been at fault. Later, I made up the story of getting hit and blacking out. That's not how it happened at all. It happened because I opened the book."

Gregori grimaced. "You were only a child," he said, though his words were barely audible. He didn't want to stop the flow of Angela's confession, but she was degrading quickly. Her energy practically curled at the edges in horror and self-recrimination. He didn't need her information so badly that he was willing to risk her mind.

Then she began speaking again. "I was a child, but I wasn't a fool," she said bitterly. "I knew what danger lay within those pages. But it didn't matter. I had taken to stealing the book out of my parents' collection and carrying it around with me. I told myself it was just to prove that I was stronger than it was. I didn't believe in evil. I didn't believe in darkness. I was a privileged daughter of two professors, and knowledge was nothing more than words on a page and thoughts in a mind, both of which I controlled. That's what I told myself. I was wrong."

She shuddered and tilted her head into Gregori's left hand, as if to draw comfort from him. But he couldn't give that comfort either. Not yet. Anything he pushed out toward Angela would serve as its own sort of wall, shoving her memories back into the dark hole out of which they were only now surfacing. He needed to let those memories pour forth, no matter how difficult it was for her. And no matter how the pain was tearing at the demon beneath his body, flaying it open, laying it bare.

"That day in the library, I convinced myself it was my own fear holding me back. That I was fascinated with the book because I'd turned it into sort of a bogeyman, giving it a power it didn't deserve. After all, I'd seen my parents open it a million times. Open it, read from it, translate it—laugh over it. The superstitions of another time, another place. The first time they did it, I about fainted with fright, but nothing ever happened to them. Nothing ever happened to Nana again either. No one seemed affected by the book at all, except me. And I wasn't going to stand for that anymore. The book had no power over me."

Once again, Angela had slipped into the outraged tones of a defiant eight-year-old, anger still winning out over the fear, but not by much. Gregori spread his fingers ever so slightly along her cheek and temple, drawing out her emotion the same way a medicine woman might draw poison from a wound. Angela's eyelids drooped, but she continued to hold his gaze as once more, tears slipped out between her lashes.

"They came after that," she whispered. "I had the book open, was even reading it, bathed in the sunlight coming through the large bay window. I could see the quad beneath me, the students laughing, talking, doing whatever they always did. I was safe. My parents were just around the corner in their own reading room. The library was full of adults. I was safe. They came anyway."

It was all Gregori could do not to ask the questions burning in his mind, but fortunately, Angela kept going.

"The same spell pulled them too," she said, her lips curving into a mocking smile. "I knew it the moment I stumbled upon it, the moment I even turned the page. I remembered. All those symbols and strange words that somehow, I'd figured out how to say. Not perfectly, but perfectly enough. Even as a little five-year-old girl. I'd learned more Serbian in the intervening years, not even realizing why. And this time when I read the words, I understood what they meant. It wasn't simply a bunch of vowels and consonants, there was a flow to the spell that made sense to me. And as my eyes raced over the page I realized it was a summoning spell, one of the many my parents had chuckled over, even sometimes reading aloud. They read them aloud!"

Her face reddened, and her eyes shot wide, fixing Gregori's with a glare. "What is *wrong* with me that when I read the words, terrible things happened, but when they read the words—when anybody else read the words—nothing happened? What had I done? What is wrong with me?"

She pushed on, saving him the need to comment. "I don't know when I actually started speaking the words. Somewhere in the middle of the text, probably, but the change happened almost immediately. I don't think I got out more than a couple of lines before the sun seemed to dim, the kids on the quad seemed farther away. Everybody seemed farther away. I was sitting in a bay window, and there were miles and miles of books all around me, corridors leading away that were far too long for me to ever run down. Then they were there. Demons. Like what you turned into. Like that...man, in the field. Oh my God... Could they actually be..."

She said this last with a sort of detachment that indicated she was no longer aware of Gregori, but searching deep within her own mind. "Horned and scaly with slavering tongues, drool dripping onto the floor, their bodies broken and disjointed. They stood around me and seemed surprised that I was afraid. I didn't realize at the time they could make themselves appear as normal people. I didn't realize a lot of things. Then there was a swift, sharp pain in my neck...and then it all went dark."

She blinked, refocusing on him. "The rest I've already told you in some way or another. They held me for eighty-seven days in a cage, they brought me out and showed me all these people, who started out normal but who changed, they would always change, turning into the same hideous creatures that I'd seen in the library, seen in my own house. Sometimes I would attack them, sometimes I would cry, sometimes I would scream. And they hurt me. Never sexually, never like that. But they struck back when I hit them. They'd bite and tear. And though I was always the one who ended up with broken bones, I think I caused them pain as well."

Angela slumped back on the couch, and Gregori held her a moment longer, until it was clear that the fugue of her confession had passed.

"Thank you," he murmured, waiting for the moment he needed. The opening she hadn't given him yet.

"I'm just...so tired," she sighed, her lids drifting shut. "I'd just like...I'd like the pain to go away."

And that was all he needed.

Kneeling as he was on the floor in front of her, it wasn't difficult at all for Gregori to bow his head and lift his hands so that his thumbs grazed his forehead while his smallest fingers rested lightly on Angela's forehead, his hands clasped together in prayer. He was no longer a Fallen angel.

He was no longer gifted with the grace of the Father to heal the most deeply broken of his children. But he remembered this much. After all the millennia of pain and punishment, he still remembered this. His great and mighty wings would spread wide as he took their pain from them and drew it into himself, suffering their agonies, crying their tears, lightening their hearts so they could be refilled with the purest gift accorded to any of His creations—love.

"Please." He offered the ancient plea not in English anymore, but in a language he hadn't spoken in six thousand years. The whispered, rustling, lyrical speech of the angels of God Most High. "Please. Bring this child peace."

And so it was done.

This newest wave of agony was by far the hardest to endure, and Gregori reared back even as Angela slumped onto the couch, passed out. He turned away from her, staggering several feet as fire and molten steel wrapped his entire body. He collapsed to the floor, his arms outstretched, and screamed in silent agony, racing through his mind, his memories, the universe itself until he reached a place where nobody could hear his cries.

And then, he wept.

19

Angela watched Gregori worriedly across the dining room table. An emergency meeting of her congressional committee had been called for later that morning, and ordinarily, that'd be no problem at all. But ordinarily, she hadn't just slept for fifteen hours straight and woken up feeling...completely reborn.

As good as she felt, however, Gregori looked like he'd been hit by a bus. He stared out into nothing, not even seeming to notice that Hellboy was on his lap, pressing eagerly against Gregori's hand. Gregori awkwardly patted the dog, his hand moving jerkily as if he'd never touched an animal before, but Hellboy didn't seem to mind. He eyed Angela from beneath Gregori's fingers with an earnest "don't interrupt him" vibe.

She pursed her lips together, but couldn't help herself. The other animals, having been returned by Joe very early this morning, hadn't ventured out of their bedrooms in the back of the condo yet, but she knew that wasn't going to last. "You sure you don't want to try this coffee?" she asked Gregori.

Gregori started, glancing down in utter confusion at the dog wriggling beneath his hand before refocusing on Angela. "I don't drink coffee."

"Well, maybe it's time you rethought that plan. Because you definitely need it."

That at least drew a grim smile from the man, but it was fleeting. His brows were drawn together in a fierce scowl, his jaw was set, and, worst of all, he stopped patting the dog.

Hellboy glared at her, but Gregori wouldn't meet her eyes. He tried, but he kept flinching away, as if she'd become disfigured. It'd gotten so bad after she'd first awoken that she'd thought she *had* been damaged, and had fled to the bathroom to make sure.

But she looked the same—better than she had in awhile, actually. She knew it wasn't simply because of all the sleep she'd just logged.

The silence dragged between them as she drank more of the incredible brew Gregori had somehow conjured up, a recipe she would absolutely be dragging out of someone before this day was over. It hurt her heart to see Gregori in such pain, knowing she'd caused it. He'd healed her before —but this was different.

"You weren't so damaged last time," she finally said, and Gregori's shoulders sagged. She realized he'd been trying to keep the truth from her, but if this was his example of a poker face, he'd never make it in Vegas.

"This time was more complete," he acknowledged, almost as a confession. He glanced up at her again, unable to keep from flinching. Hellboy's little head whipped from side to side as he tried to understand the fraught energy bouncing between them. Angela thought she heard the tiniest mew, but she didn't dare look away from Gregori.

"You're—you remember now," he said.

Her brows went up, and she stopped her spoon midway between her coffee cup and the table, then set it down more deliberately. "I remember," she agreed. She wasn't sure at first what he meant by that, but the obvious choice was that she remembered her past. The past that she'd deliberately buried for so long, it had lingered only as a hazy set of images wrapped in darkness and shame.

Only...now it didn't.

"It's all there, now." She lifted her hands to the table, pressing them against the hard wood. She felt a movement at her leg, and glanced down—Domino was rubbing against her, while Old Sir eyed her soulfully from the kitchen door. She didn't see the rest of the crew, though another plaintive mew sounded from somewhere behind Gregori.

Angela refocused on her hands, bringing them together in front of her. Everything seemed to take far longer than it should, as if she was watching herself in slow motion—everything except her mind, that is. She raced through her thoughts and memories, images and flashbacks from when she was very small, and it was all simply there. All of it uniform, all of it real, all of it accessible. The joyful memories seemed masked in a soft, hazy glow, while the terrible memories were dimmed only slightly by a gentle, cool peace.

"How did you do that? How is it I'm not afraid anymore?"

Gregori shifted, and Hellboy reluctantly jumped off his lap, though the small dachshund didn't go far. "It's never the memory that's the true horror, no matter how shocking or perverse the act that drove the memory deep into your subconscious. The human capacity to endure pain, surprise, even the madness and chaos in front of them knows no bounds. The trouble comes from the emotions you attach to those experiences. If you build up enough positive emotions around a situation, it becomes impossible for you to separate the truth from the illusion, for the heart to detach from the moment and move on. Build up enough negative emotions regarding a situation, and it becomes intolerable for the brain to process, the mind to understand, the heart to heal. These are defense mechanisms put in place to keep the fragile balance of the mortal spirit, until such time that enough distance has occurred between the event and the current moment to allow that healing to begin."

"I shouldn't have buried those emotions away so deep, the memories and everything I had attached to them," she said gravely. "But I did. And then I couldn't bring them back. Until you."

"It's what I do," Gregori said simply. He glanced down, his brow furrowing. "Ouch."

She blinked as he ducked his hand beneath the table and came up with an orange puff of fur, dwarfed in his palm. He scowled at the kitten, but Ginger merely curled into a tight ball, her head burrowing against his fingers.

He continued speaking as he tried to roll Ginger onto the table, wincing as her tiny claws dug into his skin. "I merely helped you achieve what you couldn't on your own."

"And that hurt you," Angela said. Her lips quirked a little as he tried to disengage the kitten. "Worse than you're being hurt now."

He chuckled, his large hands dwarfing the determined kitten as he pulled her away. But she got the feeling that he, like herself, found it easier to talk with the animals near, their unfettered affection a key to whatever lay locked within. For Gregori, rubbing the top of Ginger's fuzzy head seemed to be the release he needed to continue.

"I'm an empath," he said. "What that means is that I

draw on the emotions, pain and sensations of another being and take them into myself, in effect transferring the burden from the other person to within me. You know that."

She leaned forward as Domino jumped into her lap. Ghost leapt up on the nearby couch, content to survey their conversation from a distance.

"Yes, but you did this once before, this healing thing, and you weren't so wrecked. I mean, I'm sure it was no walk in the park, but this isn't the same."

Gregori grimaced, glancing up from the kitten with a new heat in his eyes. "I suspect it's because our connection is stronger than it was before."

"But why...oh." Heat swept up Angela's cheeks as she realized what he was talking about. They'd had sex. Hell, more than sex. Her entire body had been blown apart and put back together again in a new way, leaving her craving Gregori's touch, his whisper, his smile. He was everything she'd ever wanted in a man, never realizing it was actually a demon she needed. She suspected there would be some serious therapy involved with that realization, but there it was. And, as it turned out, she happened to know a very effective healer. "Are you going to get better eventually?"

That brought another wry chuckle. Gregori leaned back in his chair and lifted his gaze from the table to the ceiling, his face warmed by a shaft of sunlight. She caught her breath as the sun played over his chiseled jaw, his long lashes, his full lips. He really was the most beautiful creature she'd ever seen in her life. What had she ever done to deserve him?

There was a scramble of movement from the kitchen door, and now Hey Mister and Elvis shuffled closer, pressing Old Sir forward as they all eyed Gregori nervously. At

Gregori's feet, Hellboy yipped with satisfaction, and the dogs edged a little closer.

"I'll improve, yes," Gregori said, ignoring the dogs even as Hellboy leaned adoringly against him. "I'll get better. To get better, I also have to detach, to remove the emotions from the experience and regard the event as mere history, not some precious moment caught in time. I'm...not quite ready to do that yet."

"But that makes no sense. Why—"

He waved her off with a tired hand, even as Ginger batted at his fingers. "When you spoke of your past, there was a commonality between both times that the demons came for you."

She sighed, settling Domino more comfortably in her lap. "The book of witchcraft, the text of the Serbian witches. Before you ask, I haven't been able to locate it again. My parents long since returned it to the university library where they'd withdrawn it via interlibrary loan. Given some of the things I said during my recovery, they realized at least in part that their research books had potentially put me in danger. It created a sort of crisis of confidence in them about their work and they didn't share much of it with me for years after that. They never denied me access to their library, but at that point, I didn't quite remember what I'd done, and I didn't have any great longing to attract danger to me once again. My parents also aged all those days that I was gone, far more in some ways than I did."

Gregori nodded. "When a parent commits to loving a child unconditionally, it can be very difficult when that child comes to harm. But the book—do you remember anything about it?"

"I don't even remember its title," Angela said, grimacing. "I mean, I guess that's a good thing. I can remember some snatches of the words I said, I used them yesterday as well, but nothing cohesive enough as a summoning spell. For that, we'll need real witches."

That statement gave her pause, and she glanced over to Gregori again. "You don't think I'm a witch, do you?"

"No one is born a witch," he said. "It's a path marked by careful study and is a vocation for its adherents. Were you born with the capacity to manifest thoughts into being, a capacity that was made more real with the aid of ancient spells of powerful sorcerers? That seems more likely. You memorize your surroundings with an impressive amount of visual energy, filling in the complete picture. That visualization skill is definitely above most mortals'. The combination of your natural abilities and your unusual focus could well be all that's necessary. And it also explains why AugTech abducted witches. They're using them to summon and control the horde as they conduct their experiments."

Angela shuddered. Gregori had finally told her what the organization he worked for believed about AugTech. What she herself believed, finally, because she'd seen it with her own eyes. They weren't employing artificial intelligence units with hallucinogenic drugs floating around to trip up the unwary. These were demons. Fire-and-brimstone demons, as Gregori had called them. The scourging horde.

"I couldn't imagine willfully bringing those creatures into the world and then trying to control them," she finally said. "Why would anyone want to?"

"The reasoning for the witch-demon connection goes back almost to the dawn of humanity. There are things humans can't do, things demons can. And when one or the other party discovers a mechanism of control...it's going to get used."

"Can you get the witches away from them?"

"We're working on that." As they'd spoken, Gregori's color had gradually improved, though he was still not quite himself. The dogs seemed to realize it too. They crept out farther into the room, lying down to watch him from beneath heavy brows. Even Hey Mister remained subdued. "My associates are deploying all their resources to track down AugTech's headquarters and cell sites. AugTech may or may not know they've attracted the attention of the Syx, but their demons surely do. It's a matter of whether those demons have shared that information. If they haven't, we'll track them down today. If they have, then AugTech should already be in the wind, burrowing underground until they've received approval from your congress to proceed."

"Today's meeting," she said, filing away the name Gregori had used. The Syx. He wouldn't talk about it, but the Syx had a hold on him, she knew, a hold he wouldn't—or couldn't—break. "That's just the start, though. Anything this big will have to get approved on several levels, and that's never a fast process in Congress."

"That's as may be," Gregori said, "but I doubt very seriously that it will go through normal channels. I also doubt very seriously that most of Congress will be aware of it at all. That's the nature of the group to which you were assigned."

He flinched again, but this time, it had nothing to do with her or with Ginger sinking her claws into him. He focused briefly on the wall beyond her, then glanced back, holding her gaze. "It looks like we've found the DC cell. I have to go. I'll return before your meeting."

She lifted her brows, shifting to let Domino off her lap. "I have to leave in a little over an hour. There's no way you're going to be back here by then."

"Sure I will. It's what we do. If I'm not here, however, one of the other Syx will be. If they're not, you don't go in. Understood?"

Angela pursed her lips. "I understand you," she acknowledged, and Gregori sighed. He now knew her better than anyone ever had, and he knew she wouldn't stay put. "And I'll wait for you, but not for your team members. Whoever they are."

"I'll be here," he said.

And then he...well, he disappeared.

The cats seemed completely unimpressed but all four dogs yipped at Gregori's empty chair. Angela stared at the open space, not sure what surprised her more, that a flesh-and-blood-and-skin-and-bone being whom she'd recently *slept* with had disappeared in front of her, or that Gregori had felt so comfortable with her that he'd been willing to do that without going into another room or leaving by the front door before he went poof.

She hugged her arms to her body, chilled. Was she okay with...whatever it was Gregori was? A demon enforcer, charged with routing his own kind, possessing superhuman healing and killing and...uh, poofing skills?

"Well, I'd better be, huh?" she asked aloud, and Hellboy turned first, giving her a sharp, affirmative bark.

Angela couldn't help herself; she laughed. But even with the dog's approval, she needed to process everything, assimilate this newest information. There was really nothing else she could do but work this problem out aloud, like she'd worked every problem out, creating images in her mind and seeing them in front of her as she paced and puzzled and paced some more.

She stood. "Okay, guys," she said, addressing the dogs, who all perked up at her voice. "Gregori is a creature heretofore unknown in modern biology, presenting himself as a mythological demon. All presented evidence is consistent with this theory. He's an elite of his kind, possessing the ability to...ah...disappear. Can the others? This group of Syx? Regular demons?"

The dogs didn't have a response to that, so she answered for them. "The others can, yes. To date, based on personal observations, demons can change their appearance, as well as spontaneously travel through space unseen by the human eye. They possess varying degrees of strength, but in most cases are stronger than average humans. They possess varying degrees of intellect, some possessing intellect exceeding that of humans. They can't be killed by most humans."

Hey Mister barked once, sharply, and she nodded. "They also don't generally get along with dogs. Noted."

It wasn't all that surprising that AugTech had fixed on demons as the perfect killing machine. It was also not surprising that they elected to create the illusion these creatures were robots. There was a whole lot of religious baggage to unpack when it came to the idea of working with demons.

"Demon subjects can be controlled by witches, but that control varies with the skill of the witches and the circumstances of their summons of the demons—hey Calvin, Hobbes, how'd you get out of your cage again?" she asked, continuing her narrative as she turned to take another lap of the room and finally spied the guinea pigs now sitting beside the couch. "You poop all over the floor and Joe is going to lose his mind. Anyway—okay. Demon subjects can appear and leave without warning. Does that ability originate within themselves or is it external? Is it different for Gregori and his fellow members of...of the Syx? The Syx. A group of demon enforcers whose job it is to fight other demons. Run by who?"

There were too many questions she didn't have answers to. She'd clearly need to make more laps. She turned the corner—and the dogs went absolutely crazy.

"Guys—guys!" she shouted, but she was nearly bowled over by Old Sir, who whirled as soon as he'd reached her and was now growling with a ferocity she'd never seen in him before. Hey Mister and Elvis were in full bristle, barking and baring their teeth, and Hellboy was rushing and feinting in front of the newcomers, spinning like a whirling dervish, claws and teeth flying, his attack enough to cause the first row of them to pause.

"Get back!" Angela shouted. "I'm calling the police!"

Large, looming, and hideous, the creatures in front of her could have sprung straight out of Dante's Inferno, clearly intended to evoke a maximum response—horns, snouts, claws, and scaly skin, slavering and drooling all over the polished wooden floors.

They expected her to be terrified, but she wasn't. She wasn't! In fact, all she could think of was the dogs. And *where* had she left her phone? "Get back!" she ordered again, shifting another step toward the kitchen. "My guinea pigs will poop all over you, I'm seriously not kidding!"

Then the air seemed to shiver around her, and Angela twisted around as the dogs reacted even more wildly.

A dozen more of the creatures appeared, these smelling of sulfur and need, and they lunged at her. She wheeled back, flailing out with her hands, but something thick was shoved into her face, blocking her mouth, and a second later, she felt the prick—the same prick of a needle she'd felt all those years ago. She wasn't afraid, but that didn't matter. She was still going down, losing consciousness, and being lifted against her will as the dogs howled and screamed and fought all around her.

Could demons spirit a person out of a room bodily, she wondered, like snatching a baby from its crib?

She collapsed before she could find out.

20

"You're not going to like this," Simon the Fool warned someone at the far end of the room as Gregori materialized into the Arcana Council conference room, a second after leaving Angela's condo.

"I already don't like this," Michael returned, and Gregori's heavily attuned senses picked up on something he never expected to see in the archangel. Exhaustion.

Beyond the archangel, the other members of the Syx stood with impassive faces, watching the byplay between the two Council members. Warrick, the leader of the Syx, nodded at Gregori, while Stefan and Finn, the team's resident jokesters, appeared to be trying to gaze everywhere at once. Raum stood off to the side with his traditional quiet reserve, while Hugh watched Gregori. When their gazes met, he gave Gregori a wink, and Gregori stifled a groan. The last time he'd seen Hugh, the demon enforcer had encouraged him to act on his desire for Angela. He didn't want to have a follow-up conversation.

But for now, everyone returned their attention to the Fool as he started talking.

"So apparently, this newest run on using demons as military supersoldiers didn't actually originate within a military force. That makes it different from all the times it's happened before. Different and more dangerous."

"Because of scale," Warrick offered.

"Yep," Simon said. "Back in the day, even up to the point of the Second World War, which is the last time we saw any officially sanctioned use of demons in this way, the bright idea to conscript demons was typically born of some military type who'd had a bad encounter with demons most foul. They made a deal, or the demons offered a deal, more to amuse the demons than anything else, or there happened to be a nearby witch who traded demon control for her life. The how of the thing isn't quite clear, but it worked, though imperfectly. You needed the witch to keep everything moving, and eventually, the witch figured out how to escape. After that, the leaders of the military operation generally met a bad end. The Syx have been summoned into more than a few of those situations for cleanup, I'm thinking."

No one spoke, but no one had to. Anyone who worked with demons for any length of time eventually began believing in God. When things got out of hand, they started praying. And on this earth, only the Syx could hear and respond to those particular prayers.

"So what caused this round?"

Gregori shifted his gaze to Sara Wilde, and they shared a quick nod.

"This one is more a case of professional jealousy," Simon said with a grim twist to his lips. His fingers raced over his laptop, and a second later, an image appeared on the far wall.

"I offer up to you a warlock of some renown whose home base was Estonia up to a very short time ago. There he was part of a venerable old coven, but one that followed rigid traditions. There was only so far a warlock could ascend, because warlocks couldn't manage demons as well as witches could. That wasn't enough for this warlock, of course. He wanted to set his pointy hat for a loftier goal."

"The attack on the Serbian witches. He orchestrated that?"

"It might be too much to say that he orchestrated it, but he knew it was going to happen. This isn't some low-level tea-leaf reader. He knows his stuff. He arguably should have been the head of a coven. If he had, we might not be in this situation."

"Doubtful," the archangel murmured, and Gregori had to agree. In his experience, once a Connected mortal had run out of patience with the way the elders decreed they should follow their path, it was only a matter of time before they began chasing the shadows of other paths.

"Bottom line, he created a pretty solid plan. He knew all about the influx of demons on the planet, and he saw the potential for control, particularly with a military outfit that had the technology to extend the control of the witches in artificial ways."

"So they do use artificial intelligence?" Gregori asked. "I've seen the circuitry and gadgets, but I didn't know if those were for show or for actual use. Actual use changes things."

Around him, the other members of the Syx moved up onto their toes, their bodies tensing for battle. They had been assigned to turn back the horde for the past six thousand years, and they had done so. It had always been somewhat of a numbers game, but the numbers had always fallen in their favor in the end. Six demon enforcers against a legion of the horde made for an interesting afternoon, but little more. The idea that the horde could become super-charged, or super organized, or super anything combined with the ingenuity of human technology put a different spin on the matter.

"Most of it is for show, because, like it or not, there hasn't been a hell of a lot of experimentation with demon robotics. You can bet that's going to be changing regardless of what happens with AugTech. They were merely the group who were willing to pay the warlock the most money to bring his demon idea to market, and the ones most willing to let him run the operation the way he saw fit. There will be others."

"Are you tracking those others?" Sara asked, and Simon nodded.

"We'll know if any of them so much as sneezes. What we know about our favorite warlock is that he pitched the idea for AugTech, they wanted a demonstration, and for that, the warlock needed a witch. But he also wanted to scale up in a hurry, which meant he needed more than one just in case. It was his great good luck that the Serbian attack happened, and since I don't believe in luck, I suspect there's more to it than that.

"Either way, when the attack on the Serbian coven happened, the warlock was ready to strike. He'd already singled out several of the women who held the most potential in the coven but were not yet ascended to power. He didn't want anyone who would be noticed right away or who would be too strong for what he had planned. Collecting the bodies from the carnage went according to plan, and you can bet he left several dying coven members in his wake whom he didn't consider strong enough to be worth saving. Once he had the witches, he could go back to his friends in the private sector and make good on his promises."

"Where does Angela Stanton fit into all this?"

Once again, it was Sara Wilde who spoke, and when Gregori shifted his glance to her, he found her studying him intently.

"I went back into the case files at Justice Hall," she continued. "To see if there had been any complaint leveled on Angela's behalf. There had. Apparently, her parents are both minor-level Connected, so low that they probably never considered themselves as such. But when their daughter was kidnapped at eight years old by things they couldn't fully explain, they turned to their friends, who were more highly placed. Those friends turned to Justice Hall for help. Unfortunately, nobody was manning the store at the time, and nothing happened. Angela was left to fend for herself, which she did. But she should have had more support. Now, here she is twenty years later, in a very unique and public position to affect the outcome of demon use in a military deployment. How did that happen? Surely this warlock wasn't playing his game that long."

"The warlock wasn't, but someone was," the archangel said. "I was made aware of Angela Stanton only on the cusp of the attack in Atlanta. While her abduction and trauma was recorded to some extent, I didn't know she'd been abducted by demons until after she shared that intelligence with the Syx. But someone clearly knew."

"Yup," Simon said. "We've run the data, and all evidence points to Martin Filmore."

"No," Gregori said instantly. "Not him. There's nothing in her knowledge of him even remotely negative. She considers him a friend."

"Yup, yup," Simon agreed. "Longtime friend of the family and sympathetic supporter of their research. Took a little digging, but as it turns out, he was the family friend the

Stantons were dining with the night Angela's grandmother had a heart attack. He stayed with Angela after they rushed Grandma to the hospital."

Gregori felt his blood turn cold. "He didn't harm her." Surely he would have picked up on that.

"Nope, there's no mention of any further contact between the two of them after that point, other than the occasional get-together, up until he contacted her last year regarding her potential interest in running for a congressional seat. But what's interesting is where *his* research took him from there. A review of his internet usage from that point forward proved he became obsessed with the occult. Carefully, slowly, using computers that weren't hooked into any official networks so he couldn't get into trouble or put his political aspirations at risk. But he started doing his research, no question. There's gotta be a correlation."

"Angela told him something, something that triggered his interest, something she truly believed. Maybe there was even some evidence left behind at the scene that nobody else noticed," Sara said thoughtfully. "He goes off and starts studying everything to do with demons, and then takes a seriously wrong turn."

She turned to Simon. "Where was he during the college abduction? When Angela was eight years old?"

"Right down the street working for the Pentagon."

"And where is he now?"

"Richer than God—oh, sorry, guys." Simon shot a glance to the archangel, who remained impassive. "Seriously rich, governor of Georgia. He's an enthusiastic supporter of artificial intelligence research, and he not only was instrumental in Angela's political success, but he—you guessed it—used his clout to get her assigned to the committees she's on. She knows none of this, of course, other than that he encouraged her to run. His role with AugTech—"

Simon broke off as an alert code seared out of a nearby computer, which he immediately yanked closer to him. "We've got a break-in at the condo," he snapped.

But Gregori was already gone, the barked command of the archangel for him to leave ringing in his ears. The command, he knew, wasn't only for him. He reappeared a moment later in Angela's condo with Hugh and Raum, the three of them instantly turning around as a torrent of demons attacked. Demons and—panicked dogs?

Ambush.

In such tight quarters, the Syx didn't have the luxury of being elegant. Gregori roared an order to Angela's faithful protectors to get them out of the way—he couldn't focus on them if she was in danger.

The howling changed cadence at once, then the demons attacked, all flailing claws and teeth and knives. The Syx were compressed back toward each other with no room to move. Rage exploded through Gregori, and he lashed out, breaking through the wall of demons and creating a larger space. He was the largest of all the Syx, and he towered over the creatures as well as his brothers. He had killed his share of demons, sending hundreds of thousands of them back across the veil over the course of millennia, and for the first several seconds, he did that here too, sending geysers of black goop splattered across the luxurious furniture and cloth wallpaper of Angela's home. But once the initial curtain of rage lifted, he realized something else.

These weren't normal demons.

"Augments," Hugh growled. These were the same kind of demons that they'd run into on the field at the AugTech demonstration and that had appeared at the truck rally in

Atlanta. They smelled different and they acted with a precision that simply was not normally part of a demon fight. They'd been trained, and they'd actually taken to the training, whether by choice or more likely by force, crackling with tech, but who was controlling them? There had to be a witch nearby, right?

Even as he thought it, Gregori recognized the fallacy of this assumption. The entire point of the AugTech demonstration was that witches, or somebody, could control these units from afar. The witches they had in the field were there for precaution, but surely they'd already had some success with distance control.

He swiped at another demon, who leered at him, the demon's mouth stretched wide and its eyes manic. Gregori could tell there was something behind those eyes. None of these creatures attacking them were the Possessed, thank the Father, but there was nevertheless a focus, an awareness that wasn't normal.

And then the creature opened his mouth.

"Angellllaaaaaa..." it crooned.

Gregori leapt at him. He could hear the shouts of surprise of the other Syx, but what he was doing now, he'd never done before—had never needed to do before. Ignoring the other demons ripping at him with tooth and claw, he slammed the demon who'd said Angela's name up against the wall, his hand tight around the creature's skinny neck.

As the demon bucked and kicked, clawing at Gregori's hand, Gregori leaned in close, fixing it with his glare. The demon tried to shrink away, but there was nowhere for it to go. He was forced to stare directly into Gregori's eyes, and Gregori lifted one hand between them while the other choked the demon half to death. Tilting his head forward, he joined the two of them together—thumb to his forehead, small finger grazing the demon's brow—and saw into the mind of the creature.

It was sheer madness. But useful madness.

In a flash, Gregori learned everything he needed to know about the creature's present and past. This was not a Fallen angel. This was not even an ancient member of the horde who had lived in the shadows all these long millennia. This was one of the newest creatures that had been loosed upon the Earth, scrabbling, clawing, always hungry, always desperate, driven to experience everything this world had to offer by blackening mortal souls for power. It had already begun picking off humans, contenting itself with the weak and the infirm, like a jackal on the edge of a herd of sheep. It'd also begun hunting in small gangs, never an easy thing for demons, because so few of them were capable of controlling the others. But this demon crew had been surprisingly successful. They'd found shelter. They'd tried to hide—

Gregori tightened his grip, forcing the demon to race through its memories more quickly, and the rest fell into place. The pain that had hit it one day, the terrible pain, waking up in a cage, more pain, always more pain—then surgery, metal, and, yes, more pain. Being sent on this mission with one name on its mind, one name that it could speak with its misshapen lips.

"Angela..."

Gregori didn't see her, and the images filling his mind were nondescript, rows of cages, wide concrete spaces, rooms with computer panels. There was nothing to indicate where these images came from, but there was no denying the demon in his grip was being controlled with a current of energy. As Gregori became one with the demon's mind, he could track that energy, feel its pull. He could follow it.

Now.

Gregori squeezed, and the being exploded in his hands, gouts of black goop spraying the walls and ceiling. He turned to see the other members of the Syx fighting and realized Angela's animals hadn't fled. Instead, they still fought on, staunch and furious—Hey Mister with his teeth sunk into a demon's corded calf muscle, Old Sir chasing another demon around the room, and Hellboy riding a third high on his shoulders, his jaws clamped on his neck. The cats were in on the action as well, Ghost and Domino hissing and snarling at three demon attackers they'd trapped in a corner.

Gregori took all this in with a glance, and then he roared, grabbing another of the demons who had the stink of technology on it and squeezing it hard, feeling the energy current jump and rattle, soaring through the city.

A sudden crackle of electricity sparked at the demon's neck, sweeping through the space—

And Gregori was gone.

21

Angela woke with a start, realizing immediately that her hands were bound and she was strapped into a chair. It was almost laughable how reassuring that was. The last time she'd been taken, all those years ago, she'd woken up in a cage. A chair was a definite upgrade.

"Angela." The voice was friendly, comforting, and efficient, and one she recognized. But not one she expected.

"Martin?" she managed, trying to make sense of what she was seeing. She was in a conference room of some sort, but definitely not one of the congressional conference rooms used for committee meetings. This place was sterile, cold, and gave the impression of being underground, though she didn't know why.

Martin Filmore sat opposite her across the broad table, and notably, he wasn't tied up. The governor of Georgia was a tall, thin man, wearing his habitually too-loose, off-the-rack suit that gave him a working-man air he didn't truly merit—he was richer than anyone Angela had ever met. He had sharp, angular features and warm eyes, and he smiled easily and earnestly—the kind of man who could laugh with a group of roughneck dockworkers and take tea with a bevy of society dames with the same self-effacing good nature. He was smart and he was stubborn—but he tried to downplay both, like most Southern men used to others in politics and business disregarding them because of their soft drawl and easy manner.

Now he drawled with credible dismay. "I didn't expect things to escalate like this, and I certainly didn't want it."

"Didn't want what?" Angela asked, desperately trying to get her bearings.

He sighed, his fawn-colored eyes softening with a concern Angela almost found herself believing...except for the restraints. "Your outburst yesterday at the demonstration site was too much to ignore. We had to convince you more directly of the importance of this venture."

"By tying me up?" she asked, aghast, her mind finally locking down on what was happening here. *Martin* was working with AugTech too? "You have to know that's not going to win me over to your cause."

He smiled. With a gesture, the bindings holding Angela fell away, as if he'd hit some sort of remote. "I apologize that our methods are somewhat crude, but in many ways, these remain crude tools. Primitive, but nevertheless effective. I assure you, you never once were in any danger, and again, that no humans were damaged in the demonstration you saw yesterday."

Angela thought about the comments Gregori had made regarding the Possessed, but kept her mouth shut for another moment as Martin continued.

"When I stumbled on evidence of this technology, I didn't know what to do with it. But I was definitely intrigued. As horrifying as your experience had been as a child, it paled in significance to the idea that there were creatures who could enact a sort of mental terror on their opponents, creatures that were not things of mystery and myth but of human creation."

"AugTech is working with robots," she said evenly.

He nodded, crossing one of his legs, the crease in his gray pants just off center. "Robots."

Then he chuckled. "But you and I both know they're more than that. Don't worry."

Something gave way inside Angela, something she didn't expect. He *knew*. He'd known all this time that what had abducted her when she was very small had not been strictly born of mankind. That it had been this other, this *creature* as he called it, flesh and blood and heart and magic. All these years, he'd paid for her therapy, getting her to accept that the demons of her mind had been merely her own constructs. But he had *known* the truth. In the past, that realization might have staggered her, might have caused her to build yet another wall, but now she simply accepted it, categorized it, fit it into the puzzle as a larger piece of the whole.

"These creatures, as you call them, are dangerous," she said. "I don't think you understand exactly how dangerous, or you wouldn't be using them the way you are."

"But you see, that's where it becomes so exciting," Martin said, "because they can be completely controlled. You were the one who showed me that. I didn't realize it at first. I didn't understand, but I knew there was something there, something important that I couldn't let go. I became obsessed with learning everything there was to know about the creatures that assaulted you that night."

She stared at him, aghast. "How did you even know what assaulted me? And it didn't happen at night, it happened..."

She stiffened, because of course it all became clear now. Martin wasn't talking about the day she'd been taken by demons as an eight-year-old to endure eighty-seven long and horrible days in a cage. That wasn't the event that so excited him, because he'd been behind it. Angela hadn't mistakenly summoned the demons when she was eight... she'd barely opened the book before they'd arrived. Martin had sent the demons to abduct her.

But the first time...that's what fascinated him. The attack of demons on an unsuspecting five-year-old girl, terrified out of her mind that she had killed her own grandmother by reading words aloud from a book.

"How did you even know about that attack?" she continued, more quietly now. "Enough to get excited about anything?"

He smiled, his thin lips pressing over his too-white teeth. "By all rights, I shouldn't have, but that's how science works, isn't it? A series of coincidences and fortunate events. I was there the night you were attacked. Your parents left me there with you as they rushed your grandmother to the hospital. I was a family friend after all, more than safe as a chaperone for a frightened little girl. And, to be fair, I never intended or expect to do anything that night but babysit. But you were traumatized, as any little girl would be, and eventually, you started talking to yourself, using strange words I'd never heard you speak before. When I asked you about it, you said it was all your fault, that you had made them come and you had made them go. That's what you said over and over again, that you had made them come and you had made them go. When I asked you who 'they' were, you understandably clammed up again. But it was clear that *something* had traumatized both you and your grandmother. And eventually, I got your grandmother to agree to hypnosis."

She scowled at him. "Hypnosis? Surely you're not serious."

He shrugged. "At first, she was a little resistant, but when I explained to her that you were having nightmares, that resistance dissolved. You have always had a very loving family, Angela. Or should I call you Jane? After all, your renaming was somewhat my doing."

At this point, she knew better than to dismiss his words and posturing. "What did you do? What possible value could renaming me bring you?"

"Well, I was the one who helped facilitate it, after all. And there was a lot of paperwork involved. More paperwork than you would expect for a little girl's name. Especially if you were a professor of anthropology with your head in the clouds and your mind on everything else but the ministry of your own family. When I offered to take care of all the paperwork to execute your name change, your parents gratefully accepted. They signed every document I put in front of them too, most without giving it more than a cursory glance. From that point forward, I had unlimited access to your medical files, including your psychology reports and therapy updates. You never would accept a drug regimen for your nightmares, which would've made things a little easier, but I enjoyed the challenge."

She couldn't help herself—she gaped at him, her stomach churning. "You've been tracking me since I was eight years old?"

"I've been tracking you since you were five years old. I've been tracking you effectively since you were eight, yes. And come on, it hasn't been all bad, you have to agree." He spread his broad hands, a gesture so ingrained, so familiar, that Angela felt her mind become slightly unmoored. Was all this really possible?

But Filmore continued, easy and sure. "I helped facilitate the right introductions, the chance meetings between you and the administrators of the school you entered from junior high on. The scholarship committees as well. You had a knack for being in the right place at the right time, you see? That wasn't by chance. You could say your entire career is due in part to me, but I considered it a more-than-even trade. After all, without you, I never would have made the discoveries I have or pushed through the policies I've championed so quickly. There were some hiccups, of course. I never found the original book that you used to summon the demons and that was incredibly vexing."

This confused her. "What are you talking about? It was right in my parents' study for years. How could you have missed it?"

"I asked myself the same thing, over and over again. After all, you were there, and you were speaking a language I didn't know—and you didn't know either, certainly. It was obvious a book was involved. But by the time I reached your house that night, everyone had gathered in the drawing room downstairs, and so I assumed that's where the book would be. I never even thought you would have been given access to your parents' study. Foolish of me, I admit."

"Yes, foolish," she murmured. "So how did you figure everything out without the book?"

"Another piece of serendipity," he admitted modestly. "You see, I wasn't the only person interested in this line of inquiry. I had to be careful, I had to be subtle, but eventually, I found like souls who were as aggressive as I was in identifying solutions to our military's shortcomings."

"And you discovered AugTech."

"I did." He flashed another politician-worthy grin. "And they explained how much further along they were already, further than I'd even imagined in my wildest dreams. And I knew we were ready. There are needs that must be met and tools that have been forged to meet those needs, and it's time we accepted that truth. The rest was almost laughably easy. Starting about twelve months ago, I positioned you for the role of congresswoman, even lining you up for committees, while AugTech set about tracking down how to secure a large pool of test units."

"They're not units," she protested. "They're not human beings, but they're more than test units."

He gave Angela a mocking look. "You've seen them up close and personal, *Angela*." Somehow, his use of her adopted first name came across as a slap. "Are you trying to tell me they have rights, like we should treat them like dogs and cats? Or sacred cows?"

She shifted a little in her chair. She didn't know how she felt about demons, but she was pretty sure it wasn't her job to make that decision. Any rights they had weren't supposed to be negotiated by humans. She didn't bother saying any of that to Martin. He had clearly already made up his mind.

"So what's next? You kidnapped me out of my home. Somebody is going to notice that. You can't possibly think that I'm going to go along with anything you suggest at this point."

He sat back with clear satisfaction and excitement, clapping his hands to his knees. Another move she'd seen hundreds—thousands of times since she was a little girl. Never realizing he was watching her. Studying her. Preying on her. "On the contrary. I think you'll go along with everything that I suggest, which is why you're in the impactful position you're in. Setting aside how easily and completely I could ruin both your life and the lives of your parents, since I have absolute and total control of your entire identity and I have since you were a very young girl, there is the moral aspect to it. You've always struck me as a particularly humanistic woman. And this solution will save human lives."

She stared at him. She wasn't an idiot. She could lay out the problem as neatly and succinctly as any mathematician. Martin Filmore had her dead to rights. In large part, he was exactly correct. Anything that she was, anything that she had become, was in part the result of his careful machinations. She was at his mercy. She suspected that not too many people knew what he had done to her, and she further suspected that his control ended with her and not her parents, but that was an idle distinction. He had her, and right now, silence was her best course of action. Appearing belligerent, or, worse, that she was willing to find some workaround wasn't going to help matters. In fact, it might drive him to a proof-of-sincerity demonstration which she could ill afford.

Angela's silence appeared to be the best course. Martin's expression relaxed further. "I can tell you, sincerely, that I'm pleased to have given you pause, Angela. I suspect you've worked out all the likely scenarios. Don't feel bad, I've had eighteen years to go through those, and a significant ramping up of focus over the past twelve months. The active part of my process has really only come into play in the last five months, since around Christmas. Your swearing-in ceremony in January was a work of art."

She gave him a thin smile. "Well, you have my full attention. What is it you want me to do?"

He leaned forward. "All I'm asking you to do is to shepherd this legislation through the process and allow AugTech to continue its operations in a black box environment. You are the only person who knows the significance of what I'm proposing. Randall, Trudy, all the rest have completely bought into the artificial intelligence angle of the units and that they are organic only to the extent of appearance, not fact. We won't be able to convince Congress to use these battle units if there's any suspicion they're organic."

"Back to the dogs and cats issue." She grimaced, forcibly reminded of Ghost and Old Sir. They'd both risked their lives for her back in her condo. Were they okay? Were they even still alive?

Anger scored through her as Filmore nodded. "But I don't need this to have public approval. I need internal approval, and I need money to flow to AugTech quickly and consistently. AugTech, not me." He spread his hands. "I'm not trying to get rich off this technology, Angela. I'm trying to save lives. I'm trying to protect human lives. I'm most especially trying to make the US military once more the most effective and efficient military power in the world. We can do this, and we have a moral right to do this."

"And all you need is my support in committee?" She knew there had to be more to it.

There was.

He hesitated, then offered Angela another easy, politically savvy smile. "To start, yes. But I do need more from you. I need you to work directly with the operatives at AugTech. You have a control over these creatures that exceeds that of the witches we took from the Serbian encampment."

She curled her lip. Gregori had told her the rest of this story, too. "You mean the ones you decided didn't need to die?"

He shook his head. "We weren't a part of any of that. That was a fight between demons and witches. We simply were there at the end to take advantage and to save lives where we could."

"You mean when it suited you."

He inclined his head. "That's as may be. But I'm not here to argue with you about the ethics of this initiative. Those have already been decided. This is the right thing to do, and we're going to do it. I need you to help take it to the next level."

"Why me?"

"Because right now, you have a demon you're controlling without any spell books. He's been with you since Atlanta. We want him too."

Angela felt a chill course down her spine. "He's never going to let that happen."

"On the contrary." Martin smiled again. "He already has."

22

Aided by the archangel, Gregori followed the line of energy to its source, which was exactly what he'd seen in the minds of the demons in the condo before he'd blasted them beyond the veil. He appeared in a long, empty corridor lined with shelves, apparently some sort of underground bunker. Before he could even move, however, an enormous pressure assaulted his ears and brain, driving him to his knees. He slapped his hands on either side of his head, only to realize he wasn't touching his actual skull.

Instead, a net of electrical circuits was wrapped around his head. When had that happened? How could anybody have gotten that close? How had—

"Go with it." The archangel's voice was hollow and resolute. But Gregori was an empath and not even the highest-ranking angel of God could completely hide his emotions from him. Michael was *pissed*. Whatever Simon had finally decided these humans had done, above and beyond the kidnapping of Angela Stanton, had rattled the archangel at a very deep level. That didn't bode well for the humans. And it especially didn't bode well for him as the blunt instrument of the archangel's wrath.

"I better get a raise," Gregori muttered.

"The skullcap was supposed to be put in place by the fifty demons they sent to take you out at the human's condo," the archangel explained briskly. "None of them, of course, got close enough to do that, but there was no surveillance in the room. So we improvised."

Gregori sensed that the archangel wanted to say more, but there was no time. Doors slammed open at either end of the corridor and an onslaught of humans and demons poured out of the space beyond. The pressure in his brain was overwhelming, and he knew the tool being used. It was an ancient construct of the Greeks, a helmet into which was fashioned a sort of Sator square, a mathematical construct given over to words, where all the letters in the square mirrored each other in some way, backward and forward, up and down, the words constantly repeating with one never fully ending before the loop started up again. It was intended to distract a supernatural being so much that they couldn't focus on whatever dire intent they'd originally conceived against humans, and it worked pretty well. It certainly worked well against him. Within a few short seconds, all Gregori could think of was the run of nonsensical words that coursed through his brain.

By the time the demons reached him, he didn't even object when they laid hands on him, lifting him to his feet and shackling him with enormous cuffs. He could've told them not to bother, if he could focus on anything at all. But the archangel wanted him to go along with this charade, and fighting the constant rush and moan of words was only going to drain his energy.

Gregori allowed them to take him down the corridor

and into a large gymnasium-style room. It was clear this facility was almost entirely underground, but the space was sweeping, and he struggled to think of where it might be located. He suspected it was nearby, on the outskirts of DC. There were too many shipping and transportation opportunities in the capital city that would make launching an operation like this far easier than a more remote location.

But what was its purpose specifically?

His captors pulled him to the center of the room and attached his manacles to two posts that were driven into the concrete. The moment they did so, a beam of light shone down from above, setting everything ablaze in a six-foot circle. Despite the cacophony in his head, Gregori eyed the posts with interest. They were black, but they hadn't started out that way. Demons had been shackled here before, demons who'd been injured to the point of gushing black blood. Very few humans could make that happen, but other demons could. Which meant these people had been setting demons upon each other as part of their trials...successfully. Good to know.

A second later, a crackle of energy electrified the poles and bit into Gregori's wrists. If he'd been an ordinary demon, the pain would have driven him to his knees. As it was, he felt it well enough and staggered appropriately, having no interest in his captors amping the wattage simply because Gregori was a tough guy. A hiss of noise then broke through the words running through his head, a different voice. Male and imperious.

"What is your name? What should we call you?"

When Gregori didn't answer, the electrical prod spiked, and he screamed quite convincingly, sagging to his knees. The question came again, and he shook his head like a bull, hoping they would get the picture that he couldn't respond with all the noise being fed into his helmet.

No such luck. The question came a third time, accompanied by so much electrical firepower that this time, Gregori did feel it all the way to his broken demon body. Sweat poured off his brow, and he could see his glamour falter, the smooth skin and well-muscled arms giving way to an equally burly but diseased and gutted form. He was like a mountain after an earthquake had broken it apart, little more than a pile of rubble. He glimpsed a fleeting memory of what he'd look like before he'd been ruined. Not the glamour he showed to humans, but the figure of the angel he'd once been and would never be again. He gasped with the sorrow and pain that image brought him, having nothing to do with the electrical whine at his wrists and temples.

The moment passed, and he sagged forward. "Gregori," he groaned.

"No," the voice said. "I need the name you were given at the time of your making. At the time of your sin."

Gregori couldn't help himself. He recoiled, but there were now three voices in his head, the demanding, imperious interrogator, the hush and moan of the repeating cycle of words, and once again, the Archangel Michael seemed so close that he might as well be whispering in Gregori's ear.

"Tell them," he said without inflection. "I know the sacrifice will be great. But there is no other way to save her."

Gregori turned as if he could see the archangel. Of course, there was no one there. But he hadn't mistaken what he'd said. To save *her*. The trial that was coming was great, but it would be successful if he succumbed. If he did what they asked. He had the archangel's permission to bow to the will of these humans, but more than that, he had the archangel's directive that this was the only course. It was not a difficult decision.

"*Pónos.*" No sooner had the word slipped from his lips than a new sound replaced it, the murmur and sighing of many voices, none that he recognized. While the beam remained on him, lights came up all around him, and he saw and understood what was happening.

He was standing in a witch's circle.

He hadn't been summoned into this trap by ordinary means either. He'd walked right into it and allowed himself to be shackled. The first ever shackling of the Syx in a witch's circle, in fact, in all their long years of conflict. Anger flickered within Gregori, not an emotion he usually felt regarding humans. As an empath, he'd absorbed his share of mortal rage, dissolving it, diffusing it, absorbing it. But it was normally not his process to generate anger himself. There was more than enough of it to go around without his aid. But this was different. These mortals intended to do him harm. He knew it as surely as he knew that somewhere in that crowd of people watching him was Angela. They meant to do her harm as well, and he could not...would not allow that to happen. No matter what happened to him, she had to stay safe.

"You're different from the other demons. Explain."

Gregori tensed, waiting for the archangel to tell him to spill the secrets of the Syx. To explain the nature of the Fallen and their role within the greater horde. If the archangel ordered it, he would do it. He was bound, and he accepted that bond. The archangel, however, remained silent.

The whine of pressure increased. "You're different from the other demons. Explain."

This time, along with the additional round of pain,

Gregori felt a renewed surge of anger. It was almost freeing. Without the archangel restraining him, and given that he had already accepted that he must succumb to whatever might come, he had a curious sense of lightness in allowing himself to be irritated by humans. To not excuse their pettiness or their orders as something they had every right to feel. He...he was allowed to judge them, should they be deserving of judgment. He could never harm a human, certainly not kill one, nor could he turn away. But he could judge them in this moment, sacrificing himself to their ridiculous demands as he was. It was...unsettling.

It was also painful. The ratcheting up of the energy stream crackled across his body, making him strain against his bonds. And the witches joined in this time, raising their hands, their voices lifting in whatever cubbyholes they'd been stuck. The amphitheater-style room he stood in was surrounded by small, glassed-in observation rooms, almost like a gladiatorial arena where he would be gazed upon, cheered at, jeered by fools who didn't understand what he was. Who especially didn't know what he had been.

"You are different from the others—"

"Then why don't you ask *them* what I am?" Gregori challenged, lifting his head as he spoke. His voice roared across the open space, though not with anger or force. It was simply loud enough to fill the whole room, to echo across the concrete walls surrounding him. In its wake, the very building shook and the witches froze in their cells. Meanwhile, high above him, the knot of people gyrated quickly, clearly excited to get a rise out of him, to get anything resembling a response. They shifted and edged closer to the glass, and finally, Gregori saw her.

Angela, standing as stiff as the poles that were holding him, staring at him with her soul in her eyes.

Even through the thick leaded glass, he could feel the intensity of her pain, her anguish, and his heart leapt. She was there. She was safe. It was a start.

The voice came again. "We have tried to ask the others what you are once we realized you were so much stronger, so different. What we've gotten back has not been satisfactory. They fear you too much, even more than they fear us, no matter how much pain we can accord them, no matter that we can ensure their deaths."

Gregori smile grimly. The humans only *thought* they could ensure a demon's death. The witches they had in their employ were very strong, could even send the demons back from wherever they'd summoned them. But they couldn't send them back beyond the veil, not this group. And he further suspected the men and women who were trapping these demons didn't *want* them sent away. Why would you get rid of your army when you were convinced you could control it? All an army had to do was fall in line, and demons, for all their many flaws, had an exquisite ability to survive. But they knew they couldn't survive an attack of the Syx. It was a very delicate line to walk, but it was a line nevertheless, and one Gregori was forced to appreciate.

Silence filled the room as the electrical surge being fed into Gregori's shackles increased, then increased again. The pain that ratcheted through him was almost reassuring, grounding him in place, temporarily cutting off the impact of the Sator square helmet. Then it abruptly cut off.

"If you won't tell us, then perhaps you will show us." The doors on either side of the large space opened, and just as in the gladiatorial games, Gregori's enemies poured forth. Some of these demons he even recognized. Howling, crowing, loping toward him with blood in their eyes. If he hadn't fought them directly before, he'd fought their brethren, and they knew what he was. Even if they couldn't sufficiently articulate it to their captors. And though they knew even under tremendous stress that there were some lines they couldn't cross, they were still demons. Goaded beyond their sense of restraint. They could see him plainly locked in place while they had claw and spear and cudgel and fang and numbers on their side. Him tied up against a legion of the creatures seemed like reasonable odds. And as they rushed toward him, he couldn't fault their logic. It seemed like more than reasonable odds to him as well.

They raced toward him with naked desire and hunger in their eyes. Gregori opened his mind to them. It always made it easier, and this was no different. These creatures had harmed God's children. Slaughtered them, in some cases. They'd possessed and infiltrated and driven the weakest mortals to taking their own lives and even the strongest to the pit of despair. They'd taken delight in sowing discord and chaos, reveling in the misery of the humans caught in their net. They deserved what he would give them, even if he fell beneath their combined weight of hatred.

Some of the more enterprising of the demons didn't bother waiting to rip him with their claws. Instead, they broke apart from the group, flanking the others, and hurled weapons from afar. The blades sang through the air, and through the haze of noise and electrical crackling fire, Gregori's reflexes weren't as strong as they should be. He ducked and flinched away, but the blades hit their mark too often, searing his skin with their razor-sharp edges. And it wasn't only the cut of the blades he felt, but the telltale bubble of poison. The demons had taught their captors well, it seemed. Even with Gregori bound, they wanted to slow him down. They were worried about what damage he could wreak before he betrayed his own weakness.

They were smart to worry too. Gregori braced himself, his brows knitting together, glaring at the horde as they loped toward him, yowling their heads off with mindless glee.

Then, when the legion of his attackers was nearly upon him, his shackles fell off.

23

"Oh!" Angela lurched forward with sudden urgency as Gregori's restraints fell away. What were these people thinking? He would destroy them, he would—

"We want to see," Martin murmured, his face alight with interest, matched by the intensity of Zachary Howard's focus. "We want to see what your demon can do."

And then her demon proceeded to show them.

Gregori moved so quickly, he became little more than a blur of fury and force. Immediately, he turned to the right and yanked the pole out of the floor, fueled by his righteous anger and a very real survival instinct that he hadn't had to evoke for millennia. Raising the pole high, he swung it like a baseball bat and clocked the first wave of his attackers hard enough to send them sprawling into the second wave. Half the demons exploded on contact, leaving the next round of attackers covered in ropes of black goop.

Angela watched, transfixed. She'd never seen Gregori in action before. She'd always been in the midst of being attacked when he'd been driven to action. Watching him now, from the safe remove of this observation deck, she didn't know if she should be swelling with pride or dumbstruck with terror. To her surprise, she was erring much more on the side of pride. Her fierce and beautiful demon, mighty in his fury, was plowing through his assailants like he was on a mission from God. Which, she supposed, he was. Almost without realizing it, she pushed her way forward until she was all the way to the glass. She lifted her hands to lay them lightly on the transparent surface, as if she could reach out and add her power to his.

"He's very impressive."

She stiffened, but Martin didn't let her shift away. One of his goons stood on the other side of her, whether demon, possessed human, or merely asshole, she didn't know.

Martin continued. "The others are very definitely afraid of this one. All we've been able to get out of them is that he's a member of some sort of vigilante force within the horde itself. That implies a level of organization we honestly didn't think these creatures were capable of."

She shot him a withering glance. "Really. You've been studying demons, a kind of creature that's walked this earth for thousands upon thousands of years, for what, all of twelve months? And you don't think that maybe they're capable of a little more than you've been able to discover in that time?"

He ignored her sarcasm. "Demons have been controlled by witches for thousands of years. They've served as cannon fodder for mercenary armies for nearly as long, and some of them have proven to be quite cunning. But the idea of a team working together as a concerted, self-directed force isn't something these creatures should be able to master."

"And you know this, how? Because you've successfully killed and dissected them?" she asked, derision continuing to drip from her words as black goop splattered the window, causing most of the scientists and military types to step back. Neither she nor Martin moved.

He narrowed his eyes at her. "How do you know anything about that?"

She smiled. "Oh, you've tried, I'm sure. I assumed you hadn't wanted to kill any of the demons yourself because they were your army. Why destroy your own supply, especially when you aren't entirely sure you can keep restocking? But I underestimated you. You did try to kill them. How'd that go?"

Martin's lips thinned. "I think we're deviating from the primary purpose of this conversation."

A door slammed, and quick steps interrupted them. "Sir," came a clipped, faintly anxious male voice.

The urgency of the minion's voice drew Angela's attention back to where Gregori was fighting. Fighting... And winning. The enormous demon was now slightly less human than he had been even a few short seconds ago. The infuriated creature beneath the veneer of glamour was peeking through. Gregori's broken mountain of a body elongated and seemed, if anything, to grow larger. He towered over the other demons, sometimes three times as tall, and swept them into his enormous hands as he howled in rage, shattering their bodies into gore and spray.

The demons attacking him piled on with even more force. As attuned as Angela was to Gregori's emotions, even in this state, surprisingly, she registered something more than fury from him at this assault. She registered surprise. Gregori couldn't understand why the demons kept pressing forward, and she was smote with images of a hundred thousand other battles he'd fought before, where the demons, upon seeing they were outmatched, simply fled back to the shadows, to the caves, to the life they'd been so carefully living, until they had gained the notice of the Syx. But they weren't doing that now.

"They *want* to die," she realized aloud, drawing Martin's attention back to her. "You've done something that no other entity on this earth has managed to accomplish. You're convincing the demon horde to return to the very hellfires from which they were spawned. I don't think that's gonna make you employer of the year."

No matter what else she might think of him, Martin Filmore was a quick study. "Stop this," he snapped, his Southern drawl going hard as flint.

Zachary came forward, his voice crisp and sure as he unhooked a radio from his belt and spoke into it. "Terminate the attack."

Then all three shifted their gaze back to the war going on below, which wasn't a war at all. It had turned into a suicide mission, and only a few of the demons were hanging back.

The minion broke in again. "Sir, that's the problem. We noticed the same anomaly, took steps to redirect. But our circuits are being jammed somehow. We're not getting through. They're not responding."

Martin turned and grabbed Angela, thrusting her toward two heavily armed men. "Take her down there and set the demons on her. Get new members of the horde if we need them, but make sure you catch the alpha demon's attention. We control him, we control them."

"Sir." The nearest man nodded.

"And don't waste time. In fact—"

Angela's eyes widened as Martin moved quickly, efficiently. He reached inside his jacket and pulled a gun free, aiming it low and at an angle—directly at her. He fired, and a sudden flare of white-hot pain exploded in Angela's upper thigh.

She screamed, and a second later, a roar of unmistakable anguish exploded in the space below them. For the first time, the row of demons retreated from Gregori, and he spun, pole still in hand, a bull desperately searching for somebody new to gore.

"Get her down there," Martin snapped. "Now."

Angela didn't resist as many hands grabbed her and half dragged, half carried her out the door of the observation room, where a gurney appeared. She was hauled on top of it, and they started moving again. As four security guards raced her down the hallway, another man came out of a side room in a technician's outfit, and once they'd reached an elevator and shoved her inside, he bent to examine her.

"Through and through," he barked, though Angela didn't know if he was sharing this information for her benefit or speaking to someone on a mic. "She'll bleed out fast if we don't get her medical attention."

She didn't know whether to believe him or not, but before she could summon the energy to respond, the elevator opened again and they were in another access corridor. Screams of rage and fear echoed loudly enough from the room beyond, then the doors were thrust open and she was launched—gurney and all—into the melee.

Chaos descended around her.

Mewling with abject fear, her hands slick with her own blood as she clutched her leg, Angela rolled off the gurney as it crashed into the backs of several demons. She could almost sense when the orders came through the demons' earbuds, directing them to stop their attack on Gregori and flee—and kill her along the way.

Cowering on the floor, Angela would've laughed if it

hadn't been so horrifying. Martin couldn't have come up with a better way to play into the demons' basest fears and needs: stop attacking *this* guy and start attacking someone else and you can run free.

Not surprisingly, it worked. A full third of the demons she could see immediately turned her way, howling with excitement as they dove toward her. On the other side of the room, Gregori roared in fury, but he was never going to get to her in time, Angela knew immediately. Did Martin fully realize that? Was he counting on her bond with the demon to be so strong that upon her death, he would somehow be rendered more controllable? Or was Martin merely acting on instinct, taking advantage of serendipity, as he was so fond of saying. She had a feeling he didn't understand exactly what that word meant. She also had a feeling he was going to learn the meaning of karma shortly. But first, she needed to survive.

Traveling back on all fours, Angela slipped again on the gore-soaked floor, her own blood mixing with the blood of demons as she came face-to-face with the horde that had haunted her since she was a little girl. It was shocking how quickly all the old memories came back, and even though they weren't anywhere near as potent as they used to be, since she'd been healed by Gregori's hand, they still evoked a shadow of her former fear, and that was enough.

She moved almost blindly, without thinking, thrusting her hands in a wide arc, creating a circle that stretched at least two feet, first with the swipe of her left hand, then with a swipe of her right, while she remained inside. It wasn't a perfect witch's circle. She was pretty sure it wasn't a witch's circle at all, but it was going to have to do. With all the blood seeping from her leg and waves of dizziness starting to rise within her like a shimmering tide, there was no way she could even stand, let alone escape. Instead, she huddled in the circle and raised her hands.

And just as they had all those years ago, the symbols, images, and words that had been in the Serbian spell book sprang to her mind and lips.

She started talking. Slowly and quietly at first, feeling her way and then with rapid acceleration as the horde literally collapsed in on her. Their faces, their hands, their bodies pressed toward her, and she smelled the stink of their fetid breath, their excitement almost a living, pulsing thing. But the circle held. Sort of.

"Stand back," she ordered, her voice ringing with a sincerity she didn't truly feel. "Stand back."

Not surprisingly, they didn't listen to her, but she also realized they weren't quite reaching her either, though they were too close—too close! The circle still exerted some kind of power strong enough that their scrambling hands couldn't get hold of her body.

Angela kept up her exhortations, but she couldn't get past the fact she'd been shot in the leg and was rapidly losing blood. Unlike these creatures, unlike Gregori, she wasn't unkillable by human hands. She was weakness and flesh and blood, and she was fading.

"Kill her."

This new order was spoken by a woman, loudly enough that she could hear it crackling over the demons' earbuds, and she realized it was being spoken in the same tongue she was speaking, the ancient language of the Serbian witches, the language they'd employed to control demons since their first coven was formed at the dawn of recorded history.

Outrage kindled anew inside Angela. These were her *sisters*, her fellow humans, women being ordered to make this command. Yes, they might be brainwashed or fearing for their own lives, but to say such things, to order another creature to do their bidding in such a final heinous act, how was that even possible? How strong must the power being exerted over these women be, how strong...

"No!" she screamed back, her voice carrying over the horde. "No, you will not!"

Her anger only seemed to galvanize the demons to greater frenzy. She felt them pressing in again, and it was only with a Herculean effort that she was able to clear enough space to breathe through the torrent of words she spewed, not even sure what she was saying anymore, but throwing every ounce of her emotion back into the idea of keeping herself safe and keeping *the demons* safe too, safe from their shared enemies, instead of fixating on the outrage of her betrayal by her own kind.

The frenzy shifted, mindless rage replaced by surprise and confusion, in a way that made Angela straighten. There was something here, something important, something she was missing. A key. A memory, just a fleeting hint of an idea that she *should* recall but couldn't quite. Staring at faces inches in front of her own, she was no longer the seasoned and cynical congresswoman, but a terrified little girl no more than five years old, huddled over her grandmother and tormented by creatures she could barely comprehend.

As she peered into these new, hideously broken faces, all the old terror resurfaced, and this terror was up close and personal once again, not seen with the distance she'd captured for such a brief and beautiful time with Gregori's intercession. No. Once more, she was that little girl, lifting her hands, warding off a nightmare she finally understood deserved something more than she would ever have thought to give it. Something more than anyone *should* give it, frankly. But something she could absolutely give.

"I forgive you," she whispered. The words came out in English, but their Serbian equivalent was right there. Had she read that in the books as well? Had she learned that phrase of grace and absolution alongside the spells of domination and control? She didn't know, but it felt more right than anything else she could say. As the nearest demon stopped and reared back, she said it again.

"I forgive you."

Her words were stronger now, more resolute, and more of the demons around her flinched back from her as if she'd thrown poison at their faces. But poison wouldn't have fazed these creatures, not as much as this. Fading and weak, Angela nevertheless put forth all her energy into the words again.

"I *forgive* you," she declared, and she lifted her hands, not in a gesture of warding off but with her palms up, supplicating, no longer praying for her life to be spared, but honoring these vile and wretched creatures for their *own* lives, their own existence.

They stared at her, gape-mouthed, clearly not knowing what to do, and then they simply...disappeared. A sudden circle of space opened up between Angela and the closest demons, a breathing space she hadn't realized how desperately she needed. She hauled in a lungful of oxygen as, out of the corner of her eye, she could see movement and anger explode in one of the observation deck windows. The observation deck she'd just left. *That was good. That was right. That was—*

Another wave of demons crashed into her.

24

Gregori knew the moment that Angela's leg was shot, could feel the violation and wrongness as the bullet exploded through her leg, tearing veins, ripping through muscle, skimming an inch away from both artery and bone. His own left leg gave way, and he staggered, but that didn't stop the onslaught of demons rushing toward him. They attacked him with a renewed frenzy that was more than foolish, it was flat-out suicidal, and it had taken him clearing nearly a third of the room to understand that they were *willingly* giving themselves over to his judgment. There had been scores upon scores of demons loosed into the world, and this was the tiniest fraction. But at least he could send these assholes back beyond the veil.

Then a fresh horror struck. Angela was on the move, forced against her will into action, her pain escalating to a keening spike. There was pressure on her wound, but too little—too little! Enough to keep her alive, but not enough to stop the bleeding entirely. And she was moving down... down toward the amphitheater of death where he dispatched demons with the efficiency of a street cleaner.

She stared around blearily, and through her eyes, Gregori saw what she saw, felt what she felt, and knew something she didn't know.

He'd seen these corridors before. They'd been in the minds of the demons he'd dispatched back at Angela's condo, the long hallways lined with cabinets, with rooms flashing by. The demons had been frightened of the rooms adjacent to those corridors, had dreaded them, and as he saw them through Angela's eyes, recognizing them for what they were, he finally understood.

This was the area that held the artificial intelligence heart of the AugTech operation. This was where they took their captured demons and made them into something both more and less than how God had created them—the Augments. Terrorizing them down into their most scabrous forms with the help of the witches' spells, immobilizing them, implanting them with the chips that had served AugTech so well. These implants allowed AugTech to control these pitiful creatures and drive them to do their bidding. Only one thing could break through that hold, it seemed: the hope of escape from their torture at humans' hands. Even the wrath of God was more palatable than that.

And it had all started in these halls.

Gregori couldn't see enough to get a fix on the true nature of the technology in the rooms Angela was racing by, but all of them were lit with a blue metallic glow, and as Angela passed lab after lab, he got a sense of how massive the operation was. Now, at least, he understood that AugTech's hold on both the horde and the witches they'd enslaved was more impressive than he feared. How many witches had they stolen from their home covens and pressed into service to manage such a force? How many more were they subjugating to summon additional demons to the front? There was an endless supply of the horde, after all. What they couldn't find on earth, they could find beyond the veil.

They had to be stopped.

At that moment, though, as the doors to the amphitheater swept open, Gregori's thoughts exploded into a million shards of crystalline agony. He could feel Angela's energy shoot into the room, her terror and resolution as she rolled off the gurney and hit the floor.

He wasn't the only one. The demons could literally smell fresh blood, but beyond that, the wailing tenor of the witches surrounding the amphitheater changed, and with it, so did the demons' focus. They didn't have to go beyond the veil anymore. They could escape—truly escape—if they killed the wounded human.

Gregori would have laughed at the simplicity of the plan if he could breathe past the sudden knot of fury in his throat. No demon truly wanted to return beyond the veil, to face the Father's judgment or their own permanent eradication. That it had seemed a better future than the ones provided them as prisoners had been telling, but temporary. Far better to simply kill, destroy, then retreat to the shadows. The demons were so damaged at this point from what they had endured, they believed what they were being told as simple truth.

You could push a demon too far, but the humans didn't know that. There were a lot of things the humans didn't know.

Such as, you could push a Syx too far as well.

Gregori hefted the pole that had bound him to the concrete, and brought it crashing down—only this time, he didn't slam it into the horror-struck faces of his opponents, he struck the floor. The sound of metal hitting concrete sounded like the breaking of the world, and it had the effect of sending all the demons into a renewed agitation. The humans as well. Then he heard Angela's voice loud and strident over the howling, though he couldn't understand what she was saying—still, it was all he needed. He turned to where her voice had come from, straining to see...

The lights went out.

If anything, the screaming of the demons only got louder as Angela's shouted words lifted above them, but instead of being disoriented, Gregori was able to continue tracking Angela's location with one horrifying marker: the smell of her blood. He surged forward, clearing demons from behind, sending them to their judgment beyond the veil with increasing brutality as he struggled to reach Angela. There were too many demons, though, and only one human—and all the demons were focusing on her. Yet Angela's voice remained strong, if muffled, resolute. She kept shouting. As long as she remained shouting, she was alive.

It took him a few precious seconds to realize she was shouting in Serbian, and an electric kind of joy lit him from the inside. She was remembering, recalling the powerful words she'd spoken as a child and she was no longer afraid of those words. She was willing to use them to save herself and give him the precious extra moments he needed to reach her.

Pride suffused his entire body, almost literally giving him wings. He bolted forward, disintegrating the demons in front of him to ash, and finally reached Angela. In the glow of the emergency lights high above, he could see her plainly. Her dark hair, normally so perfect, was snarled and hanging in clumps over her shoulders, coated in demon blood and gore. Her pale skin was flushed, her hands and face marred with a dozen different wounds. Blood oozed from one thigh, staining her pantsuit, and she stood with her weight balanced on her other leg, well within the glistening circle of blood swept around her by her own hands. She turned and turned again in a pained, jerking movement, holding off the band of demons that lurched and lunged toward her, mad beyond all reclaiming.

She was beautiful, terrified, and terrifying.

She was *his*.

He stepped inside her circle.

"Gregori!" Angela gasped, whirling to him. And then her arms wrapped around him, her face on his chest. Only it wasn't his chest anymore, it was the chest of the creature he'd been made into at the moment of his demonization. His scaly, rotten skin, his ragged scars, his claw-like hands. She didn't seem to care. She didn't seem to see anything except some image she had of him in her mind that was true and right, special and good. He knew this because he knew her. Her emotions were completely intertwined with his, her mind and his were linked, her heart and his were one. The way she saw him was nothing short of a miracle.

"I know the answer," she blurted. "I know how to break free!"

No sooner had she spoken than another sound assaulted them from the far wall. A crease of light appeared, and new demons surged into the room, wild with terror. Gregori leapt forward, even as Angela cried out, "No!"

But Gregori didn't stop to think. He rushed forward, only to realize it was a different kind of assault he now faced. Not demons anymore, not exactly. These creatures were the Possessed. God's children, trapped and enslaved by the horde. He couldn't kill them. He didn't want to hurt them. But at the same time, extracting the demons from within them, which he was morally charged to do, would take more time than he had. He might be able to grab three, even five, but the rest would get by him. The rest were also going directly for Angela. There was no solution here. There was nothing he could do but defend her.

He fell back to his original position as quickly as possible, gratified to see that the circle of demons surrounding Angela had widened enough for him to step inside. She beamed up at him.

"You came back," she gasped, the moment seeming caught in time.

He stared at her, startled. "I'll always come back."

In a flash, the connection between them expanded so dramatically that he rocked back on his heels. Once again, he had a glimpse of the being he'd been so many millennia ago, a creation of light and magic. A creation worthy of the love that now shone in Angela's eyes.

The first of the Possessed reached them. Angela's shout turned from surprise to horror as she recognized the creatures for what they were. These were humans. Seeing them through Gregori's eyes, experiencing his emotions, she could perhaps still see the demon within them, but she more recognized that these were her *own* kind, bent on attacking her, attacking him.

She tried to stand—couldn't. "*Zaustaviti!*" she cried in Serbian, her voice strident with pain. "Stop!"

But whatever she thought her exhortation would accomplish, she was wrong. The creatures kept coming, and Gregori reached over her, protecting her with his body as he dispatched them one at a time. He was on the fifth when he noticed the horde had begun to falter. He was on the tenth when Angela slumped against him, then slid to the floor. He crouched down, protecting her, and realized there were no other demons left on the floor—only him and collapsed humans.

"Angela!"

"Gas..." she whispered, and finally, he scented the wrongness in the air. You couldn't kill a demon, but you could kill a Possessed human—or at least incapacitate it for a short while. It appeared that AugTech had figured out a way to get the demons back under their control. If they were smart, they'd also identified a battle unit the Syx wouldn't kill.

The reality of this horror struck him hard. The Syx wouldn't be facing purely demon soldiers—but Possessed human soldiers, humans they couldn't outright blast beyond the veil. He'd inadvertently given AugTech the tools they needed not only to take down their mortal combatants, but to stymie the Syx as well.

"Forgive them," Angela murmured. "It's...it's the only way."

Even as she spoke the words, he rejected them. The same way it wasn't his place to judge God's children, it wasn't his place to forgive them. And it certainly wasn't something he had any interest in doing now. Rage boiled through him as Angela choked in his arms. He could heal her and let the others die, but that was no solution either. And the archangel remained maddeningly quiet.

He was a demon, not a Fallen now. He could not forgive. He could not impart the grace of the Father—and he could not heal as he once had. It was forbidden.

But he hadn't forgotten how.

The gas pumped with greater force, and without even making a conscious decision, Gregori placed his hand over Angela's mouth, over her eyes. Drawing on abilities he hadn't used in millennia, he quieted her heart, slowed her lungs, ignoring the renewed scream of pain that pounded in his skull. These were not his powers to use anymore. These were not his abilities to command. This was not the grace a demon was accorded, and there would be literal hell to pay when all this was through.

But not yet.

"Rest, child of God," he murmured. "Simply rest."

She slumped to the floor.

His shoulders shuddering under the pain that assaulted him from all sides, Gregori staggered back, then stood, tilting back his head to stare blindly at the lights blasting down from the ceiling, illuminating the carnage all around him. "What is it you want?" he demanded.

"You," came the response over the loudspeaker, immediately. With his heightened awareness, Gregori knew what the disembodied voice was saying. He was the supersoldier they craved. He was the one they continued to think they could control. He was the one they thought they *had* controlled, with the lever of Angela Stanton and the Possessed, whom he wouldn't harm. They wanted him in turn as a lever against the Syx, against any who might oppose them or interfere with their plans. They were humans, and they were making use of every opportunity, every break, every strategy.

He'd have to give them something more to keep them busy.

"You want me?" He growled the question. "Come and get me."

He scooped up Angela, then ran toward the one thing the owners at AugTech cared about even more than their stable of demon soldiers. Their technology. And as he did, he opened his mind once more. Not to pray...but to summon.

"*Shemael, Barzac, Mithra,*" he whispered, calling the demons he'd freed from Angela's parents. He had a job for them to do, and he was sure they would do it. "*Mortain, Rickmalid, Zehim.*"

Gregori followed the direct trajectory that both Angela and the Possessed had taken, tracking their steps backward to the doors that had most recently opened onto the amphitheater. If this was where they housed the tech systems for their AI, it was reasonable to assume there would still be humans working in the section. Doctors, technicians, he didn't care. The moment he blasted open the door, those humans would be at risk of inhaling the same gas that was currently flooding the amphitheater. That meant the assholes high above would cut it off. Maybe.

The door was electrified, but it served as merely another layer of pain that barely raked across Gregori's senses. He burst through the barrier with the force of a charging bull, ducking his shoulder to protect the fragile body he clasped in his arms. He stumbled, then staggered into the bright lights, recognizing immediately the same corridor that he'd seen both in Angela's eyes and in the minds of the demons he'd attacked. He was close. Alarms sounded all around him, and an initial row of charging, armed soldiers collapsed, none of them wearing masks.

Gas.

More alarms blared, and he ducked into a side room where a bed on wheels sat pushed against the wall and monitors lay quiet and dormant all around. He laid Angela onto the bed and raised his hand, sealing her safety with a benediction that made his fingers bleed, then raced back out, knocking two more soldiers flat before they could get their guns up. These ones were wearing masks. But they were fully human, and he wasted no time with them.

Now that his plan was set, his attention focused on only one thing. The machines. A second later, the demons he'd summoned blasted into being beside him, and together, they became a full demon wrecking crew, grabbing up whatever was closest at hand and trashing the electronic bays in every room. The fact that Gregori was here, that he had eyes on this equipment, meant there was more damage he could do than simple brute destruction too. Though brute destruction was working pretty well. No, the Fool of the Arcana Council had made sure to outfit Gregori with his own tech, and was doubtlessly seeing what Gregori was seeing. If that meant Simon could figure out how to get into the network of this abomination, to keep them from ever setting up such a foul operation again, so much the better.

All Gregori knew was that he had to destroy as much as possible before they caught up to him. Because they *would* catch up to him and set on him once again with demon-infested humans, too many for him to combat without more bloodshed, more murder. And then he would be forced to do the unthinkable, what Angela had exhorted him to do before she'd lost consciousness.

He would be forced to play the god that he was not, and he would burn for it.

25

Angela came back to consciousness with a jolt of fire and pain. Chaos surged all around her, but not directly attacking her, which she supposed was a good thing. The demons racing past the doorway paid no attention to her, in fact. Thank heavens for small favors.

Her gaze shot to her leg and the shreds of her pantsuit. She pulled aside the ripped material, shocked to find her skin unbroken, a starburst of bright pink, healthy skin replacing the scorched hole that'd been there before. Blood still streaked the skin around the wound, but as she bent forward and ran her hands down her thigh, her leg felt normal, healed as if it hadn't been pierced with a metal slug. She twisted her leg to see the exit wound, but once again found only smooth, healthy skin beneath its veneer of dried blood. Her head spun, her stomach roiled, and she fought the urge to vomit from adrenaline and fear, but she was okay. She was whole.

She was healed.

"Gregori?" she asked aloud, but the enormous demon was gone. She thought she heard a violent crashing sound from far off, and she half limped to the doorway as more demons raced by, heading down the hallway for the exit— she assumed¹ it was an exit—where she'd been pushed through minutes earlier. Had it only been a few minutes? She'd lost all sense of time.

But where were they going? Another resounding crash in the distance drew her attention, and she saw more demons racing out of the darkened amphitheater, while others seemed to be destroying everything they could in the labs farther down the hall. She needed to join the fleeing demons, to leave before the last one ran screaming through the exit. She couldn't wait until they'd all gone, or Martin Filmore or his thugs would come for her.

"Hold!"

Too late.

Angela whirled to take in the woman who'd appeared in the hallway—only it wasn't one woman, it was three, holding their hands up as if to constrain her. The first woman was the tallest, an imperious Amazon with dark red hair falling over her shoulders, her sturdy body encased in a long tunic and pants with embroidery at the edges, some- where between a lab tech's scrubs and ceremonial gear. The women behind her, both pale-skinned brunettes, were far shorter than the first woman and wore the same style scrubs. They all held their arms high, shouting at her in a language she couldn't understand.

What was the point of that? Angela wasn't a demon. She wasn't even a witch. They couldn't hold her.

Ignoring the women, she turned to run, but she found she couldn't move. Her eyes snapped wide. "You have no power over me," she gasped.

The redheaded witch merely grinned at her, a terrible and manic expression. More demons writhed just behind the trio, crouching against the walls of the corridor— new demons. They acted wrong—or more wrong, anyway. They twitched and jittered. Angela could see the spark of electricity at their necks. Indicator lights? What fresh hell was this?

"Take her," breathed the head witch. Angela stiffened with renewed fear as she realized she was talking to the demons. Gregori was gone. She was alone. She had no more protection against these demons than any human—other than the witches, anyway.

Other than...

"No." Angela held up her hands as well, the ancient book of witchcraft and its dictates once more springing to her mind. Back in the amphitheater, she'd believed in the circle and so it held power, but these witches clearly didn't need the circle to perform their magic. They hadn't needed it in the field when the demons had attacked the "hostage" next to AugTech's van, and they weren't standing in a circle now. Which meant it was only the *words* she spoke that were important. The words and her belief in them.

She began reciting the words of warding she could remember, her hands held high, her focus intent upon the first of the demons who stepped past the witches, swiping for her, raking the air in front of her face with its long talons. But it came no farther. It screamed as it faltered, but Angela could no longer see it, nor could she see the Serbian witches. Instead, she saw what she always saw when she invoked the words of that terrible night—words, symbols, glowing in the darkness, leaping off the page. Billowing outward with crackling, hissing smoke.

"You *dare*," the red-haired witch seethed. Angela hadn't just been imagining it—there *was* real smoke in the corridor. The demons cowered, screaming in frustration and pain, but the women stood firm.

"Me?" Angela raged right back. "Who the hell are you to be doing this to *any* living creature on this earth? Your pact with the horde is to summon them to do your bidding. Your bidding, not the commands of people who would use these creatures to kill for personal gain. I don't know what code or creed you aspire to, but there can be no honor in what you do. You shame your order and you shame your sisters."

"You know nothing of what we do and why we do it," one of the shorter, paler women retorted, her voice cold as steel. Her hands were down now, her arms spread wide, almost as if she was trying to balance herself. "The horde has overrun the world above, and only we can stop them."

Angela gaped at her. "What are you talking about? The horde isn't overrunning the world. You are, by helping AugTech turn them into supersoldiers."

"No," the witch gasped, her hand fluttering to her neck as she shook her head. The other two did the same. Smoke billowed all around them, and the demons continued howling in rage and pain. If anyone reviewed a video feed of this corridor, would they assume the witches were doing their jobs?

"How long have you been here?" Angela demanded. She spoke in Serbian, she realized with surprise. It had been the language of her captors when she'd been held as a child, the language the demons knew. Were these women the same ones who'd held her all those years ago? Surely not —and yet...

"It has been fifty years since the horde overtook the light and everyone died," said the red-haired witch, her voice ringing with truth. "Fifty years that we've fought to regain control. The demons here are our servants, a lone outpost to turn the creatures against themselves, now that the enforcers have abandoned us."

"*Not* fifty years," Angela countered. "Try a few months. And the enforcers did come. You tried to kill one of them right here, in front of my eyes. The demons went after him rather than remain in your control."

"False," the women all said, their voices almost mechanical. The hand of one of the shorter witches fluttered again to her neck, and Angela grimaced. They were bound in some kind of neurological thrall, and together, they were stronger than her. She might have been able to stop the demons from reaching her—she had the same spells they did, and more strength with the fire of Gregori's healing upon her, but she...

She blinked. Was *that* the answer? Could she take the energy Gregori had given her, the energy of the empath, and turn it on these women?

"You've been lied to," she said quickly, putting all the emotion she could into the words as she still felt the surge of energy from the Serbian spells whirling around her. "Your sisters are crying out for you, believing you to be dead. Don't you remember the fires of Ahriman? Don't you remember the horde ripping through your homes, your families? That wasn't some long-ago memory from a barely remembered time, that was just months ago. Months when the attack of Ahriman foretold for centuries finally came to pass, and you gave all you could to withstand him."

"Death—so much death—" moaned one of the short, pale witches.

"But you *weren't* killed. You were terribly hurt. Taken, held against your will, poisoned with lies and pain. Your beautiful words twisted to serve a darker purpose, the demons that you called bent to hideous service."

"No..." the women said, almost as one, but their hands shook, and the demons edged closer—to the witches, not Angela. The women noticed, and fear slid across their faces.

"The pact of demon and witch has lasted throughout time," Angela said. "Yet now you need technology to hold them to your will? Since when was that required?"

"False," the red-haired witch hissed, but the others seemed more uncertain.

"You can escape," Angela said. "You only need to break through the hold AugTech has on you. You can do it. I can help you. I can...heal you. Take your pain as my own." She had no idea if she could or not, but she reached out for the women, and the nearest one grabbed her hand.

Angela staggered back. The pain was overwhelming, dirty and dank, filled with shame. She hadn't realized that was the key, but it was with these witches. On some level, they'd known of the atrocities they were committing against their will. They'd always known.

"I forgive you," she whispered. "Fly."

The witches turned and raced back through the throng of demons—while the demons themselves fled forward, past Angela toward the potential exit at the top of the hall.

Holding her breath, Angela dashed up the corridor, following the demons, trying to vault over as much of the blood as she could, though the floor was coated in it. She faltered on something wet and slippery, and her stomach lurched again, but it wasn't her own blood she skidded through. Instead, pools of black goop glistened on the concrete, the thick spatter of sludge tracking chaotically all around. Gregori had definitely been here. She didn't think any of the demons had been ordered to turn on themselves, which meant it'd been him standing alone against all of them. How had that even been possible? Just how fierce was the mighty demon of the Syx?

Steeling her guts, she started moving down the hallway —tentatively at first, and then with greater speed as she realized the throngs of demons were rapidly diminishing. Was this seriously an exit for them? Or if not, where were they all going?

There was only one answer, of course. They were going after Gregori. There must be something that AugTech wanted from him that was worth losing their precious army...or, worse, they'd figured out something else to use against him.

"No," she whispered. She passed doorway after doorway, instantly knowing that Gregori had come this way. Each room she passed looked as if a tornado had blown through it, and the wreckage left behind crackled and burned. The smears of demon goop continued as well, and ahead of her, the fleeing demons shifted away from the walls and danced across the floor. Clearly, they were aware of the danger they were racing toward, and yet they couldn't stop. The control that Filmore and the witches enslaved by AugTech exerted over the horde overrode even their inborn drive for self-preservation. How strong that must be! And how in the world could anyone break an instinct like that?

She stumbled past the next room, then stopped abruptly, startled to see it was occupied by a woman roughly her age, wrapped in the same woo-woo scrubs as the witches who'd attempted to hold her. The woman turned as soon as Angela hesitated, and her eyes caught Angela short. They were far darker than they should have been, given her skin and hair color, and her hands seemed to be smoking.

"Witch," gasped Angela.

The woman swayed. "I...I don't know what's happening,"

she whispered. Blood stained her clothing. Slight and almost translucently pale, with soft blonde hair cut brutally short, she kept blinking those jet black eyes that threw off her whole appearance. "But I...I was told your name. Told to come for you. To protect you."

Gregori? Angela wondered, then immediately doubted herself. More likely another trap laid by Martin Filmore.

"Why should I trust you?"

The woman smiled sadly, wincing as she raised her hand to rub her neck. "You shouldn't. I think a demon, um, *forgave* me up in the corridors above, so clearly I've gone insane. I was supposed to control the electronically enhanced demons there, but...but instead, I was sent down here to get you. I do know the way out, though. Beats getting attacked down here."

Something in her voice made Angela exhale. It had to be Gregori she was talking about. But she also knew something the woman didn't.

"First things first." She dashed over to the trashed medical cabinet, searching and finding what she needed: a scalpel. When she turned back to the witch, the woman's eyes were wide.

"You want to be free? Free of whatever's inside you?" Angela demanded.

"I can now. I didn't..." The woman shook her head. "None of that matters now. But I can take the pain. There's a spell we used at the beginning, before we lost the sense of ourselves—"

"Then use it." Angela moved toward her, gripped in the thrall of Gregori's abilities—Gregori's, not hers, which allowed her to see the woman as a creature of light and beauty, with one very unbeautiful anomaly in her neck, beeping and gyrating like a living thing. She didn't hesitate but sliced through the woman's skin and popped the device free. It fell on the ground, quivering, and the woman stomped on it, her hand going to her neck as her eyes squeezed shut, her mouth moving quickly. A second later, she opened her eyes again, and they seemed far clearer, sharper. Aware.

"Come now—quickly," she said, and raced from the room.

Together, they ran up the hallway, and with each step toward Gregori, Angela felt better, stronger. They blew right past the elevator and instead followed the tracks the demons made up an access staircase, the trailing goop proving far more resilient than the demons themselves.

To Angela's surprise, the witch didn't hold back and instead joined the ranks of the demons, who shifted and shuddered away from her. "What are you—"

"No time." The woman waved her off. "Shh."

A moment later, the crowd of demons slowed down, even as their excitement ratcheted up. Angela strained forward and noticed something else. There was something different about these demons. They retained their human forms even though their brethren would have long since converted to their demon forms. But though they appeared human on the outside, she could see, smell, breathe the heavy pressure of demon around her.

"What are these things?" she muttered, and the witch beside her turned, her gaze flashing an expression of utter despair for the barest moment before shifting back to flat resolution.

"They're the Possessed," the woman said. "They're humans, but taken. An abomination that should never have been allowed." As she talked, she continued pushing through the crowd. The creatures started huffing, shifting back and forth, their howls and moans building.

"Why aren't they bothering us?" Angela whispered. They passed more of the Possessed, and the nearest man turned to them, his nostrils flaring as his wild eyes tracked them. He was practically quivering with excitement, but he didn't move.

"Their instincts are being overridden twice over. First, they're not attacking us, though we're fresh meat and in better condition than some of the humans they're possessing. Second, they're way too eager to tangle with a Syx. Except a Syx is the only thing that can hurt them."

"But they did that before," Angela said. "The regular demons were attacking Gregori even though they didn't stand a chance against him."

"That was different. Those demons were controlled by AI and had made the realization that there is, in fact, a fate worse than death. This group is human at its core. The host doesn't understand what a Syx is, but its demon does. They're not being controlled by AI, they're being controlled by witches and..."

The woman stopped so abruptly, Angela swung her gaze to her. "What?"

"They're human," she breathed, stricken. "A Syx can't kill a human, even one rotting from the inside due to its demon controller... *Shit*. This is bad."

The witch fell silent as they finally reached the door and squeezed through, and Angela realized they were on the first floor of the facility, the doors opening onto some kind of lobby. Escalators, tiled floor, and collections of sitting areas belied the frightening scene that unfolded before her. Gregori, standing in the center of the group, surrounded by demons that were not quite demons, all of them huffing and stomping, building themselves up to an attack. They growled, they yowled, they pressed toward him, while Gregori stood in the center of the group—and bent his head forward, lifting his hands wide in apparent absolution of his soon-to-be attackers.

Martin Filmore's voice broke over the crowd.

"Now," he said.

The creatures rushed forward.

26

Gregori pounded through the last set of metal doors, then skidded to a stop, his arms windmilling to slow his forward motion enough for him to get his bearings. He was in some sort of lobby—on the first floor, thank everything holy, and he would have wept to see the sun again if he'd had time. The nightmare he'd seen belowground at this facility had made him wonder if there was anything but darkness left in the world, but as it had since the world had first begun, the appearance of the sun restored hope to a faltering soul.

Even his.

He turned, coming to grips with this new battlefield. It was filling rapidly, and he could tell at a glance that the humans had learned as quickly as he had from the demonstration below. There were virtually no true demons in the crowd that faced him, augmented with artificial intelligence or otherwise. Instead, he faced a throng of Possessed, their eyes wild, their breathing labored. Some had clearly been possessed for a while, ground down under the weight of their demon infiltrator, but some were freshly taken. Both types were dangerous in their own right. A newly Possessed was erratic, impossible to predict, particularly if the human host continued to resist. A worn-down Possessed moved like it was broken, but in truth, it was stronger than steel, willing to subject its body to startling pain at the urging of its demon. It would have grown numb to everything but the will of the evil that possessed it.

It was that will that Gregori would be facing now.

He'd done so many times before, but never alone. With the Syx at his side, he could dispatch even this horde with relative ease—doing some damage, inevitably, but far less damage than the horde would inflict if allowed to stay inside their human hosts. But that wasn't an option with this group. He couldn't betray any information about the Syx to these humans. And, though the archangel remained silent and apart, Gregori knew why.

So far, the humans didn't know anything about the Syx other than what they'd been able to pull out of the demons they'd interrogated—demons they could torture eternally and not kill. But demons knew nothing but lies and would say anything to avoid pain. They also could manipulate the humans who were torturing them. Eventually, the humans here would have figured out that their intelligence was useless. The witches would provide them with more data, but their data was also hearsay—the covens and the Syx interacted very rarely. Which meant that if the humans wanted legit intel, they had to take down Gregori.

That wasn't going to happen.

He eyed the Possessed surrounding him, knowing what was to come. They would rush him all at once. It was their only move. The first ring was largely made up of the more long-term enslaved, those humans that could be pushed into a roaring blaze without much effort, but the second consisted of the wild-card Possessed, those new to control. Gregori had to be prepared for them to attack at once, clawing through the first ring to reach Gregori and destroy him.

And that was their goal, he realized. Their goal, not their human overlords'. The humans wanted him alive but incapacitated, but the demons didn't so much care about that. For the first time in their existence, they had a chance to kill a Syx. And they would sacrifice their human hosts in a heartbeat to do so.

Fire of *God*, this was going to be tricky. He had released his own summoned demons after the destruction of AugTech's labs was finished, but...he might be needing them again.

Something shifted in the distance, and Gregori stiffened, knowing immediately that Angela was there. Angela and another human, damaged but not possessed. The knowledge that two of God's children still stood against their oppressors made him straighten with pride and hope, renewed energy pouring through him. He might not survive the coming trial, but he had done this, at least. Two of the blessed now stood shoulder to shoulder, their fire and resilience reaching him over the hunched and shuffling backs of the Possessed. He couldn't kill a human, but he could set them free to fight their own battles, even as he fell.

"Now." The order came through the overhead speaker, and the effect was immediate. The entire group rushed forward, the long-term Possessed quickly overtaken by the humans more recently violated, their panic and pain much more intense as it swept over Gregori well in advance of the bodies hitting him.

Born of long habit, his initial reaction was to remove the demons from the Possessed and cast them across the veil, and he was able to do that for the first several that attacked. Black goop flew as humans toppled, their screams of horror and bewilderment cresting over the howls and yammering of the other Possessed. Some of the horde naturally strained back, their overwhelming compulsion toward self-preservation momentarily overtaking their orders, but with a crackle of electricity, they too joined the fray, the renewed frenzy of their attack pushing the closer lines forward until too many spilled into Gregori's reach for him to attack quickly.

At that point, he knew what he had to do. There was nothing for it. He had no option but to do the unthinkable, what Angela had offered up with the guilelessness of a human who had ever and always been one of God's beloved children. Among all his other treasured gifts, the Father had given humans the power of his own almighty grace, a grace they so rarely used.

Forgiveness.

Gregori set his feet wide and braced himself for the wave of demons, his hands held at his waist, palms up, as he dropped the last of his barriers against the onslaught rushing toward him. There was the pain that he expected— human and demon alike, twisted and frightened and confused—that pounded through him with a strength that took his breath away. How could humans, in their frail and fragile bodies, feel so much? How could their hearts grow so full, their minds so frantic, their eyes peeled wide to see everything that was real and so much that wasn't real, but which loomed so large in their imaginations? How was it possible for them to withstand day after day of this pain, anxiety, and terrible, overwhelming worry?

But it was the second wave of pain that caught him off guard.

Why?

With the humans overtaken so completely by the demons, it was only because there was an amalgam of them in such a tight space that the word could even be pieced together, a hundred thousand shards of pain and misery coalescing into that startling, agonized word. *Why?* What had they done to deserve this painful path, where had they fallen from the grace of God, what was it about them that was so miserable, so base, that the Father had so completely abandoned them. Why were they being punished?

Gregori staggered back.

He didn't have the time to explain to the humans how their paths had been initially set, how they'd walked once among the stars and chosen tests to raise them in their own power, to fill them ultimately with grace and goodness and joy. This was not the time for those conversations, and they were in no place to understand them anyway. In truth, if any words like that were directed at the humans, the demons within them would scramble and snarl, their own jealousy and rage blocking all light intended for the fragile souls they drove forward.

Instead, Gregori's words were not for God's children. They were for the creatures of the damned. He caught the first human as he flailed toward him with eyes peeled wide in inarticulate horror, and Gregori saw the demon within immediately. With the ability accorded to all the Syx and every Fallen, he could name that demon as well.

Then he did something not accorded to the Syx. That was forbidden, in truth, the violation of an ancient creed older than Gregori himself.

"*Morkadelei*," he murmured. "I forgive you."

The effect was immediate and devastating on both sides. The power of grace that surged from Gregori's own broken body, beneath the veneer he still maintained, ripped through him like a jagged knife. Morkadelei, deep within his human host, gasped and shuddered, but he was an old demon who had seen the Fall, and had swept into the world under the wings of the condemned. His place among those banished souls was never to be forgiven, and yet with these simple words, Gregori did exactly that. Morkadelei burst from the human with a blinding, golden light, and was gone.

The screaming took on a new tenor almost immediately, with the demons and the mortals in their thrall recognizing that something very unexpected had just happened. With the second demon Gregori forgave, his knees buckled. With the third, he fell to the ground, kneeling as he lifted his hands, bowing beneath the assault only long enough that he could feel the tattered remnants of his half-remembered wings once more spread across his back. It was an illusion, a false memory, but it gave him the strength to lift his head and meet the eyes of his oppressors. They seemed to think his wings were real as well and approached him from the front, as his unassailable armor blocked him from the back and the sides.

And so they came, and so they stared full into his eyes, and so he forgave them one after the other, each forgiveness driving a nail through his hands, his temples, his guts, his heart. He was convicted over and over for the crimes of these creatures, and not only the demons' crimes, but those of God's children as well, some petty, some grave, all contributing to the weakness and separation that had led to their possession. No demon could attack a human uninvited, after all, even if the mortals didn't understand the opening to darkness they'd provided.

"I forgive you," he gasped again and again, and it was as if the waves of his oppressors flowed more quickly with each given grace, until they were little more than a blur in front of his eyes. And still they kept coming. Gregori could hear the wail of sirens, the loud orders ripping over the speaker system, but he couldn't make out the words. He had eyes only for the mournful stares of the afflicted, ears only for the cries of the oppressed and the damned. At first attacking him, then, almost pitifully stumbling toward him to receive the grace they didn't deserve, the grace that killed Gregori a little more with each approaching soul. It was the only way he could save the mortals and destroy the demons at once, each new ray of light signaling their departure from this plane.

Where they went, he had no idea. Their judgment remained a contract between them and the Father that would have to be reconciled. But they would go to that confrontation with the knowledge they'd been seen, they'd been heard, they'd been forgiven, their sins transferred to Gregori's own shoulders, their horrors stripped away to blacken his soul.

It was enough to clear them from their human hosts, and the bodies of the afflicted either collapsed around him or staggered away, confused and dazed, rushing toward the doors, where men with guns flinched from their pressing panic.

Until, at last, it was done. No more demons came forth, Possessed or otherwise. No humans remained with the screams of the damned ringing from their throats.

Of course, that didn't mean there wasn't any screaming.

But it was only Gregori's voice raised high unto the heavens.

When Gregori's vision cleared again, he no longer saw the lobby, the piles of humans, the unnaturally bright light surrounding them, all that was left of the demons who'd been torn from their mortal hosts.

Instead, he saw a desolate wasteland.

He'd never been here before, but he recognized it all the same. It was the field of the lost, the hell that was set aside for those fallen from God's grace. Not a plane of fire and brimstone as so many mortals needed to believe, but far, far more hopeless. Empty, forsaken, with a howling wind that never ceased, a chill that never tired, a bleakness that was worse than either of the other two torments combined. The wind seemed to wail his punishment in ever-expanding waves. *Forgotten, abandoned, cast out.*

Gregori collapsed to his knees, and tears flowed from his eyes. He had given all. He had remembered, and he accepted what was to come. It was worth it to have saved the demons from their own perfidy. They would be judged, yes. But they would go to that judgment knowing the power of grace along the way. It would likely not be enough to turn them from their path. That was not his to say. Just as it was not his job to have done what he did.

Though he'd paid the ultimate price, he was glad he'd done it. And he prayed that God in his grace would bring Gregori's own end soon. He was close, he thought. Very close to that end. His bones remained alight with fire, his blood had dried to dust, his skin had burned away. There was nothing left of him but the tattered memory of wings and shattered hope.

He bowed his head, once more dying a thousand deaths for each act of grace, remorseless waves crashing on an empty shore.

"*Pónos.*" The voice was quiet and seemed to come from a far distance. Gregori lifted what was left of his face, as the wind scoured over his sunken eyes, ruffling the tattered rags of his skin. He couldn't see anyone. There was no one here. He dropped his head again.

"*Pónos.*" Again the voice came, more insistent this time, and Gregori did not see so much as feel the presence beside him, turning him over, cradling him in his arms. He slit his eyes open to see the archangel gathering him close, but an archangel like he had never seen before—his skin warm and filled with life, his eyes no longer pale and ghostly but flashing with fire. He stared down at Gregori a long moment.

"*Pónos*, you have done the unthinkable, taken power not yours to take and poured it out for the children of God and for creatures beneath disdain. You gave a life that wasn't yours to give. You gave the ultimate grace that wasn't yours to grant."

Gregori drew in a ragged breath, disgrace lancing him anew. "I—" He struggled to speak, but no more words would come.

The archangel lifted his hand to Gregori's brow and bent, his forehead touching his thumb as his small finger brushed against Gregori's ravaged skin. With a graceful flap, the archangel's magnificent wings spread wide, bathing them both in radiant light.

"Blessed warrior of God," the archangel murmured, his words as soft as a sigh. "I forgive you."

27

Angela watched with wide, horrified eyes as Gregori disappeared, then whirled on the dark-eyed blonde beside her.

"Where did he go?" she demanded. "What have they done with him?"

"No time!" the woman shouted, shoving Angela into the throng of stumbling, shuffling humans. "Go, go, go!"

Together, they ran back into the same corridor they'd recently exited, the place still slick with black demon goop and mortal blood. The woman pushed Angela into the nearest trashed laboratory, then pointed frantically at the back of the room.

"There!" she said, and a moment later, they were stuffed into a supplies closet barely larger than a cabinet.

"What are you doing?" Angela asked, bewildered.

"Buying us some time," the woman said. "They'll come for us almost immediately. If we'd stayed in that lobby..."

Angela nodded, understanding. But she couldn't get past the last image she'd seen of Gregori. Her throat ached from unvoiced sobs, her eyes burned. She'd never felt so lost. "What happened?" she finally asked again.

The woman merely stared with her strange, haunted eyes, her expression implacable. "I don't know. There was so much light. I've never seen that kind of light when demons are returned to their creator. It's not supposed to happen that way."

"Did somebody return Gregori too, somehow?" Angela persisted. "He was there, then he wasn't. Did we miss something?"

The woman flinched, then her eyes cleared, a flicker of hope springing to life in the charcoal depths. "I can't help you. Not with that."

Something in her voice made Angela's focus sharpen. "With what, then?" she asked.

The witch straightened her narrow shoulders, tilting her head. Her close-cropped hair looked roughly cut, Angela realized, old wounds still visible at her nape. Had she been *shorn*? And if so—what did that say about her...and her captors?

The woman's hard gaze never wavered. "There are over two dozen of my sisters being held in thrall to these monsters, forced to order demons to perform whatever AugTech wants. If we leave now, AugTech will simply rebuild. Their technological infrastructure is astounding. The money it must've taken to assemble this facility..." She shook her head. "I don't know how it was ever possible."

Angela set her jaw. She knew how it was possible. All it took was an open-ended black box budget that never saw the light of day, certainly not the light of congressional over-sight. Whether it originated with the President, the Pentagon, or some office she didn't know about, it was all too easy to see what was going on here. And to think she'd likely been complicit in all this, had helped to ensure safe passage for the money to keep flowing...

But if she wasn't involved, if she walked away, it would happen all over again. AugTech would simply start over, with no oversight, no awareness. Or worse, they could go overseas to someplace completely unregulated. They wouldn't have the credibility of a US installation, but there would be plenty of buyers on the international stage. Which meant Angela not only needed to stop what was going on here, she needed to control it going forward.

She studied the witch. She looked a little too fried, too traumatized to take on the next task, but they had no other choice. "What do we need to do to release your sisters?"

"Ideally, we'd remove their implants, the same way you did mine," she explained, waving vaguely at her bloodied neck. "But there's no time. So we'll do the next best thing. We'll short their implants out."

Angela blinked, startled. "You can do that?"

"Not alone. But with two witches, it's easier than you might think. Something we were able to keep from our oppressors should any one of us escape. Sadly, they're not complete fools. Their leash on us was kept very tight."

Angela sighed. "Well, that's not really going to help us out, because we only have one witch between us."

The woman regarded Angela with her smudged-charcoal eyes, waiting.

Angela's eyes popped wide. "No, no, no. Don't get ahead of yourself. All I know I learned from a book that I haven't read since I was five years old. I have a pretty good memory, and necessity proved to be all the motivation I needed, but all I know is how to summon demons, I guess, and how to defend myself against them. I don't know how to create some sort of tech hex."

The woman waved fingers streaked with soot, the skin blackened around the nails. She'd already suffered much. Who was Angela to deny her this? "You don't need to. All you need is to repeat the words after me. Are you an auditory learner or just visual?"

Angela tilted her head, responding automatically. "Primary visual, secondary auditory, tertiary kinesthetic. I tested it once. Auditory is best only for short-term."

"Short-term is all we're going to need. I suspect I'll have my hands full explaining even that to the coven." She grimaced. "What's left of the coven, anyway."

"I don't know how many are left," Angela said quietly. "But we will find them, I promise you."

"We'll find each other," the woman corrected. "My sisters will be enough to start over, once they break free of this place."

"Then I guess you'd better start talking."

The woman reached out and grabbed Angela's hands, interlocking their fingers as they made a human circle and paying no mind to her own damaged digits. When she spoke, her words came fast and furious. She uttered several words, and Angela repeated them back, and then she started over from the beginning, each time moving further through the spell, making sure Angela knew it completely before she continued to the next section. Angela spoke the words back rapidly, and she almost thought that this layered approach charged the air around them, each pass building the spell's power. So maybe the woman's repetition wasn't so much for Angela's ability to learn, but to prepare the space for the strength of the spell to come? She didn't know. But...maybe.

When the woman completed the last new lines, she nodded. At that moment, the sound of heavy footfalls pounded through the corridor, jarring them both.

"Now," the woman nearly shouted. "Go."

They began the spell. Their hands gripped tight together, they ordered the sacred words with a gradually increasing cadence, their voices lifting and falling according to a music long since gone from the world. An electrical charge swelled between them, and when the woman reached out with their joined hands and pressed them against the metal door, she jolted. Literally. The bolt of electricity that passed from their bodies into the metal infrastructure of the building created a shock wave of pain that practically lifted Angela off her toes and felt like it set her hair on fire. Then, as quickly as it had begun—it ended.

The two of them sagged against the wall, the woman grinning as the authoritative shouts of the men in the corridor beyond turned to alarm and anger, then outright fury.

"They're fleeing," the woman said with satisfaction. "The demons. They're returning to the shadows from whence they came. My sisters too...gone. Flying and gone."

Angela scowled at her. "Seriously? But won't their handlers know how to find them? Won't they simply catch the women and control them again?"

The woman shook her head. "We've been waiting for this opportunity for too long. AugTech could control our magic, they could control our conversations, but they couldn't control our hearts or minds. We've worked too long together as sisters, and we felt the pain of those who came before us who were so long entrapped. Even though we weren't broken by their service, we bowed and scraped beneath it like any animal pressed into service without hope of relief or release. But unlike those animals, we had something more. The memory of our coven and its strength and its freedom. So while we didn't hold hope, we held a certainty of what once had been. That was enough."

Angela took in her calm resolution, her quiet strength. She knew what she had to do.

"Teach me," she said, the words firmer than she would have expected. "Even if I'm not a witch, exactly, teach me to control the horde like you do. Teach me what I need to know to keep this from happening again while making AugTech believe that I'm helping them."

She saw immediately that the woman understood what she was asking. Her eyes narrowed thoughtfully. "The horde is not a computer, no matter how much AugTech wanted them to be. Demons don't simply take orders like a program and execute consistently every time. It doesn't work like that."

"Show me," Angela said again. "I only need to know enough to make them believe."

She didn't explain that by them, she meant both the demons and the men and women of AugTech, but she didn't have to. The witch took her hands again, but this time she placed them against her forehead.

"Kinesthetic may be your third preference, but think of it less as learning by touch than simply opening the channel to your visual centers," the witch informed her. Then she bent forward, pressing her forehead to Angela's fingers. A flood of visions assaulted Angela—images, words, ideas, symbols, history. So much information transferred so quickly, it was as if she were the computer being programmed, and yet the experience was so visceral, so emotional, no computer could hope to duplicate it. And when she was done, the woman stood back, visibly shaken.

"I don't know who you are, Angela Stanton," she said. "You believe yourself not to be a witch, and in truth, you've had no training, but there's far more to you than you realize. Far more for you to give."

Angela sucked in a quick and shaky breath. She felt unsteady, unmoored, her natural propensity for learning stretched far beyond its limits. She tried to resettle herself as the woman put her hand on the door and pushed it open. "Where will you go?" Angela asked, then blinked as she realized she knew the woman's name. "Cara Night, right?"

The woman turned back, flashed her a small smile. Her eyes, still jet black, blazed with new purpose. "I'm going to find my sisters. And you're going to find your calling." She nodded to Angela one last time. "And when your demon returns to you, please give him my thanks."

Then she was gone.

Angela waited a full minute after the woman left before she peeked out of the lab and into the destroyed corridor. She knew exactly where she needed to be.

Moving swiftly, she dashed down the corridor and reentered the large amphitheater where Gregori had fought so many demons. As she suspected, there was still a large group of people milling around in the observation deck above, doubtlessly kept there while Governor Filmore and Zachary Howard's crew tried to lock down the facility and perform damage control. They didn't notice her at first, but she didn't need much time.

She ran to the center of the room, the only area unmarked by demon gore, and quickly surveyed the mess around her. Sucking in a tight breath, she slid her hands through the muck to ensure there was no unbroken surface to the circle of blood and goop. Then she stood, her hands dripping with demon ichor, and lifted her chin, her hair flowing down her back. And she cried out to the demon horde.

Her summons was as old as time, offering the ancient words of partnership and payoff, respect and understanding. The bond between a witch and a demon always favored the witch, but that didn't mean the demons went away empty-handed. That was what Filmore and his crew failed to realize, and what the witches were wise enough, despite their terror and torture, not to share. The demons were bound to come, yes. But that wasn't enough. Angela needed them to obey. Willingly.

And not even for very long.

Fortunately, the horde wasn't unaware of what had just befallen their brethren. Their response to Angela's call was quick and absolute. Within a few short lines of her summons, the first demons appeared, shifting easily between their humanlike glamour and their hideous demonic forms. They were terrifying to see, even to Angela, who'd now met so many of their kind that they were practically old friends. But their display had the desired effect in the rooms above the amphitheater. Activity in those spaces picked up immediately. Phones were placed to ears, hand waving and shouting followed, and within a few short seconds, she saw the man she needed to see: Zachary Howard. And standing beside him, the man she knew now as a betrayer, Martin Filmore.

It was Martin whose voice echoed over the huffing and stamping horde, nearly five hundred strong. "Angela?" he asked quietly. Just that one word. But really, there was nothing more for him to say. She had all the control.

She met his gaze through the glass. "Martin. Hello again."

"Angela, what are you doing?"

"I'm doing what needs to be done. If you'd come to me at the beginning, we could've saved ourselves a lot of time and the good people at AugTech a lot of money. But either way, there are needs that must be met and tools that have been forged to meet those needs, and it's time we accepted that truth."

He didn't miss her echoing back his own words, and the people around him straightened as well, their excitement almost palpable.

"You'll help us?"

"I'll help you." She had no intention of doing anything of the sort, but she needed to get out of this building alive, and there was only one way that was going to happen. What Martin didn't know wouldn't kill her. "You don't need a cadre of terrified witches to do your work for you. There are better ways, ways that I know. Ways that you'll only have access to if I'm running the operation from inside the committee."

Martin scowled. "You're only a junior congresswoman. There's only so much sway you're going to have."

"Then I guess it's a good thing I have friends in high places. And low places as well."

On cue, the demons lifted claws and wings and talons, howling in agreement. Martin's jaw dropped, and beside him, Zachary Howard appeared stricken for a moment with excitement and greed. She suspected the witches had never secured that level of cohesion from the horde.

She was right. "How?" stammered Howard, his gaze sweeping over the fresh unimplanted demons, who were still shifting between their human and demonic forms.

"It's amazing what you can accomplish when you ask nicely," Angela said dryly.

But Martin knew her arguably better than anyone in the world, her trusted confidant, friend of the family. He narrowed his eyes suspiciously. "Why are you doing this?" he asked. "What's in it for you?"

"Fortunately, that's not something you need to worry about," Angela said. "It's a one-time deal. I help secure the safety of American troops or I don't. Good luck finding your next cabal of witches, though. Because once word gets out about what you were doing, you can bet they're going to see you coming long before you get there."

Martin frowned, but Zachary Howard leaned forward. "We can work together. There's so much we can do."

"Yes." Angela nodded. "Now that we understand each other, I'm leaving."

Martin started, "But the demons—"

Amanda cut her hands dramatically, and in the space of a breath, all five hundred of the horde disappeared, laughing as they went. "They'll be here when you need them and not before," she said.

But she'd taken it a step too far. Martin's eyes narrowed sharply, and he said something beneath his breath that she couldn't catch. A hiss of smoke immediately flowed through the room, and Angela's heart squeezed. *Shit!* She'd forgotten about the gas. How could she have forgotten about the gas?

A second later, there was the softest flutter of a breeze, and somebody else stood next to her, his body immense and bathed in white light, his wings arcing above and around her.

"No," the extraordinary being breathed. "No, and never again."

Gregori wrapped his arms around Angela and carried her home.

28

Gregori stepped quietly through the living room of Angela's condo, though nothing stirred. The place had been cleaned, he could tell, but...how bad had it been? And what had happened to—

Angela, now healed and purified of the battle she'd waged, stirred in his arms. He stumbled over to the couch and gingerly laid her down. He knew she wasn't injured bodily, but when her eyes flickered open a second later, there was no denying the shock and fear that crossed her expression. Gregori instinctively flinched back, but she grabbed his arms, bursting into tears.

"You're back! You're back and you're safe and you're here!"

As if on cue, a single bark sounded deep in the condo, and both Angela and Gregori jerked in surprise as a soaring roar of animal happiness billowed forth from the back of the condo—animal—and men's voices too.

"What the—"

"Gregori, my man!" Hugh of the Syx strode into the living room from the back of the condo, holding a bandaged

Hellboy, who was doing his level best to wriggle completely out of his arms. Raum followed, cradling the smoky-gray cat, Ghost, who regarded them imperiously from his perch. The other animals cavorted around their legs, with Hey Mister bouncing straight up into the air, easily clearing three feet every time, as if he was wound on a spring. "Angela Stanton, Hugh and Raum of the Syx. Demon enforcers and dog watchers, at your service."

"Oh, thank you—" Angela began, still clearly a little disoriented, then her gaze fell on the dogs. "Oh my God. Old Sir!"

She pulled herself up on the couch as the greyhound trotted happily over, straining forward to lick her face as the other dogs, Elvis and Hey Mister, quickly followed. The black-and-white cat sat off to the side, licking her paws, and the beanbags sat happily beside her, tearing into two large lettuce leaves. "You okay, good boy?"

"Your dog is a menace," Hugh informed Gregori as Gregori stood, then crossed the room in a few long strides to reclaim the dog. "He about bit our faces off before we could assure him of our good intentions. Raum knew some sort of dog spell, and boom, we were good, but it was close."

"What happened to him?" Gregori asked, staring down into the dog's soulful eyes. Hellboy's tongue hung out of his mouth as his lips pulled back in a goofy doggy grin.

"Singed a little—wouldn't let us get near him, not even to heal him, so we had to get him to a vet. A vet who may have fallen in love with Raum here," Hugh cracked, while the quieter demon merely shrugged. In his arms, Ghost shrugged too.

"Oh, Gregori." Angela's voice had him turning, and there —with his demon brothers watching—she threw her arms around Hellboy and him, hugging them both close.

The emotion that poured out of her swamped Gregori like a crushing tide. But for once, he didn't shrink away from the deluge of grief, relief, joy, and something else. Something he'd never experienced before.

Before he could say anything, Angela spoke again, pulling away. "What did they do to you? What happened? All I saw was you in the middle of...all those creatures. They were the Possessed, weren't they? Demons inside of humans, and there were too many of them to fight without..."

"Yeah, spill it, home slice," Hugh said. He snagged a chair closest to Domino, then reached down to scratch the cat behind the ears. After a moment, he also ruffled the fur of the guinea pigs.

"There were too many," Gregori said as Angela clung to him. "Too many to fight, too many to do anything but what you suggested. You helped me know how to remove as many of them as I could without harming any more of God's children."

"But none of them died," Angela said. "The humans, I mean. They all seemed okay. Messed up a little, maybe, and I wouldn't want to see the therapy bill, but okay." She was babbling, her voice hiccuping with emotion, and she moved her hands from Gregori's arms, to his shoulders, to his hair to his face, as if she was trying to convince herself that he was really there. That he was real. His own chest felt unaccountably tight, his heart swelling as tears swept down Angela's cheeks and fell over his hands.

"It's okay, it's okay," he assured her. "Don't cry." When that only seemed to make her sob harder, he furrowed his brow. "Are you all right? Did they harm you? Is there something wrong?"

Angela shook her head, but she still couldn't speak. He

grabbed her shoulders, suddenly even more afraid. "What's wrong?" he demanded.

"You...you came back for me," she whispered, her voice still choked. "You didn't have to do that. There's so much work left for you to do, and I'm only one human. And you—came *back* for me."

And in that moment, Gregori understood. This wasn't Angela Stanton, junior congresswoman, who was speaking now, not entirely. This was the five-year-old little girl, summoning and then dismissing the creatures of darkness to save her grandmother on her own. Eight-year-old Angela abandoned by everyone she trusted and knew, held in a cage to be poked at and prodded by demons. This was a little girl who'd broken her own arm in two places to escape, somehow knowing that was what she needed to do to get home. This was a woman who'd never been rescued. And who couldn't believe it was happening now.

"Of course I came back for you, Angela. I'll always be here for you." It was only the newest in a line of hundreds of promises Gregori had made this very day, promises of grace and forgiveness he had no right to make, but, as with every one of those promises, nothing felt more right for him, nothing felt more true than to lean forward over this miracle of grace and strength and give of himself until there was nothing left.

"But what about you?" she whispered, her eyes lifting to meet his gaze. He was transfixed by the need or desire in them, and he didn't understand it. "Who will take care of you? Who will stand with you in all your battles? There will be so many battles, my beautiful demon, so many terrible battles to come."

He sharpened his gaze on her. "What do you mean?"

Her hands found his and gripped them tightly. "I spoke

with the Serbian witches. I saw what they know. I understand something of what you'll be facing. And you would do it all *alone*."

Gregori shook his head gently, and Hugh and Raum straightened, Hugh once more coming to his feet. "I'm not alone. I have my brothers to stand and fight with me."

"He does," Hugh said quietly. "I swear it. We all swear it."

"You have me too," Angela said, her eyes burning bright. "I know I'm only human. I know I'm weak, but you have me too. I'll stand with you and fight. I will!"

For a moment, Gregori could only stare at her. She seemed so impossibly frail and fierce at the same time—her hair a tangled mess, her skin tracked with tears, her large, cloudy eyes far too full of things no human should ever have to endure—but the emotion that radiated from her was all-encompassing. "That's not your place," he began, but her chin came up, her shoulders squaring.

"It *is* my place," she insisted. "It is. I'm nothing without you."

The impossibility of that statement was so strong that Gregori clasped her hands together, giving her a little shake. "*No*," he said fiercely. "You walk in the light, Angela. I do not. That's not my path."

"But I love you!" she said with such ferocity that it took his breath away. "I love you, and I want nothing more than to fight by your side. For your battles to be my battles, Gregori, your life to be my life."

Gregori closed his eyes against this new fresh torrent of pain that assaulted him. He was what he was, and Angela was worth more than a thousand of him put together. But he knew she wouldn't—couldn't understand—

"Don't you *dare* think that," she said, as if he had spoken the words aloud. Gregori's gaze snapped to meet hers, and he found in her eyes a steely determination. "I didn't just talk to the Serbian witch, Gregori. I *learned* from her. She taught me. I summoned the horde to buy the witches time to escape, and also, I hoped, to save my own skin." She smiled a little ruefully. "I didn't do so well with the last part of that equation. So thank you for that."

Gregori went completely still, while his brothers stiffened. Ghost, disconcerted, jumped down from Raum's arms. "You summoned the horde? In front of the others?"

She bit her lip. "It seemed to be the only thing I could do to keep their focus on me."

"You could've been *killed*. If not by the demons, then by the AugTech directors."

"And?" She shrugged, her reaction so quintessentially human it made his heart ache. "If they'd found me and you hadn't come back for me, I would have been dead anyway. There's no way they could manage the liability of a member of congress knowing what they were trying to do with federal tax dollars, completely without any meaningful oversight. Even now, I probably have a target on my back."

Gregori rumbled a laugh. "I can guarantee you won't. I'm not completely without resources when it comes to interacting with humans, even though it's our charge to protect, not terrorize them. There are times they can benefit from a deeper awareness of the full extent of the Father's creations."

She narrowed her eyes at him. "You're going to scare them?"

"I'm going to make sure you're protected, blessed child of God."

"No," she said, and her sudden certainty shook him again. "I'm more than that. I'm the woman who loves you,

Pónos. I'm the woman who will fight to the death for you, and I am claiming you as my own."

"WE'RE OUT, MY MAN." Hugh's abrupt announcement reminded Angela that the other two members of Gregori's team were still present—people she hadn't properly *met* yet —but before she could even turn to them...they were gone. The animals, startled at their sudden disappearance, tore off for the back of the condo in hot pursuit, except for Hellboy, who made no fuss as Gregori laid him gently on the side chair.

"Sleep and heal, brave warrior," Gregori murmured. Angela's heart nearly burst as the dog sighed happily beneath Gregori's fingers, then let his eyelids droop. A second later, he was snoring.

Gregori turned back to her, his face more beautiful than anything she'd ever seen—strong, caring, certain, true. His dark hair clung to his skin, his brilliant green eyes were exhausted now, his arms were covered with rents and tears, but to her, he would always be...

"Perfect," she sighed.

He grimaced. "Hardly that."

"But you are," she insisted. She hadn't missed the way Gregori flinched every time she told him that she loved him, but she couldn't help herself. She felt like she was crawling out of her own skin, desperate to join with him no matter the consequences.

There was something else about his response that triggered something deep within her, something she could barely wrap her head around. It was as if, after all this time —all these centuries of being part of one of the mightiest teams of warriors the planet had ever seen—he still doubted his own worth. She'd seen him clear demons in his hideous and fearsome form, she'd seen him bent beneath excruciating pain as he forgave those who had done nothing to earn that right except exist as part of God's creation, she'd seen him study her with fear and wonder in his eyes, as if she was a miracle beyond his reckoning.

Yet still, he doubted.

She couldn't allow that to continue a moment longer.

"Gregori," she murmured, and his eyes shifted to hers. Those dazzling eyes, that focus that made her feel like no one else existed in the world. She caught the sudden flare of worry in his glance, and she smiled despite herself. He was so quick to want to ensure everyone else's comfort and safety that he'd gone centuries—millennia—without ensuring his own. "You can't keep doing this without healing yourself as well. You know that."

"I don't know that," he grumbled.

"You do. You were made to heal the world, but you can't do it every moment of every day."

"I was meant to fight."

"Not only fight." She caressed his cheek. "You were meant to wage war, but you were also meant to heal. You were always meant to heal. It's your greatest gift."

"Angela..."

She didn't give him a chance to say anything more. Just hearing her name in his rumbling, tortured voice unlocked something inside her. It was no longer the time for words, but the time for connection. Pushing him onto the couch, she climbed into his arms, the weight of her body pressing him back into the cushions until she rested her hands on his chest, her legs straddling his hips. She stared down into his eyes for a long moment.

Clearly, he was letting her do this. She wouldn't have been able to move him a centimeter without his permission, she knew. And that gave her hope. For him, for her. For the two of them together. She didn't care in that moment if their relationship was appropriate or allowed. She didn't care about anything but the feel of him beneath her.

Angela leaned forward and brushed her lips against his beautiful, perfect mouth. Even though she knew there was a broken ruin beneath the glamour, she kissed him. She now could see all of him with the benefit of the witch's teachings. Gregori was the ultimate destroyer and destroyed, and he was *hers*. For as long as she could help him, he was hers. She gave a little sigh, groaning as Gregori responded to her simmering want. He put his hands on her hips, and she pressed against him. Just that quickly, the emotion between them turned from gentle absolution to fierce need.

"Yours," she insisted, though he hadn't said a word. "I am yours, I will always be yours and I want nothing more than for you to be mine."

At her words, Gregori stiffened for only a breath, then his arms tightened around her and he crushed her to him, a growl starting low in his throat.

"Yes—yours," he said, and it was as much a declaration to the heavens as it was to her in his quiet and certain voice. "Only yours."

He rolled her until she was beneath him, his hands tearing frantically at her clothes as his own clothes fell completely away. He surrounded her with his body in all its glory and all its tragedy just beneath the surface, and she wanted every part of him.

"Always," she said, surprised to hear the word spoken with such fierce certainty, but there was no going back now. She would live, she would die, she would do everything that needed to be done no matter the pain, no matter the loss. And she would do it with him by her side.

Gregori shifted, and she could feel the additional pressure of his shaft at the junction between her thighs. She fell back, every part of her turning to liquid heat to accept him into her, to let them join together as one. With a rumble that was half gasp, half sigh, Gregori pushed into her, filling her completely. But this time was different from when they'd made love before. This time, she better understood who he was and who and what she was. So as his healing energy flowed through her, healing pieces of her she didn't even realize were still broken, Angela sent a return energy back into him.

Now it was his turn to shudder in surprise, and, emboldened, Angela intensified her focus, moving against him rhythmically with her body as her mind and her heart sought out all that was broken in this extraordinary being. This incredible creation that humanity certainly did not deserve, but with which they'd been gifted nonetheless.

Gregori pressed back slightly to stare at her, his eyes as green as emeralds flashing with a deep and silvered fire. "What are you..."

"Kiss me," she demanded, she ordered, she begged all at once. "Please."

She didn't have to say anything more. Gregori pressed his mouth to hers, joining them anew, and as they moved together, they sought, they found, they healed. Until there was nothing but a perfect circuit of energy running between them and through them and back around again, with each passage redoubling their strength and connection.

Time seemed to pass away and go somewhere else, but as their bond built, a new sense of urgency rose within Angela, a need she couldn't deny. She gripped Gregori's shoulders, her fingers digging in, her heart beating even faster, and he lifted his face once more to meet her eyes. An echoing need built within his emerald eyes as her own intensity increased, until she felt the climax building inside her. Their gazes remain locked on each other as they both crashed over the edge, caught up in a whirlwind of sensation that circled around and back again, over and over, never ending. Perfect, powerful, complete.

And together, they were enough.

29

Gregori stood in a place he almost remembered, the wind rushing around him, the endless gray landscape barren and lost. He vaguely remembered being here before, but with only the shadow of the sadness he'd felt before echoing through his memory. He'd come here broken and condemned. But he didn't know why he was here now.

A figure appeared beside him.

It was the Archangel Michael, as of course it had to be. Gregori wanted to speak, but the archangel lifted his hand. His expression was unlike anything Gregori had ever seen before. "Thank you, *Pónos*, for all you've given. You have done well."

Gregori looked sharply at the archangel. There was something different in his voice as well, something almost sad. It immediately put him on the defensive.

"You will not take her from me." Even as he made the impossible demand, Gregori heard a different tenor of strength in his voice that hadn't been there before.

To his surprise, the archangel merely shook his head. "I

will not take her from you," Michael agreed. "But her way will be long and filled with pain. And if you would love her as you already do love her, you have to know the sacrifice."

Gregori stiffened. When the archangel had summoned him from Angela's arms, he'd gone automatically, without hesitation. But even in that short breath where he had passed through the realm of humanity and into this sacred space, he could tell the difference. There was a harshness, a keening edge to the mortals' cry he hadn't felt in six thousand years. He was still a demon, but something had changed. Something he didn't understand.

The archangel settled his wings more tightly against his back. "You are not once more a Fallen...yet," he confirmed. "But you are closer to that already than any of your brethren. You have, perhaps, always been closer to that than any of your brethren. You need to be careful."

Gregori snorted. "Since when have you cared about any of our safety?"

The archangel's expression never changed. "The fight grows harder from here," he said, his words little more than a sigh in the wind. "Your brother Hugh will be tested next, and..."

When the archangel paused, Gregori's entire body jolted with alarm. He was, after all, an empath. He could read emotions as easily as any language, and not even the archangel of God was hidden from his view.

"He's as strong as any of us. There's no test you can put before him that he'll fail. Don't mistake his manner for his truth."

"It is precisely Hugh's strength that will be his undoing. The demon he fights is unlike any that has been fought before, for it's no demon at all."

"He'll stand strong."

"He will," the archangel agreed, his wings once more shifting, as if eager to pull the warrior of God away. "And you must stand with him, stand for him, receive his broken body when it returns to you. You must heal him as best as you can with the strength you have received from the child of God, for without that strength...he will never survive the test."

And with that, the archangel disappeared.

ANGELA WALKED into the congressional conference center, nodding at the security guard as he scanned her. She smiled ruefully as she set off the detectors. "Pins in my wrist and shoulder," she said, pulling out documentation. In truth, she was wearing embedded tech supplied by Gregori and his team, which would allow her to record everything she heard and serve as a tracking device for the Syx, should she ever be hunted again.

The security guard grimaced. "That sounds painful," he said.

"It wasn't my best day," she agreed.

She'd spent the last three weeks since fleeing the AugTech facility in isolation, first in the hospital and then back at her condo, though she hadn't truly been injured. The subterfuge had allowed her to access the resources she needed. Resources she'd actually turned to her parents to help provide. They'd been surprisingly forthcoming, never asking her what had transpired between her and Governor Filmore, but knowing something had changed in their daughter, the way thorough anthropologists always knew something had shifted in a species they studied but didn't quite understand.

Behind her, Joe moved smartly through the security gate, murmuring a greeting to the guard as well. Gregori wasn't with her, not here. Not physically. Yet she felt his presence like a glow of comfort as she moved through the cold and sterile halls. They'd been together for most of the last three weeks, and even now, she could feel the touch of his heartbeat at her fingertips, the warmth of his sigh against her skin. Their fight would continue separately, but they would be together. Forever.

"Randall," she said as she entered the conference room lobby. He eyed her steadily, his expression unreadable. But Angela hadn't just spent the last three weeks with the greatest empath on the planet without having picked up a few tricks. She could sense Randall's emotions rolling off him no matter what his face didn't betray. He was nervous but not afraid. Resolute, but not angry. He hadn't survived this long in Congress, nor ascended so many levels in back-room politics and black box operations, not to know how to adapt to a new world order.

He had his instructions, and his handlers. As long as she didn't cross either of those, he was willing to go wherever she directed him to. And she would definitely be doing some directing. Within the next six months, she would be running this committee, and within a year, she would have her hands on every installation of demon technology and artificial intelligence operating in the world. Because the US might have been the most advanced, and would continue to appear to be the most advanced, but they were by no means the only players in the game. And through her involvement, Angela could help the Syx hold the line as long as it was needed. As long as it took Gregori and the other members of the team of enforcers to return the world to a safer place.

They all filed into the room, where she met Randall,

Trudy, and Bob, accepting their condolences for her injuries, answering their questions of concerned interest. But as they settled into the day's work, she felt the softest brush of pressure against her neck, the whisper of warmth at her ear.

"I love you, bright light of the angels, precious song of the stars," Gregori whispered in her mind. *"I will always love you. And I will always be yours."*

Angela lifted her chin, blinking quickly to stave off the sudden rush of tears that rose to her eyes. *I love you too,* she thought fiercely.

And then she opened her folder and went about the business of saving the world.

THANK you for reading **Demon Ensnared**! I sincerely hope you enjoyed Gregori and Angela's story. If you did and you'd like to help other readers find them, I truly appreciate you leaving a review for the book wherever you purchased this copy!

WHAT'S **next for the Demon Enforcers?** While Hugh of the Syx has spent the last six thousand years as a master of deception, his silver tongue may not be enough to save him as he's asked to pull off the greatest deception of all...serving as the world's hottest, most conflicted guardian angel. Visit my website or sign up for my newsletter to learn more about the Demon Enforcers!

BOOKS BY JENN STARK

The Demon Enforcer Series

Demon Unbound

Demon Forsaken

Demon Bewitched

Demon Ensnared

Demon Betrayed *(coming in 2020!)*

Immortal Vegas Series

(series complete!)

One Wilde Night (prequel novella)

Getting Wilde

Wilde Card

Born To Be Wilde

Wicked And Wilde

Aces Wilde

Forever Wilde

Wilde Child

Call of the Wilde

Running Wilde

Wilde Fire

Wilde Justice Series

The Red King

ABOUT JENN STARK

Jenn Stark is an award-winning author of paranormal romance and urban fantasy. She lives and writes in Ohio. . . and she definitely loves to write. In addition to her Immortal Vegas and Wilde Justice urban fantasy series and Demon Enforcers paranormal romance series, she is also author Jennifer McGowan, whose Maids of Honor series of Young Adult Elizabethan spy romances are published by Simon & Schuster, and author Jennifer Chance, whose Rule Breakers series of New Adult contemporary romances are published by Random House/LoveSwept and whose modern royals series, Gowns & Crowns, is now available.

Visit her online or sign up for her newsletter to keep up with all the latest information about upcoming releases and special events!

facebook.com/authorjennstark

twitter.com/jennstark